WHEN NEW FLOWERS BLOOMED:
SHORT STORIES BY WOMEN WRITERS
FROM COSTA RICA AND PANAMA

WHEN NEW FLOWERS BLOOMED:
SHORT STORIES BY WOMEN WRITERS
FROM COSTA RICA AND PANAMA

Edited & with a Prologue by
ENRIQUE JARAMILLO LEVI

LATIN AMERICAN LITERARY REVIEW PRESS
SERIES: DISCOVERIES
PITTSBURGH, PENNSYLVANIA

YVETTE E. MILLER, EDITOR

1991

The Latin American Literary Review Press publishes Latin American creative writing under the series title *Discoveries*, and critical works under the series title *Explorations*.

Library of Congress Cataloging-in-Publication Data

When new flowers bloomed: short stories by women writers from Costa Rica and Panama / edited & with a prologue by Enrique Jaramillo Levi.
     p. cm. -- (Discoveries)
    Includes bibliographical references.
    ISBN 0-935480-47-1
    1. Short stories, Costa Rican--Women authors--Translations into English. 2. Costa Rican fiction--20th century--Translations into English. 3. Short stories, Panamanian--Women authors--Translations into English. 4. Panamanian fiction--20th century--Translations into English. I. Jaramillo Levi, Enrique, 1944- . II. Series.
PQ7488.W44   1991
863'.01089282--dc20   91-26038
                                                 CIP

ACKNOWLEDGEMENTS

This project is supported in part by a grant from the National Endowment for the Arts in Washington, D.C., a federal agency.

The translations of the stories in this anthology have been published by permission of the authors and/or translators.

The original Spanish title of the collections from which the selections was made, and the publishing house appear at the end of each story.

Our thanks to Lisa Fedorka-Carhuaslla for her careful editing of the manuscript.

When New Flowers Bloomed: Short Stories by Women Writers from Costa Rica and Panama may be ordered directly from the publisher:

Latin American Literary Review Press
2300 Palmer Street, Pittsburgh, PA 15218
Tel (412) 351-1477 Fax (412) 351-6831

For the valiant and gifted writers of Costa Rica and Panama, who honor their countries with their talent.

For the new generations of women writers of Costa Rica and Panama.

In memory of Sabina Lask-Spinac, the translator whose unselfish contributions form an important part of the English version of this anthology, and who died tragically just days after finishing her excellent work...

Whence the blue expanse
and the word
to make fertile the world?
....

Along the way
some voice to remind us
and to tell us clearly
and to extend us throughout
the world.

Leonor Garnier
"Rostro", in *Agua de cactus* (1985)
Costa Rica

Woman: point in time, hub of the infinite,
as fertile in your gifts as the seed in the furrow:
through you the centuries pass in the genuflection
of the secret rose.
Scepter of sun, full red flame of fire,
whirlwind on high, both sides of the coin!

Stella Sierra, in
"Mujer, sexo dolido",
Libre y cautiva (1947)
Panama

TABLE OF CONTENTS

Women Writers from Panama

PROLOGUE

Enrique Jaramillo Levi

I

Central America has for several years been the focus of a great deal of international media attention, as the world has become aware of its social and political problems, its peoples' struggle to survive adversity and misery, and because of the violent conflict over ideology and power. Both historically and geographically considered the "back yard" of the U.S., especially from the North American perspective, the region is a boiling pot of pulsations desperately seeking some breathing room as well as a sovereign self-identity which might be made permanent.

Hunger, exploitation, armed struggles, civilians who flee the war and become refugees in neighboring countries where they increase the unemployment in those new zones. Each and every one of the large and small anguishes which these situations create in the life of the men, women and children of Central America, have often been turned into a cause (public or private) for artistic creation through works of literature (novels, short stories, drama, poetry). They have inspired chronicles and newspaper reports which Guatemalans, Salvadorans, Hondurans, Nicaraguans, Costa Ricans, and Panamanians have written since the beginnings of the twentieth century, and especially, during the last thirty years.

But the fact remains that the tragic social and economic underdevelopment which smothers the region does not permit art to develop to the fullest, or reach the oppressed people, its logical public. This condition is largely the result of the inhumane exploitation exercised by oligarchical families and classes, and the new wealthy military leaders, at the expense of the large masses of workers and farmers. Those groups are stirred up, openly and not so openly, by the North American empire in its diverse forms of expression. And the repression exists despite the enormous wealth of literary talent which has always existed in Central America.

The two authors who are most widely known internationally, who enjoyed wide distribution and recognition during their lifetimes, and who still are enormously popular, are the Nicaraguan, Rubén Darío (1867-1916), one of the best poets in the Spanish language; and the Guatemalan, Miguel Angel Asturias (1899-1974), winner of the Nobel Prize for Literature in 1968. Asturias is one of the most outstanding novelists of the continent, especially with his works *El Señor Presidente* (1946) and *Hombres de maíz* (1949). But currently, other writers are beginning to find acceptance outside their countries: the Guatemalans Luis Cardoza y Aragón and Augusto Monterroso (1922), who have lived in Mexico for many years, the first a great poet and essayist; and the second, an extraordinary short story writer, author of *Obras completas y otros cuentos* (1959) and *La oveja negra* (1960); three Nicaraguans: Pablo Antonio Cuadra (1912), Ernesto Cardenal (1925), both excellent poets, and Sergio Ramírez (1942), an important novelist and short story writer; the Salvadorans Manlio Argueta (1935), a novelist, Alvaro Menén Desleal (1931), a short story writer and dramatist; José Roberto Cea (1939) and Claribel Alegría (1924), both poets (she is also a novelist)—Three other Salvadoran writers who during their lifetimes were beginning to gain a certain international prestige were the poets Roque Dalton (1935-1975), Hugo Lindo (1917-1985), and the short story writer Salarrué (1899-1975). Another important writer is Carmen Naranjo (1931), a Costa Rican novelist and short story writer of the first order, who is, along with Ramírez y Argueta, among the best known Central American writers in international literary circles today.

Numerous books exist, literary histories of the region or of a specific country, as well as critical anthologies which document and explain in Spanish the surprising achievements realized over the years in Central American literature, beginning with the cultural production of the ancient Mayas in Guatemala and in parts of what is now Honduras and Mexico (Chiapas and Yucatán). The most widely distributed study of the novel is *La novela centroamericana. Desde el Popol-Vuh hasta los umbrales de la novela actual* (Río Piedras, Puerto Rico: University of Puerto Rico, 1982), by Ramón Luis Acevedo. An earlier work, *Indice informativo de la novela hispanoamericana.* Volume 2: *Centroamérica* (Río Piedras, Puerto Rico: University of Puerto Rico, 1974) is very informative. One of the few historical and textual analyses of the novel of a specific country of the region is that of Seymour Menton: *Historia crítica de la novela guatemalteca* (Guatemala, Editorial Universitaria, 1960), an important work if one takes into account that Guatemala is, along with Costa Rica, the country which has produced the most numerous and the best novels of Central America (with the exception of some isolated cases in Nicaragua, El Salvador, and Panama). Given the great richness and variety of the literature of Guatemala, and its extremely important pre-Hispanic origins, it is worthwhile to consult other works, specifically the two volumes by the Guatemalan researcher and critic Francisco Albizúrez Palma: *Historia de la literatura guatemalteca*, whose co-author is Catalina Barrios y Barrios (Guatemala: Editorial Universitaria, 1981-1982) and *Grandes momentos de la literatura guatemalteca* (Guatemala: Editorial de Pineda Ibarra, 1983).

But, the genres of the short story and poetry have flourished in Central America, even though some critics and translators have only recently begun to give them the consideration which they deserve. The most representative anthology of short stories from the region is that of the Nicaraguan writer Sergio Ramírez: *Antología del cuento centroamericano*, 2 volumes (San José, Costa Rica: EDUCA, 1973). Recently two other anthologies, which have helped expand the appreciation for works from the region, have appeared in translation in the United States: *Clamor of Innocence. Stories from Central America* (San Francisco: City Light Books, 1988), by Barbara Pascke and David Volpendesta; and *And We Sold the Rain. Contemporary Fiction from Central America* (N. Y.: Four Walls Eight Windows, 1989), edited by Rosario Santos, with an introduction by Jo Anne Englebert. Moreover, the anthology which I have compiled for the Institute of Latin American Studies at the University of Texas at Austin, and which will carry the English title *To Tell the Tale. Short Story Writers from Central America* will be published in Spanish as *Para contar el cuento (Cuentistas de Centroamérica: 1963-1991)* by Editorial Costa Rica, San José, Costa Rica. The present anthology of works by women short story writers from Costa Rica and Panama will help draw the attention of North American readers and critics to the excellence of our contemporary prose writers. The same interest is occurring in the field of Central American poetry, thanks to the many anthologies which are beginning to circulate, the most important of which is, at least in the United States, the bilingual edition by Zoe Anglesey: *Ixok Amar-go. Central American Women's Poetry for Peace* (Penobscot, Maine: Granite Press, 1987), with 616 pages.

Although the greatest number of literary works from the countries of the region has been written during this century, esteemed poets and short story writers were already emerging in the nineteenth century. They were writers who, in general, ascribed to the various movements in vogue in certain epochs: romanticism, modernism, naturalism (with its variations: regionalism, *criollismo*, *indigenismo*), which were in some cases to extend well into the twentieth century. The principal tendency has always been to be conscious of social problems, and of the exploitation and injustice which they imply, and to condemn such situations with patriotism and dignity. Although works of denunciation do not always reach a necessary artistic level, they remain a sensitive testimony to their historical moment. One of the most interesting and accomplished sources concerning this predominant type of literature of the region is by Panamanian poet Esther María Osses: *La novela del imperialismo en Centroamérica* (Maracaibo, Venezuela: Universidad de Zulia, 1986). In this study the preeminent interests of the United States in the social, cultural, political, economic, and military realms of the countries of Central America occupy a principal role in the twofold cause-effect of the endless misery afflicting it.

But it is essential at this point to mention the existence of an important body of pre-Hispanic literature, which would have its influence on the thought and artistic production of writers and painters of the region. I am referring, fundamentally, to *Popol-Vuh*, *Chilam Balám*, and *Rabinal Achí*, three of the most important works of the indigenous Maya-Quiché past. Albizúrez Palma and Barrios y Barrios in their above-mentioned work state that:

> The remaining indigenous Meso-American manuscripts are endowed with a value which is more documentary and historiographic. Reclamation for rights violated by the conquistadors, descriptions of genealogies, the documentation of traditions, testaments of customs, make up the principal contents of these works. In them, there is not the epic vitality of *Popol-Vuh*, the lyric density of *Chilam Balám* nor the plasticity of *Rabinal Achí*. They are the result, as is *Popol-Vuh* itself, of authors raised already within colonial conditions, assimilated to the Hispanic culture, who, in our alphabet, pour out the meaning and the sounds of their native language...Moreover, one must point out that a large number of them have not survived, whether it was because they deviated from the common practices of the times, or whether it was because they were destroyed by the missionaries. (p. 19)

Among the collections which have been made of pre-Hispanic poetry of the continent, the one which best reveals to us the splendor of Meso-American art is by Miguel Angel Asturias: *Poesía precolombina*, Second Edition (Buenos Aires: Co. General Fabril Editora, 1968).

II

The short story has been, in Latin America, the most successful of the genres. Beginning in the nineteenth century, newspapers and periodicals published them from time to time, and, from their initial appearance as a romantic expression of the period, their vitality and charm were well received among their readers, a feeling which prevails to the present day. Later, the modernist short story appeared. Outstanding poets such as Rubén Darío, and the Mexicans Manuel Gutiérrez Nájera and Amado Nervo, among others, cultivated this genre assiduously, and, through their original images (semantic and phonetic combinations, and technical methods associated with poetry), the Spanish language acquired a new artistic category. But social realities, brutal and unavoidable in every country of the region, were to impose themselves in the end, as a motif which still subsists in the great variety of realistic or naturalistic short stories which fill the publications of the twentieth century.

Often, nevertheless, there appeared a psychological, existentialist or magic interest in delving deeper into the conflicts presented, and into the profound being of Latin American men, women, and children, converted by the power of words into representative personages. Fantastic, mythical, and lyrical stories gained relevance. Much has been said, about "*realismo mágico,*" about "*lo real-maravilloso,*" and even just "*lo maravilloso,*" as prototypic stamps of the narrative prose of our continent. And critics, not always in agreement, have expressed their judgements concerning the importance and the limits of such labels. Nevertheless, it is the important to point out that Latin American narrative (including that of Brazil, written in Portuguese), and, above all, the artistic jewel of a good short story, has always shown the world, through literary themes and applications which are profoundly idiosyncratic and original, the apparently simple labyrinths of everyday living which afflict our countries. And in that sense, the short story of Central America also can make unique contributions to raise the reader's social consciousness and esthetic taste.

Many of the great Latin American novelists are also outstanding short story writers: Rulfo, García Márquez, Carpentier, Fuentes, Cortázar, Donoso, Onetti, Roa Bastos, Benedetti, among others. But even earlier in our history there were masters of the short story, a large number of Argentines, Uruguayans, Chileans, Brazilians, Mexicans, Cubans...I am thinking, for example, of the great master of the genre, the Uruguayan Horacio Quiroga (1878-1937). We must recognize the excellent short stories of Argentine poet Leopoldo Lugones and the Uruguyan Felisberto Hernández, who was only appreciated posthumously. By the same token, one must value the stories of the Dominican Juan Bosh (1909), the Venezuelan Arturo Uslar Pietri (1906), and the Mexicans Juan José Arreola (1918) and José Revueltas (1914-1975), among many others. In fact, one could easily compose a list of several hundred Latin American short story writers whose works would merit re-discovery, study, and translation to other languages. So vast and complex is the reality of our *mestizo* continent, and so powerful are those talents which, through the short story, have been able to captivate and to communicate!

III

Central America has also been a fertile land for the short story. The stories of Rubén Darío were collected by the Nicaraguan poet Ernesto Mejía Sánchez in his important work: *Cuentos completos de*

Rubén Darío (Preliminary notes by Raimundo Lida; Mexico-Buenos Aires: Fondo de Cultura Económica, 1958); those of Asturias in: *Obras completas de Miguel Angel Asturias* (Prologue by José María Souvirón; Madrid: Aguilar, 1968, several volumes), although they can also be found in his own works such as *El espejo de Lida Sal* (1967) and *Weekend en Guatemala* (1956). But perhaps the most distinguished and best known, at least among those who are familiar with the literature of the region, is the Salvadoran, Salarrué (pen name of Salvador Salazar Arrué: 1899-1975), the author of excellent collections of short stories with regional themes, and also of anthologies with universal motives (fantastic, exotic, spiritualist) such as: *Cuentos de barro* (1933); *Eso y más* (1940); *Cuentos de cipotes* (1945); *Trasmallo* (1954); and *La espada y otras narraciones* (1960).V

IV

It would be impossible to speak of past centuries of writing in the Spanish language without mentioning names such as Sor Juana Inés de la Cruz and Santa Teresa de Jesús; in the present century those of Gabriela Mistral, Alfonsina Storni, Alejandra Pisarnik, Rosario Castellanos and Sonia Orozco, among the Latin American women poets, and Elena Poniatowska, Julieta Campos, Clorinda Matos de Turner, María Luisa Bombal, Martha Lynch, Silvina Bulrich, Marta Traba, Silvina and Victoria Ocampo, Luisa Valenzuela, Elena Garro, Isabel Allende, Rosario Ferré and Cristina Peri Rossi, among the Latin American women writers of prose. But these are only a few of the names, and the works of even these women continue to be little known in a broader context. In the past twenty years, a large number of talented women writers, particularly in Argentina and Mexico, have appeared and are attracting attention. Central America is also beginning to give the world outstanding women writers of both poetry and prose. Among the writers of prose, one must mention the names of Claribel Alegría (1924), Matilde Elena López (1922), Mercedes Durand, Yolanda Martínez, Maura Echeverría, and Jacinta Escudos from El Salvador; Rosario Aguilar (1938) and Irma Prego from Nicaragua. One must add, however, that Nicaragua also possesses a wealth of women whose poetry adds quality to our daily lives.

In general, the characteristics which predominate in the narrative work of the women short story writers from Costa Rica and Panama represented in this anthology are the following: a struggling will to accept, an authentic commitment to life itself, to their countries, and to art; the creation of new, original literary arenas and terrains; the search, at times anguishing and alienating, for self-identity as part of their status of being a woman in a class and "*machista*" society; the attainment of effective narrative techniques and of a language which is appropriate to the material narrated, reflections always of a deep sensitivity and of a superior intelligence. And the themes, presented with artistic refinement and deep sense of social responsibility, are multifaceted and complex; they include the desperate necessity to love and to develop all of the human potential of which they are capable, even if renouncing social, family or personal situations which, in a determined moment, are recognized as absurd or grotesque. Such situations are confronted stoically or handled by seeking some permanent form of liberation.

It has been widely discussed whether literature written by women has special characteristics which are different, whether it possesses nuances or presents unique or particularly distinctive textures, in contrast to literature written by men. There is a feminist attitude which rejects any type of gender distinction because women aspire to the ideal of seeing themselves as a part of that wider dominion of ART—without being catalogued sexually in any way. Nevertheless, that same emphasis on the feminist phenomenon is what has produced individual studies in the fields of psychology, sociology, culture, and even literature, explorations of the role of women in history and in today's world, as well as numerous anthologies, newspaper articles and interviews which seek to separate and distinguish the changing coordinates of "what is feminine." I must say that I am clearly in agreement with the premise that establishes that a work is simply art or it is not—well founded criteria exist for evaluation and individual "tastes,"—independent of who created it, their ideological affiliations, their sexual status or their age.

The fact is that until just a few years ago, women did not have equal access to means of mass communication, to publishing houses, to periodicals and cultural supplements, and, therefore, to the reading public. With women's access to the multiple gifts of education and culture, with their "liberation," first in the decade of the twenties and again in the sixties, and above all with the impressive explosion of their diverse talents and initiatives in the last few years throughout the world, and specifically in Spanish American literature, it would be, in my opinion, not only narrow-minded, but truly impossible, to close one's eyes to the works which they have generated. A natural tendency toward justice, plus a strong dose of human sympathy and solidarity, impels researchers and anthologists to single out the literary production of women on our *mestizo* continent, rescuing it from the immense sea of novels, short stories, poems, which in ever greater quantities and quality emerge from our long-suffering countries, with the goals of bearing witness, of protesting, of recreating, of dreaming of the possibilities of the impossible...

V

Literary activity in Costa Rica and Panama

Throughout their history, Costa Rica and Panama have been the Central American countries which have produced the largest number of short stories and novels, as well as the best women writers. They have also managed to maintain the greatest political stability and are the least poor. The political and economic situation in Panama, nevertheless, began to deteriorate drastically in the final three years of the recent military dictatorship as the corruption of the regime accelerated, as the civil and human rights of the opposition were systematically violated, and as the multiple aspects of already latent social and moral inconsistencies were exacerbated; although democracy returned to the country after the North American military invasion on December 9, 1989, the social inconsistencies continue, and economic bankruptcy is still quite predominant, resulting in the most difficult economic crisis in Panama's history.

The two countries share a border (Paso Canoas), and a constant flow of mutual visits as well as commercial and social interchanges have long existed between them. Although Costa Rica has a more developed and varied cultural tradition, thanks to the greater interest of its leaders in education and due to the organization, promotion, and diffusion of its cultural values, it as well as Panama has given artists and writers to the world whose unique genius supersedes national borders.

Among Costa Rican artists, those who have gained the greatest international prestige, are, in my judgment, Francisco Amighetti (painter, engraver, and muralist), Francisco Zúñiga (sculptor and painter, resident of Mexico), and Rafa Fernández (painter, now highly esteemed in Europe). Among the Panamanians, the painters Guillermo Trujillo and Manuel Chong Neto, and the composer Roque Cordero, among others, enjoy recognized international fame, as does the "salsero" Rubén Blades, in the field of popular music. And among the writers of Costa Rica who have international standing, José León Sánchez (novelist, living in Mexico), noted author of: *La isla de los hombres solos* (1971), and *Tenochtitlán* (1986), both published in Mexico; Alfredo Cardona Peña (poet and short story writer, living in Mexico); Fabián Dobles (writer of short stories and novels); Joaquín Gutiérrez (novelist); Samuel Rovinsky (dramatist, novelist, and short story writer); Laureano Albán (poet); and Carmen Naranjo (novelist and short story writer). Panamanians of international repute include Rogelio Sinán (novels, short stories, poetry); Joaquín Beleño (novels); Tristán Solarte (novels and poetry); Gloria Guardia (novels and essays); Enrique Chuez (novels and short stories); Bertalicia Peralta (poetry and short stories); Dimas Lidio Pitty (short stories, novels, poetry); and Enrique Jaramillo Levi (short stories and poetry).

In spite of the talent of an impressive number of poets and short story writers, Panamanian literature has developed slowly, largely because there have been no publishing houses in the country to promote the production of books, and because the state has never had, except during very brief periods, established a clear and permanent policy of cultural diffusion. Nevertheless, it is interesting to affirm that at no time have its writers stopped writing, and that many authors have managed, through their own efforts, to be published both inside and outside Panama.

The literature of Costa Rica, on the other hand, has always been able to rely on the formal and moral support of the state, as well as on the stimulus of several private publishers and numerous cultural institutions. The two large publishing houses which promote the maintenance of the national culture and the diffusion of new values are: Editorial Costa Rica, which relies on a state subsidy (thanks to the "National Publishing Law", created in 1959, which is the principal organism which fosters national literature, and a model worthy of imitation by other small Spanish speaking countries), and Editorial Universitaria Centroamericana (EDUCA), an organ of cultural diffusion of the Consejo Superior de Universidades Centroamericanas (CSUCA), headquartered in San José. (This second enterprise publishes national works as well as those from other countries of the region.) But without a doubt, the publisher which has distributed more local authors, with diverse collections of books, literary prizes, promotional activities, and the uninterrupted publication of a large quantity of works in the last thirty years, is Editorial Costa Rica, whose administration is partially responsible to the Sociedad de Autores de Costa Rica. Several of the national universities also publish books, although in limited numbers, often on specialized themes.

The most significant efforts in Panama to create small editorial houses whose principal goal, with no interest in profits, has been the diffusion of local authors and the rescue of the Panamanian identity, have been realized in this century by four writers: Guillermo Andreve (1879-1940; politician and man of letters), both while in public service and as a private citizen; Rogelio Sinán (1902), as a public servant; and Enrique Jaramillo Levi (1944), as a private citizen: his Editorial Signos, a modest one-man enterprise, published, first in Mexico (1982-1983) and later in Panama, thirty books in two and one-half years, and twelve numbers of the cultural periodical *Maga* (1984-1987), besides creating literary contests and organizing numerous activities for the promotion of culture. Also, writer Pedro Rivera (1939), at the University of Panama, has in recent years managed to publish a small number of works by national writers.

In Costa Rica, the cultural periodical *Repertorio Americano*, which writer Joaquín García Monge directed for many years, was a constant haven of great continental prestige for the diffusion of vanguard ideas of the Central American region and because of its familiarity with the creative efforts of a large number of authors from Costa Rica and other Hispanic countries. In more recent years, other periodicals have appeared, such as: *Revenar*, the organ of the Sociedad de Autores de Costa Rica; *Kañina*, of the University of Costa Rica; *Andrómeda*, of a group of young authors; and *Escena*, dedicated to promote the production of national theater. And in Panama, the Instituto Nacional de Cultura sporadically published for some years the periodicals *Itinerario* and *Revista Nacional de Cultura*. Another state publication is *Lotería*, this one with many years of uninterrupted activity (but it dedicates only a small portion of its contents to literature). Several writers themselves have founded short-lived magazines, such as *Quijote 20* and *El Pez Original*, and more recently the already mentioned *Maga*. And for some time, the University of Panama published *Humanidades*, and later *Imagen*, while the Catholic University, Santa María La Antigua publishes *Antigua*. In Panama there were important literary magazines at the end of the nineteenth century, and sporadically during the first fifty years of this century. At present, the economic collapse of the country is so severe that only *Maga* continues to publish, with great difficulty.

VI

The Short Story in Costa Rica

The first short stories, works of local color and poetry with a regional flavor appeared in local newspapers around the year 1884, and their author was the priest Juan Garita (1859-1912). Other important writers of short stories of that epoch were Carlos Gagini (1865-1925), with his works *Chamarasca* (1898) and *Cuentos grises* (1918); and Ricardo Fernández Guardia (1867-1950), with *Hojarasca* (1894) and *Cuentos ticos* (1901). Other authors who made notable contributions to shaping the literature of Costa Rica were: Jenaro Cardona (1863-1930), with *Del calor hogareño* (1929), and his novel, *El primo* (1905), which brought him renown; Manuel González Zeledón (known as Magón) (1864-1936), considered to be the founder of Costa Rican *costumbrismo*, with *La propia y otros tipos y escenas costarricenses* (1912); and, Aquileo J. Echeverría (1866-1909), known throughout Latin America for his *Concherías* (1905), and *Crónicas y cuentos míos*, published posthumously in 1934.

The place of honor in Costa Rican literature is occupied by Joaquín García Monge (1881-1958), based primarily on the publication of his novel, *El moto* (1900); another important work is *Las hijas del campo* (1900) and the short stories anthology, *La mala sombra y otros sucesos* (1917). His broad cultural vision and his interest in promoting new values were to form an integral part of his work during forty years as editor of *Repertorio Americano*, the best periodical of Central America (1919-1959).

There are other authors of realism, of course, and some who cultivated modernism in the early years of the present century, and who form an essential core of Costa Rican letters. The most predominant is Carmen Lyra (1888-1949), pen name of María Isabel Carvajal, known for the juvenile novel *En una silla de ruedas* (1918), *Las fantasías de Juan Silvestre* (1918), and her stories for children, *Los cuentos de mi tía Panchita* (1920). Her works *Relatos escogidos de Carmen Lyra* (1977), and *Los otros cuentos de Carmen Lyra* (1985) were published posthumously, thanks to the efforts of Costa Rican writer, Alfonso Chase. Another interesting narrative writer is María de Noguera (1892), *Cuentos viejos* (1923) and *De la vida en la costa* (1959).

Since 1960 the short story has enjoyed a resurgence in Costa Rica. Several writers who were later to become important began to publish in periodicals and local newspapers. Worthwhile books of short stories and novels begin to appear, with very diverse techniques and thematic orientations. And women began to take a leading role, on the same level in these two narrative genres as in poetry, in the development of the literature of their country. Julieta Pinto (1922) has published, among other works, the following short story anthologies: *Cuentos de la tierra* (1963); *Si se oyera el silencio* (1967); *Los marginados* (1970); *A la vuelta de la esquina* (1975); *Abrir los ojos* (1982); and the novel *La estación que sigue al verano* (1969). Carmen Naranjo (1931), the Costa Rican woman writer who is best known internationally, has published the following collections of short stories: *Hoy es un largo día* (1972); *Ondina* (1985); and *Otro rumbo para la rumba* (1989); as well as the novels: *Los perros no ladraron* (1966); *Camino al mediodía* (1968); *Memorias de un hombre palabra* (1968); *Responso por el niño Juan Manuel* (1971); *Diario de una multitud* (1971); and *Sobrepunto* (1987). She has also published poetry and essays.

Two women writers who have added to the prestige of Costa Rican fiction from their residences in the United States are Rima de Vallbona (1931) and Victoria Urbano (1926-1972). The collections of short stories of Rima de Vallbona are: *Polvo del camino* (1971); *Mujeres y agonías* (1982); and *Cosecha de pecadores* (1981), and her novels, *Noche en vela* (1968) and *Las sombras que perseguimos* (1983). Victoria Urbano published a book of short stories, *Y era otra vez hoy*, and also wrote drama and poetry. The erudite essay and literary criticism are also forms which both cultivate.

Eunice Odio (1922-1974), one of the outstanding poets of Costa Rica, also wrote interesting short stories, as well as a large number of newspaper articles in newspapers and periodicals in Central America and Mexico, where she lived for many years, and where she died. Her prose has been collected and studied by Rima de Vallbona in *La obra en prosa de Eunice Odio* (1981).

VII

The Short Story in Panama

The Panamanian romantic poets began to unite as the voice of what will be the first generation of national poetry around the year 1849. They also represented what can be called its first literary generation. All of these writers also participated, in one way or another, in the cultural and political life of the country, a Panama joined, as it was between 1821 and 1903 with what was originally La Gran Colombia, and then remaining as a part of Colombia.

Manuel T. Gamboa, who was very active in cultural journalism during that time, is considered the first Panamanian literary critic and holds the honor of having founded, in 1866, the first literary newspaper in Panama: "El Céfiro." In this context, it is important to point out that civic, social, political, and cultural life does not begin, as is often believed, with the advent of the Republic and the subsequent construction of the Panama Canal by the North Americans (1904-1914). After the construction of the railroad (1855), and later with the promise of the French Canal (1882)—which was to fail because of bad financial management and the many worker deaths from tropical diseases—, the Isthmus experienced an economic boom and a diversification of culture.

Panamanian novelistic literature was born in 1849, with the serial publication of *La virtud triunfante*, by Gil Colunje (1831-1899). In 1888, *Mélida*, by Jeremías Jaén (1869-1909) appeard in New York. Salomón Ponce Aguilera (1868-1945), founder and co-director of *La revista gris* (1892-1896), published his first short stories in 1892; he was considered, therefore, the first national writer in this genre. His short stories are circulated in newspapers and periodicals of the era. Darío Herrera (1870-1914), valued in his time as a modernist poet, was the first Panamanian to publish his short stories in book form, although it appeared in Buenos Aires: *Horas lejanas* (1903). Both of these writers created excellent short stories. And that same year, Julio Ardilla (1865-1918) published in book form the best novel of the epoch: *Josefina*.

With the advent of the Republic, the country began to develop in all areas of life. The general prosperity created by the construction of the Canal by the North Americans, the guarantee of a national territory, and the emphasis on public education were factors which contributed to the growing prosperity of Panama. For literature, the creation of the Imprenta Nacional in 1911 was an essential development. Many of the national leaders were humanists and men of letters, through whose efforts scholarships were established, and a climate sympathetic to intellectuals was facilitated. The most distinguished writers of those years, besides those already mentioned, are: León A. Soto (1874-1902); Adolfo García (1872-1900); Simón Rivas (1868-1915); Nicole Garay (1873-1929); Hortensio de Icaza; Alberto Dutary; Guillermo Andreve (1879-1940); Ricardo Miró (1883-1940); and Gaspar Octavio Hernández (1893-1918). Several from this group founded literary periodicals, not totally removed from the political scene; but the most tenacious and outstanding in the realm of literature were Andreve, with *El Cosmos*, *El Heraldo del Istmo*, *La Prensa*, and the publications of his *Biblioteca Cultura Nacional*, and later Miró, with the periodical *Nuevos Ritos*. Many of these writers were poets, but also wrote short stories, almost all of which were published in the newspapers and periodicals of the time. Only those of Miró have been collected, in the book—*Estudio y presentación de los cuentos de Ricardo Miró* (1957) by Mario Augusto Rodríguez—an outstanding writer of short stories in his own right.

For many years, Rogelio Sinán (1902), who is also a novelist and poet, has been considered the most renowned Panamanian short story writer. His books of short stories are: *La boina roja y cinco cuentos* (1954); *A la orilla de las estatuas maduras* (1967); *Cuentos de Rogelio Sinán* (1971); and *El candelabro de los malos ofidios y otros cuentos* (1982). He also penned two notable novels: *Plenilunio* (1947) and *La isla mágica* (1980).

Among the authors of the new generations who have had an impact primarily with their short stories are: Moravia Ochoa López (1939), also a poet, with *Yesca* (1963) and *El espejo* (1968); Pedro Rivera (1939), poet, with *Peccata Minuta* (1970); Bertalicia Peralta, poet, with *Largo in crescendo* (1967), *Barcarola y otras fantasías incorregibles* (1973), and *Puros cuentos* (1988); Bessy Reyna (1941), poet, with *Ab Ovo* (1977); José Antonio Cordova, poet, with *Con Irene y otros cuentos*; and Enrique Jaramillo Levi, poet, playwright, and essayist, with *Catalepsia* (1965), *Duplicaciones* (1973), *El búho que dejó de latir* (1974), *Renuncia al tiempo* (1975), and *Ahora que soy él* (1985), as well as the anthologies of short stories *Caja de resonancias: 21 cuentos fantásticos* (1983) and *La voz despalabrada* (1986); Raúl Leis (1947), poet and playwright, with *Viaje alrededor del patio (Cuentos de vecindario)* (1987); Roberto Luzcando, poet and essayist, with *Relatos sobre dipsómanos, orates y otra gente rara* (1977); Jaime García Saucedo, poet and essayist, with *De lo que no se dijo en las crónicas y otros relatos* (1982); Julia R. de Wolschoon (1953), poet, with *El que tenga ojos que...*(1975); Pedro Correa Vásquez (1953), poet and essayist, with *Donde viven las bestias* (1975); Reynaldo Barría (1951), poet, with *Los casicuentos* (1980); Giovanna Benedetti (1949), lawyer and essayist, with *La lluvia sobre el fuego* (1982); Ernesto Endara (1939), playwright, with *Cerrado por duelo* (1977), *Las historias de Pitty Mini,* and *Un lucero sobre el ancla*; Ricardo J. Bermúdez (1914), one of Panama's most important poets, with *Para rendir al animal que ronda* (1975); Víctor Manuel Rodríguez S. (1949), poet, with *Al margen de la vía* (1975); as well as Beatriz Valdés and Lidia Emir Castillo, both essayists, and whose short stories have yet to be published.

Another group of Panamanian short story writers consists of Pantaleón Henríquez Bernal, journalist, with *Cuentos de acá y allá* (1986); Griselda López (1938), with *Piel adentro* and *Sueño recurrente*; Héctor Rodríguez C., also a novelist, with *El mar océano* and *De retratos y ventanas y otras ilusiones*; José Guillermo Ros Zanet, one of the most distinguished Panamanian poets, has also published short stories; Herasto Reyes (1952), journalist and poet, with *Cuentos de la vida* (1984) and *Cuentos en la noche del mar* (1989); Jorge Turner (1922), lawyer and journalist, with *Viento de agua* (1977); Benjamín Ramón (1939), poet and short story writer; Juan A. Gómez (1956), poet and co-author of *El puente* (1983) with Digno Quintero Pérez (1957); and Isis Tejeira, with *Está linda la mar y otros cuentos* (1991); and Consuelo Tomás, with *Cuentos rotos* (1991).

Claudio de Castro (1957) is one of the few Panamanian authors who exclusively cultivates the short story with a febrile talent. He has published *La isla de mamá Teresa, el abuelo Toño y otros cuentos* (1985), *El Señor Foucalt* (1987), and *La niña de Alajuela* (1985), *El juego,* and *El camaleón* (1991), as well as numerous "short shorts" in national newspapers and periodicals.

Although there are no private publishing houses in Panama, and despite the limited amount of literary output published by the state (with the exception of the annual prize-winning books in the national "Ricardo Miró" contest), there is a rather impressive production of prose writing, albeit anarchical and of various levels of quality.

VIII

The production of short stories in Costa Rica and Panama is only a fraction of the impressive variety of literary works which their writers have created. The same could be said for the rest of the Central America, although other countries of the region have found themselves chronically involved in situations of conflict, exploitation, and misery, indignities suffered by their proud, hard-working peoples. The selections of short stories by these women writers of prose from Costa Rica and Panama give us an idea of the high degree of artistic mastery and human sensitivity attained by their creators. As is the case of all anthologies, this one does not pretend to be exhaustive let alone, definitive. Other short stories and other women writers—both published and unpublished—could have been included.

I would like to thank the Costa Rican writers Carmen Naranjo, Rima de Vallbona, Carlos Cortés, Habib Succar and Luis Bolaños, as well as the Panamanian writers Rodrigo Miró, Rosa María Britton, and Isis Tejeira for their help and their moral support.

I would also like to thank all of the translators for their unselfish participation in the English version of this anthology, without which its publication in the United States would have been impossible. They are, in random order: Elizabeth Gamble Miller; Leland H. Chambers; Birgitta Vance; Clark M. Zlotchew; Linda Britt; Irene del Corral; Julia Shirek Smith; Don Sanders; Virginia Edwards; Zoe Anglesey; Gloria Nichols; Robert Kramer; Marinell James; Bessy Reyna; Sabina Lask-Spinac (who died in a tragic accident on June 7, 1990, just days after sending me her translations of the short stories of Emilia Macaya); and Samuel Zimmerman, who translated this prologue. The arduous work of such altruistic people makes it possible for the enormous wealth of Latin American literary talent to be circulated in other arenas.

IX

This anthology was prepared while I was Professor of Spanish and Spanish American Literature in the Department of Foreign Languages and Literatures at Oregon State University, in Corvallis, Oregon (1989-1990). The preliminary investigation was done at the University of Texas at Austin, Texas, where I was working as a Fulbright Scholar (1987-1989).

My deepest appreciation to the Latin American Literary Review Press for the publication of this book, and to the National Endowment for the Arts for the financial support which has made it possible.

Translated by Samuel Zimmerman

GARABITO
THE INDOMITABLE

Delfina Collado

Garabito, a distinguished man in his town in the Indian lands, defended his race, scattered in their tragic destiny, with blood, toil and ashes.

Of untamable courage, noble bearing, a gallant air, haughty, impetuous, battlescarred and handsome; with a narrow forehead, prominent cheekbones, small and fierce eyes, straight black hair, a coppertoned burnish in his elastic body, as tense as an arrow about to be shot, made of stone and mountains, he bellowed his dissatisfaction with his lack of freedom.

He, Garabito, wanted no obligations of tithes or *primicias*—the gift of the first fruit to the church—nor did he care to be at the service of the friars and soldiers who arrived with the Conquest.

Faced with the violence of the whites, he had first offered passive, peaceful resistance so that his people could survive as men and not as beasts.

His world was in his land, his home, and in the woman he loved, fragrant with perfumed herbs, in his corn and cacao, the sun, incense, songs and the rain.

His hierarchy and rites helped protect him from uncertainty and change. But now even the Proclamation had reached him, wherein a student of Salamanca, the future governor of Costa Rica, Juan Vazquez de Coronado, advises him that he had begun a legal process against him. It said: "Garabito, the rebel chief, is condemned to death. Make war against him as is the custom with a person who has rebelled."

This edict obliges the chief to become a fugitive. In this condition he fights furiously against the strangers who are trying to take over his lands. His heroic attitude had been made a crime.

When the Spaniard learned that Garabito had taken refuge and sworn vengeance, along with one of his captains he formed a plan to kidnap the chief's adored wife and keep her hostage.

The plan was accepted and the mission was entrusted to Captain Pereira.

Feathers, broken clay pots and a forgotten arquebus. Traces of a fight. His wife, the beautiful and skillful woman, had been captured and taken to the Spanish town.

With his nerves tense, his face contorted with rage, Garabito heard a howling scream of criminal desires of revenge, anger and agony. He ascended the palisade and walked through the town.

He felt a coldness in his heart and in his bones. Again a scream rose from his bowels and was heard throughout the jungle. His wife was not waiting for him within their home.

A new roar of almost insane anguish and jealousy rose from his wounded heart and stirred the sleeping air among the foliage, and awakened the river and the forest.

His heart died within his chest.

Garabito thunders the bitterness of his agony in the midst of the dark valleys. He drinks the chicha fermented in pain, crying out in loneliness. He, who would have liked for the nights to have forty-eight hours in which to make love to his beloved...

He drinks, and drinks, and drinks; in the midst of his suffering and drunkenness he seeks her and calls out:

"My wife, my love for you is like the full moon.

I love you, I cry, I shout, I think and feel for you in my heart.

Woman, you are my narcotic to make me forget so much iniquity, shame and sacrifice.

You cleansed my soul with the waters of love.

My beloved, who makes me forget everything outside when you wrap around me like a liana vine.

My love, life is nothing but ashes in my mouth since you are no longer here.

Now I am only the shadow of my spirit.

Knives of cold silver slash my heart.

I walk among clouds and fog and suffer like the wind and sea.

Ay! woman, who left with the wind."

The chicha runs, the fires go out, the wooden flute is quiet. Garabito keeps on drinking...the memories embroider intricate cloths with the bitterness that paralyzes him.

"Women, why do you leave me alone,

why did you go without me?

Will I no longer hold your hands within mine?

Who will warm me on cold nights?

Treasure of my hidden corner, where are you?
You who gave me dew and honey to drink, who gave me orchids and moonlike sedge, you are no longer here."

His sun: life of his life, flesh of his flesh, subtle and beautiful, with the body of a musk deer, skin like rosy coral, black eyes of shining jade, hair as dark as the black jacaranda, crystalline smile, nightingale in a dream, protection of each other in the shadows, warm sweetness in the corner.
"I feel frozen and cold as water in the canyon.
I am living, although I have already died.
These white human beasts with perverse souls whose claws reach farther than the tigers or the wild boar have taken you from me.
I want to live! Why can't they let us live!"

Black doubts blind him, he has to defend what's his, and he will form his plan of attack.
Raising his hands, he asked the Sun God for infinite strength and power.

Sweat and the blood of suffering beneath a green suspended moon. The knifelike cold of the air cuts the body and rasps the throats of the Indians gathered around the bonfire, united by the same anguish, looking at one another in silent expectation.
An Indian took up his wooden flute, letting the sad music flow... The newly fermented chicha began to pass from drinker to drinker.

Garabito, overcome with nostalgia, continues to lament:
"How much pain without you.
Woman, one can finish off a wounded deer, but no one puts a sick human being out of his misery.
Princess, even the river that sees my suffering is weeping.
Ay beloved wife! A broken jar can be replaced, but a man without his other half suffers the most brutal pain that can exist. Gold can be replaced, but never your heart!
Come back.
My heart and my body lie waiting in desire for your firm young woman's flesh.
Beloved, I gave my heart for your beauty.
You are liquor in my mouth and your hair has the perfume of herbs.
Your arms drive away my loneliness, they are my home."

"Like fermentation in the chicha, like yeast raises up the bread, like the torrents of rushing water rise in winter, like weeds invade the fields, like the parasitic red-flowered vine slowly grows up the trees, like the bones of the living grow, like the hair of the dead grows longer; thus hate, vengeance, the desire to bite and kill grow within me.

I am corn, rootstocks, blood, heart and arrow: I will grab my bow, my courage and mind, and driven by wild sorrow, with a thousand thorns that rip red blood from me, I will not let my lineage end and my loneliness becomes perpetual.

Death. Death is preferable to worthless life without your love."

He would be drenched in laughter when he dealt death to the paleskins and the land became soaked with the blood of those foxes, with their houses, necklace, feathered hats and bells.*

With determination painted on his firm visage, Garabito approached the circle of his men: he directed few words to them, for he had become a lonely sunflower of silence and sadness.

"It is my will to demolish the Spaniards and recover my wife.

Before midnight we will depart, fording the rushing stream to avenge the insult to our race."

The lightning shone strangely and the wind snaked through the forest. In the darkness, under the shadow of the trees in the mountain brush, in the midst of the thickets, among the rocks, dark silhouettes began to slip by. An Indian for each ear of corn waded through the river on a savage night. They are going in search of the town, where the foreigners grow rich, fat, where they rob and kill others.

The military staff of the conquistadors passed the time giving orders. At night under the shed they played cards and drank or tossed and turned in their beds or on the grass, until the first rustles of dawn.

Only a few kept guard.

Thunder rolled, and then another and still more booming and deafening claps of thunder followed. A new thundering, harsher and raging, broke through the night.

Cold knives of rain began to fall on the bodies and planted fields, flooding the earth and making the rivers rise. The owls blinked trem-

---

*Translator's note: The feathers refer to the type of Napoleonic hat that was the fashion at that time, and the bells, to the little bells Spaniards tied to their children's shoes so that they could find them even if they were too young to answer. Also, the Spaniards wore spurs that made a jingling sound.

bling, toads and crickets joined their cries to implacable, fiendish Nature.

Sheets of water and wind fell like a whirlwind onto the underbrush, which became charged with hatred.

The protests of the heavens increased, still more harsh and deafening, obliging the troops to seek refuge while they slipped in the mud and fell, muttering imprecations, prayers, exclamations and curses. The waterspouts ripped the branches off trees and made tattered clothing stick to the skin.

One soldier said to another:

"I thought I saw an Indian go by."

"Idiot. On a night like this."

"Something moved," he insisted.

"What did you see?"

"Moving shapes."

"Come on. You're just afraid."

The storm increased still more. It punished the black, silent earth numb with cold. The conquistadors silenced their talk, prayers, imprecations and curses.

The fury of the untiring tempest drowned out the voices of men and screeching of birds.

The white men moved about in a stupor at the mercy of the elements.

The water rose above the land, passed over the cliffs, and filtered through the wild cherry trees in the forest, along the rocky peaks and river beds.

Wild, untamed water, risen over its banks, swirling with howls, cries and laments in that cross-shaped land.

Dreams and nightmares roar.

The woman sensed the arrival of her man.

Love had guided her life. She could not live without her husband, who shaped her with his love.

On feeling him approach she tried to get up and could not.

Garabito gazed on her copper sweetness, her nude and slim silhouette curled up and sleepless on the ground. On seeing him she revived, lifted her hands and spoke: "Without you, my soul was lonely."

He broke open her shackles violently. Still exhausted, overcome with fatigue, he took her in his arms. His. She was his again.

"My love, my love" is all he could say.

With the agility of a jaguar, and his wife in his arms, he mounted the first horse he could find, carrying an arquebus that he found on the ground.

They must go farther, ever farther, to the loneliest places in the mountains.

The rain fell from all sides, even from below. Man, woman and beast disappeared at the gallop of a heartbeat and went to live in the huts built on the mountain tops, like eagles' nests, in search of freedom and work, under a sentence that was never carried out and a war that in spite of the centuries would be never-ending.

Translated by Virginia Edwards

From: Collado, Delfina. *Tierra Intima.* San José: EDUCA, 1985.

THE INDIAN MUMMY

Delfina Collado

After many years of married life with no children, the old Borucan* woman felt a new life move in her womb. That night, after lighting the incense and praying to her gods, she had a dream.

In the dream she saw her daughter in the stomach of a great anteater. A long procession of ants bearing tiny white flowers led the way for the animal that carried her child within it.

Her offspring would be eternally beautiful and, as endless as the sky, would never die.

The Borucan mother wondered: would her descendent be denied entrance to heaven and its nine stairways with ninety nine steps? And the chorus of sorcerers answered: "Thus it is. Thus it is."

In the yellow glow of the bonfire, beside the golden corn, under the copper flashes of lightning, the little girl was born who was laid on a golden tiger's skin.

The spirit that protected her accompanied her by night in the form of a bat, and by day it was a rose-colored heron which served as her fan.

The Newborn girl was cradled among goblets of cotton and their bone-colored tufts; her hair was brushed with butterfly wings.

When she grew up, the woman who cared for her took her to the river bank, where she amused herself with the arrival of the deer and trilling of the birds; she watched small floating islands carried along by the current, where the mottled serpents travelled as they slept.

Later they taught her to dance the ritual dances and to play the flageolet with its sad holes through which the cane cries. She also learned to sing wonderful and prophetic songs of strange white men who arrived in homes floating on the sea and like the parrots flying above, shed their finery: their shirt, their cape, their hat and shoes.

When she bathed in the stream, the butterflies formed precious garlands, like flying orchids, to adorn her.

*Translator's note: The Borucas, also known as the Bruncas, are Indians who live in Southeastern Costa Rica.

In the afternoons, the young maiden knitted tunics for the priests from feathers of hummingbirds and birds of paradise. Her beauty had increased, and soon thereafter she was taken to the temple as a priestess.

She would never marry. Breasts as small and firm as lemons beat beneath her beautiful clothing of quetzal feathers. She would never grow old.

Everything stayed the same during the first twelve hundred moons. Then, little by little, changes began. She began to fade, to lose her beauty. The freshness of her skin began to tarnish. Her shining eyes began to dim, and the night-like blackness of her hair became dull.

She began to wrinkle, to shrivel up more and more, until she could no longer walk or even stand, or drink, or eat.

Her movements were slower. She no longer sang. Her voice became no more than a murmur. She could not scale the steps of the temple, much less dance; it was an atrocious dwarfism.

She was turning into a dwarf mummy, but she could not die, according to the prophecy.

What did it matter, to die or not to die, if those who came after her would take her place? It is harsh and difficult not to die.

The priestess thought: "Thus it is. Thus it is."

Many moons passed and no one took notice. The Indian, a living mummy, had disappeared. Then it was known that one of the great priests had gathered her up and placed her in a tortoise shell lined with feathers.

Many years later, another priest took her delicately within his fingers, fearing to injure her, and placed her within an inflated anteater bladder which he hung from a beam in the temple.

The priest brought her food no more than once every moon. She did not move, and rarely opened her eyes. Eventually he served her queen bee honey only every twelve moons, using a snail shell.

Night of the full moon in the year of the tapir: The priest remembered the dwarf-Indian-mummy that was in the temple. He went to get the honey and snail shell and, approaching the bladder, opened it: There was no longer anything inside. Only an air bubble came out.

The chorus of sorcerers said, then the echo repeated: "Thus it is, thus it is."

Translated by Virginia Edwards

From: Collado, Delfina. *Tierra Oscura*. San José: EDUCA, 1985.

RAMONA,
WOMAN OF THE EMBER

Carmen Lyra

> Do you understand, do you under-
> stand, sir, what these words mean:
> "to have nowhere to go." No? You
> still do not understand this!
>
> *Crime and Punishment*
> F. Dostoevsky

She was called Ramona, like many of those village women you often find along the road—overworked and humble as they complete daily chores—her limp hair gathered up in any old way, in a hurry. She's shod in twisted, unfashionable shoes, which merely cover her feet; the toes are turned upward as if praying with resignation to God. Ramona, a good name for a stone on the street! There was no time for the mothers of the village to read novels, not even romances, and they gave their children the name of the saint of the day they were born, and rarely did they get it into their heads to decide between Juliet or Roxanne, Marco Tulio or Roland. Their spontaneous, obscure reasoning advised them to give the children the sturdy, simple or foolish names that filled the calendar, the names of martyrs who endure injustices. Most likely, these women suffer through an existence similar to those holy ones, although no one will ever canonize them; even if, upon digging them up, it were discovered that death had respected their bodies more than life did. Their image surrounded by a halo will never appear on any altar.

Anyhow, this creature was called Ramona and she was one of the many heroic shadows that pass through life enduring almost in silence the weight of Holy Poverty, that frugal, hypocritical old woman with bones and cloak of lead. No one knows how she could have found favor in the eyes of St. Francis of Assisi.

For Ramona it had already been fifteen years of marriage and ten childbirths, which had turned her into a faded and wrung-out creature. Maternity had squeezed from her body its youthful charm and form; now all that was distilled into those eight little human pitchers, into her eight children, the oldest, thirteen. The only thing the miserable woman had left was her courage.

She got up before dawn in order to cope with the hustling that ten bodies demand and to carry out the task of washing and ironing other people's clothes. So many nights she did not know what it was to lay her head on the pillow, because she was rolling cigarettes on commission or selflessly ironing. All that, regardless of the times her legs were as swollen as banana stems. There was nothing else she could do, because that idiot husband of hers was lazy and indolent and was incapable of going forth with similar resolve.

Yes, he always slept the nights away, from curfew in the neighborhood until the whistle at the Atlantic station blew at six a.m.

But her husband did not take into account his woman's sacrifices; and although he was unable to work as he should, given the eight mouths always ready to gobble up food, he certainly had strength to insult his woman at every opportunity and even to abuse her if it struck his fancy. And on top of all this, the mother-in-law, good God!, who couldn't even see the writing on the wall, because she believed that her son had descended from the throne of the Most High to the deep abyss where Ramona had been born, just to marry her. If you only knew about the wicked cunning the old so-and-so used to wheedle her son! She was always cat-fighting with her other daughter-in-law, who was really a lady, of the same class as them all, if not a little bit higher.

And this life of work and torment, along with a certain nervous irritation due to the numerous childbirths, had wound up embittering Ramona's character. It took effort now to speak gently to the children; she shouted threats at them over nothing and beat them for no reason. The older ones held a grudge about it, declared themselves her enemies and when she punished them, they threatened to go and live with grandma. They were drawn to the grandmother because she made a good living. They never went hungry there, and their aunt, the daughter-in-law, a woman to whom God had not given children, spoiled them. This always infuriated Ramona.

Oh, that old thief and that other useless woman who'd been married for nine years without knowing what it is to bring a child into the world! All she could do was try to steal someone else's!

Every lunch and dinner hour was stormy: her man shouting, she herself crying while hysteria convulsed her, the little ones screaming and fleeing like little chickens.

He had said good riddance to her many times:

"Get out, get out of here. You're unnecessary. The little ones will be better off with my mama and with Lola than with you. We don't need you here."

"Okay, all right, it's better to split!"

This is no way to live, and a bad example for the children, she thought. Let them be taken away, let them abandon her! She knew how to work, it could be arranged!

And she went outside, screaming. The children watched her in terror and not even little Pedrillo, who was the most attached to her, nor Juancito, the youngest, who always hung on her like an earring, wanted to come near her. They watched her from a distance as if she were a stranger.

When she calmed down, she went back into the house and found everything in chaos. Her husband was loading the heaviest objects in a huge crate: the table, the dresser, the four chairs, the children's beds, their double bed. The bed where her ten children had been born!

How lucky the two dead children were! Look what they had escaped! The lucky ones!

The children were carrying out the smaller things. She went to the door to watch them leave. None of them said good-bye. They went away one behind the other; they looked like a little row of ants: some with the paintings of the saints, others with bundles on their heads. Even Juancito carried something: the tin-plated candlestick, with a stump of candle still stuck in it. The candle that last night had illuminated her final vigil at the children's bedside.

They walked slowly with their burdens because Juan—clinging to Maria, who was the oldest daughter—couldn't walk any faster.

Pedro was at the front of the troop, and his little red head bobbed like a flame that was lighting the way.

"Pedro, Pedrito!" screamed Ramona.

Pedro stopped and wanted to go back, but Nicholas, the oldest, pinched him and the little boy took off running and disappeared.

"Nicholas, Nicholas!" yelled his mother. The boy did not even turn his head, and he hurriedly crossed the street, because he was already worried about appearances and he didn't want people to see him leading this bunch of brats.

"Juancito, Juancito, my little one!"

The little boy started crying pitifully and didn't want to walk. Maria dragged him along; and Ramona could see the dirty little face turned toward her until they crossed the street.

She entered the house with her head in her hands. Her husband went out with a few last tools. He said ironically,

"I'm leaving you with what you had the day we got married."

The house was empty. She'd had nothing the day they got married.

She was so poor! And her youth and her vitality had been tangled up in the thorns along the way.

Night fell. The rooms filled with silence and shadows.

Ramona went into the kitchen and sank onto a stone left in the corner. The only living thing around her was an ember that glowed among the ashes in the hearth. The poor woman's glance clung anxiously to that feeble light and her spirit stretched out, like an animal wounded by the cold, toward that little lump of heat that burned in the darkness.

A whirlwind spun in her head. She was a tree, the wind had blown off all her leaves, which danced dizzily around her. Her teeth chattered.

How cold it was, my Lord, Jesus Christ!

Somewhere—where?—a row of children's heads....

One had red hair and looked like a little torch. That was the one that was closest to her, among the ashes.

In the silence, eight pairs of little feet pattered as they walked over the pavement.

But wasn't the pavement inside her, within her heart?

The ember snuffed itself out among the ashes.

Translated by Marinell James

From: Correas de Zapata, Celia and Lygia Johnson. *Detras de la reja.* Caracas: Monte Avila Editores, C.A., 1980.

ESTEFANIA

Carmen Lyra

On the endless, deserted beach that runs from the Tortuguero to the Colorado sandbar, we found the rough wooden cross, once black, now almost completely bleached and faded. Along the length of the cross-beam, a name, and perhaps the first letter of a surname which will soon be completely illegible. Estefania R. Perhaps Rojas, perhaps Ramírez or Ramos.

You can travel many miles without finding anything that breaks the monotony of that landscape: the sea and sky to the right, the sand of the beach in front and to the left the vegetation of cocoa-plums, almond trees and palms. Suddenly, there's the blackened cross stuck in the sand, the arms extended before the blue vastness. The sea had carried it that far.

Estefania R....

What had the woman with that name been like?

And a row of feminine silhouettes like the ones found on the beaches or on the banana plantations began to march by through the imagination: pale figures, withered, burned by the sun, fevers and man's sensuality, amoral and innocent as animals. There is one who stands out from the suffering frieze: could she be Estefania? The name has been erased from memory. Her face is a dark triangle within a commotion of black hair; sclerotic, and with very white teeth, naked feet, strong and wrinkled, very long arms.

How did she arrive at the banana plantations from the lowlands of Reventazon and Parismina? Life brought her rolling along from the Guanacaste. I think that in Santa Cruz, the judge who later became an honorable magistrate in the Court of Justice gave her a little boy-child when she had scarcely entered adolescence. Of course, afterward the esteemed gentleman never remembered the insignificant affair. She left the child at the next well-off household and began wandering around. Then another man, she didn't remember his name very well, left her pregnant and she continued wandering, wandering. A girl was born. The woman was like those bits of wood that you see in river currents. Life deposited her, baby girl and all, on a banana plantation near the

Atlantic. And in this way she went on from plantation to plantation, today with one man, tomorrow with another, until the poor thing even found herself with the mestizo owner of a commissary, and the baby girl always stuck to her like fungus on a broken branch.

One occasion she took up with a Honduran and she went with him to a plantation where they admitted only single men. She was the only woman there. One night all the laborers got together and stormed the Honduran's house to take away his woman. They stabbed him and did what they pleased with her. No one knows why they didn't get rid of the little girl, who at that time would have been about three.

On the plantation where I met her, the woman was the cook, faithful as a dog to the owner's son. The boy was handsome and kind and she would have killed for him. The boy came every month to the ranch to inspect the crops and these visits made the woman as blissful as a saint is at the visits of an angel descending from heaven. For his sake she endured the drunken binges of the plantation foreman, who beat her as well as her daughter and her little dog; and for him, she did not allow one cent to be lost at the commissary, nor allow a single egg to vanish, nor allow a stick of firewood to be carried off.

Meanwhile, in the city, the plantation's profits enabled father and son to be members of the Union Club; enabled the wife, who had bunions and callouses, to remain in her car; and enabled the daughter to dress in the latest fashions and go each year to Europe and the United States to bring back dresses and lingerie that caused envy in her best friends' hearts.

The woman served there several years, but when she fell ill with malaria, no one did anything for her. She had to take her daughter and her belongings and go to the Saint John of God Hospital. Who knows what she did with the little girl...because I don't think that in a charity hospital they would admit her with a little child and everything. And the good young son of the plantation owner, in the city, did not even remember his poor, sick servant. As regards the wife with bunions and her distinguished daughter, they were unaware of the very existence of that woman who stayed awake so that on the plantation they wouldn't lose an egg, or even one cent. These vigils had humbly contributed to the purchase of a car, to trips abroad and to the daughter's fine lingerie.

I saw the woman for the last time upon her return from the hospital, on one of the trains on the branch lines that go out from Siquirres, in a car full of black men who guffawed and black women dressed in flashy colors, who shrieked with smooth voices like Nicaraguan parrots. She always had the little girl stuck to her, the child now wrinkled like an old woman, and so serious, one wondered if laughter had ever played on her lips. It grieved me to see this little girl whose eyes were hard as pebbles and with a mouth so dry it made me think of land where it has never rained. The mother travelled dressed in blue and the child, in yellow, in glittering fabric. Why had they put on these showy clothes? Within these clothes the sadness of their lives acquired a painful absurdity.

Who would have guessed that the woman had barely turned twenty-five? She was so skinny that it looked like she was sucking her cheeks in. On her skin, which was a greenish-black, sclerosis shone a sinister yellow; and at her cheeks, shoulders and elbows, the bones almost broke through her skin. When she spoke she made a grimace that revealed discolored gums. Weakness had yanked out those white, beautiful teeth with the same indifference with which a hand plucks a daisy.

When we arrived at the station, she descended laboriously, supported by her daughter, and disappeared into a group of people that had awaited the arrival of the train. From there she went to seek a place with the other passengers on one of the mule-drawn platform cars that run along the network of lines furrowing the plantation, and transports the fruit. Where was she headed? She sat down with her little daughter among piles of sacks and huge boxes. It was obvious that she had trouble breathing. It's not surprising she was tubercular.

The mule-driver cracked the whip and the mule began to trot, pulling the car behind it along the rails. At the back of the narrow line along which the car ran, the living stain formed by the clothes of mother and daughter trembled, and was plunged once again among the banana plantations.

From which humble cemetery among those villages of Linea did the flood of a river or the waves of the ocean tear away the lowly cross?

Estefania R....

One of so many women who have passed through the banana plantations.

Behind us the cross remained, sowed in the sand, its arms opened toward the vastness of the sea. Above it, twilight was beginning to fall.

Translated by Marinell James

From: Lyra, Carmen. "Bananos y hombres." *Repertorio Latinoamericano*. San José, 1931.

ALCESTIS

Emilia Macaya

"Apollo: The Fates agreed to release Admetus from the hard trance of death that was threatening him if in his place I could bring another dead man to hell.... No one wanted to die in his place except for his wife, Alcestis...."

(Euripides, *Alcestis*.)

I never thought I could do it. It's more than that. I never felt capable of it. Too many years of thinking but not acting in order not to notice things too much. Or seeing but not acting. Perhaps I didn't dare to look completely. You force your life to remain in *chiaroscuro*. Until one day more light from the story filters to you. Or someone filters it to you. It's a fight between your conscience and your courage. Or rather between conscience and the lack of courage. In spite of not being a man, you have sufficient intelligence to see with clarity. But you can't act. Yes, maybe I'm one of those incomplete women—Will I finally convince myself that he's right?—I have a head but not a will to act. To be a complete woman it's not enough to realize that Western civilization keeps a foot 30 centuries long upon your neck. You also have to act, reject, rebel, be a target, and be ready for them to destroy you. You are strange, hormoneless, inhibited, frustrated, frigid, insatiable, a nymphomaniac...and who knows what else. But no, you attend the university, you study with the enthusiasm so characteristic of a woman who studies—We fight to the last—until the apparent man of your dreams crosses your path, when you are most vulnerable.

At first it's a matter of flattery. Of the most intelligent sort, the one who fulfills all aspirations, an intellectual, the one with whom you can hold interesting conversations, be independent, capable of working and being useful. Because he is a man of ample intellect and rejects absurd forms of dominance, wants a companion and not a slave, respects the incorporation of women into the labor force—in this country we're underdeveloped, we don't need worse things—so you marry. Then everything turns upside down. The woman who was known and supposedly loved for what she was, now turns out to be a monster of intellectuality, of self-sufficiency, who must be changed and compared to feminine ideals, surfacing now as if in an alchemist's stone, each time it's necessary to put you down. So you begin to die every day. Or better said, the endless task of your annihilation begins. Fatal vengeance when you've been considered a threat to the integrity of the man of dignity, a sin for which you have to suffer until one day you fall dead from fatigue in the middle of the road. That day he'll pick you up, place his hand on your forehead, look at you with redeeming eyes and—miracle of miracles—you'll be reborn as someone else. From that moment on, you'll have to dedicate yourself with a radiant and doll-like face to serving his friends, to appearing impeccably dressed at parties, weddings, wakes and baptisms. What a good living Mr. So-and-So must make, look at his wife—doesn't she look like a model out of a magazine—to keep dinner and bed ready, warm, and tasty for him, to nurse his illnesses while hiding yours, to keep his house looking like an illustration and his children looking exquisite. This, yes, without leaving work, because your salary has become indispensable, and, indeed, it you've studied and you're a professional, it should be for something, we don't need worse things! If, on the contrary, you are not able to change, if you're bent on keeping yourself dangerously whole, you'll find that each day they'll cover your forehead with ashes—Beware! This woman is condemned—They'll give you a free kick in the behind and order you to atone, second by second, for the terrible sin of your irresponsible foolishness. And what was my first penitence? I remember it well. More than that. I will never forget it. Because it's a matter of wounding where it hurts the most, in a place where the wound is most easily made, so that it will be ready for the moment when it's time to add a little more salt.

We were going to have our first child. I announced this to him with the tender naivete of a 20-year old. This child is not mine—he answered. It couldn't be mine. He continued eating his soup with absolute impassiveness.

I'll never forget it.

It was then I began to die.

After that my job went—Sure, here you are, surrounded by men, which is what he likes. You make up your face for a couple of hours; you dress to provoke them, and the old goats flatter you thinking you're so great. A bunch of sissies! And what's more, lazy bums.... Reality began to sketch itself so sharply that it became impossible not to see it. I was becoming aware of the inexorable process of extermination carried out by him while I—who had been until that moment the happy 20-year old, the mother full of illusions, the professional who was productive and appreciated at her job—was to end up converting myself, already at the lowest of levels, into the supreme negation—a mannish woman! I even put on a tie yesterday. A tie and a tie pin, if that weren't enough.... They exterminate your sex, your body, your soul, you convert yourself into that degraded being that constitutes the tiresome burden of poor Mr. So-and-So—What an unjust world, with him so good, and that disgrace of a woman that became his lot—to remain crossed out, blotted out, and finally substituted by those "whole" and "perfect," those you should have been and could never be.

"Did you notice Estelle? Did you see how she sat on Ferdinand's lap? There is a loving wife, unlike you. It should have made you feel ashamed."

Ferdinand, that dear friend, the one I ran into one night with his secretary in the village hotel, where I was sent on business and while Estelle was travelling in Europe.

"Did you notice how lovingly Eugenie prepared a plate for Luis during dinner?"

Eugenie, I know you haven't forgotten how I found you in Adolph's arms that time I didn't feel well and went up to look for an aspirin in your bedroom.

"And Carmen, how affectionately she spooned the dessert into Rodrigo's mouth?"

Carmen...the one who so often used to put God knows what else in her mouth.

Have I ever been unfaithful? No. Not once. Though I didn't lack opportunities or the desire. And I've asked myself many times why I didn't take advantage of them, since love, naturally, would have played a very little role in all of this. The reason may be several related things. Cowardice in the face of censure by others, apprehension for the children, fear in the face of risk. What do I know? As I said, it was a little of everything. You can't deny that society puts pressure on you. The fear of censure and rejection is immense. Because you've heard it so often, you've probably begun to believe, without meaning to, that that which is a light slip for the man when it comes to us constitutes authentic prostitution.

Moreover, even if you're ready to dispense with etiquette, you always worry they'd call you bad names in front of your children. The power of men! They convince us from childhood of our maternal saintliness. Your mother is always a perfect being, with an angelic halo. And this is exactly how you want your children to see you, to repeat history from one century to the next. We know that even career women possess maternal vanity. You try to be honest, to not betray yourself or others. You defend or pretend to defend this thing called morality. You'd even sacrifice yourself for a very high principle—

doubtful in most cases—even though your mental and physical health end up destroyed. And the truth is, considering all of this very pragmatically, is there perhaps some guarantee that the lover will be different? He'll be able to dissimulate a little longer because you won't see him as often or as regularly, although sooner or later the truth will come out when you least expect it. However, yes, I must confess that I did once think about playing around just for revenge. But I was so tired, so fed up with existence, that I believe I didn't have the strength. Or perhaps all those values of our beloved and notable Western culture acted up in me. Who knows? Finally, the only thing I'm sure of now is that I've talked a great deal, and I'm feeling quite better. To the point when I'm ready to joke. I never thought I could do it. More than that, I never felt capable of it. I'm amazed to see how today I've had the courage to open my mouth. Perhaps because the light is so dim, doctor, and I find this couch of yours so comfortable....

Translated by Sabina Lask-Spinac

From: Macaya, Emilia. *La sombra en el espejo*. San José: Editorial Costa Rica, 1986.

EVA

Emilia Macaya

"This premonition of an early death influenced
in a decisive way the spin which Eva Peron
imparted to her existence.... Her conduct was
less gentle, her sentiments fuller, her actions
intensified, and her passion profounder."

(Alfonso Crespo. *Eva Peron Alive or Dead.*)

An acrid medicinal odor permeated the humid passage. The floor
boards, already loose from so much hustle and bustle, emitted sad
sounds each time a footstep managed to crush them anew. To the
outside world the small yellow facade showed no distinctive features
other than a red light whose appearance managed to create, thanks to
the dust particles suspended in the air, a curtain of the same intense
color. Thanks to it, two worlds were kept separate: the dark interior of
the house, and the narrow brightness of the sidewalk, illuminated
weakly by the neon light and the red-hot cigarette ash on the lips of the
still undecided clients. Inside the entrance, along the sides, the place
was filled with rooms whose doors, closed or half-open, depending on
what was happening, were linked like cells and led to a living room of
average size, a corner bar, fairly well stocked, and a jukebox, forever
repeating the whining notes of "Gardenia Perfume." Several couples, in
close embraces, were dancing, bending their bodies in such a way that
the law of gravity imposed a search for a bed.

A woman in a tight-fitting dress, with burning eyes and a voluptuous body, advanced through the street until she reached the door;
reluctantly she greeted the men leaning against the wall and entered the
house. Upon her entrance, a rain of reddish particles, arising from the
luminous curtain, darkened her crimson skin. Under Rosa's feet the
floor boards trembled again. She looked around for a chair in the room
crowded with dancers, sat in it heavily, and asked the bartender for
something strong. The doctor's words, along with the jukebox's sounds,
echoed in her ears:

—Nothing can be done. It's a matter of three months, maybe six, if we're lucky.

It seemed absurd that a small delay in the hour of death could be called lucky. An empty anguish rose sourly from her stomach to her throat, cutting her saliva, swiftly followed by the ascent to her head of a heavy cloud of inevitable memories oppressing her temples: the child-hood surrounded by manual laborers; the delicate beauty which surfaced before its time and in an unusual way in those places accustomed to plumpness and reddishness; the love of Luis Antonio; the unwanted child and the terror before the parents—place a sharp-pointed stick against you and pierce until it hurts, until you bleed—the secret ready to be uncovered by the uncontrollable hemorrhaging; the trip to the city. Afterwards, everything became a whirlwind: withered beds, violently urgent men, venereal diseases cured and contracted again, repeated abortions on the midwife's cold and bitter table. If only she had let the baby live....But the fear returned, Luis' stare of accusation, the difficult solution. She closed her eyes and tried to let herself be carried away by the music.

"Your body is perfumed with gardenias...."

A hefty man, smelling of rancid sweat and pent-up sex, grabbed her to lead her to the center of the living room. Rosa, vanquished in his arms, began to rock her body with growing abandon at each new movement; as the dance progressed she appeared more as booty than a complete human being, trapped as she was against the chest of her incidental companion.

When the music stopped, the two headed toward the bedroom, and, on the way, certain murmurs in one of the rooms captured her attention. It wasn't the first time she had heard such sounds. While the brutishy couple, lunging and lurching, gave free rein to their needs, Rosa, her ear attuned, tried to transform the whispers into compre-hensible sounds. She remembered having seen those mulatto men many times, with their bags and suitcases even more suspicious now, especially upon noticing that they never had solicited female company, only drinks, pencils, paper, or some food left over from the previous day. On another occasion, she had accidentally opened a door and stumbled upon a web of maps and strange drawings lying on the floor. The young men must have protested because José, the bartender, reprimanded her nervously, and the room was never again left un-locked, whether its occupants were in it or not. Something important must have been happening between those four walls. And as the evidence grew with time and inquiries, Rosa became all ears whenever the mysterious clients came through the door. Using whispers, silent gestures, and promises of absolute secrecy, even more details were obtained. Two of them, foreigners, had crossed the border illegally, led by a doctor engaged in the battle after leaving the hospital for life in the mountains; the police, it seemed, were on his trail; there was a matter of robberies or kidnappings—the versions kept changing—someone managed to involve the group in the planting of a bomb in the embassy a few days earlier. Quite an interesting life those guys led!

Since the meeting room shared a wall with a bathroom closed in the last health inspection, Rosa had a stupendous site to find out major things. Sitting on the tank of the broken toilet, among the vapors of the urinal, her forehead leaning against the boards through whose joints was filtered the essence of the conversations, she heard unknown words, fulfilled senses until then ignored, which, in the mouths of the men, were transformed into magical possibilities greater than whatever she had experienced up to that moment.

By accident or providence, a kick to the chamber pot led to her discovery during one of those sessions; and no more than two seconds passed before four voices, embodied in very concrete faces, appeared in the doorway to the hideout. Who is there, where did she come from, what should we do with her? She knows too much, she'll expose us. Only José, who had jumped across the bar as soon as he had heard the tumult in the bathroom, was able to calm the anger with his explanation.

—She's a good girl. I'm sure she was there only by accident.

The bartender must have had a great deal of influence, for thanks to his intervention, the relative initial tolerance toward Rosa soon turned into full acceptance by the group. She then got the job of copying the map's routes for everyone; later, because of her non-suspicious appearance, she was sent to get a good supply of tacks, nails, staples, and nuts; another time they ordered her to obtain photographs of a certain public building situated downtown. Her sick body and the burden of those lowly beings she had to tolerate every night were lightened the day's labor. She barely slept a few hours. With genuine fervor, she listened to the discussions about revolution, liberty, and brotherhood, while she went around depositing nails and glass shards into their assigned containers. In the midst of such feverish activity, the prognosis she had been given three months earlier became but a weak echo in the depths of her mind. There was no time to think since there was so much to do in this world. Her personal anguish became nothing, immersed in the scream of the entire human race.

The increase in her companions' habitual anxiety had to be great for Rosa to finally notice it, absorbed as she was in her devotion to her duties. No doubt, by the signs, what was being prepared was special. The operation, which called for a deep foray into enemy territory, raised the risks to their maximum level. On the maps it was possible to see a bridge, long like a sleeping alligator, and three explosives marked in red, distributed in strategic places along the immense length of the animal. The whole thing would have to be blown into a thousand pieces—she thought—before the alligator and its guards awoke. The passion with which she participated in the planning raised the possibility of her inclusion in the operation. Finally, during one of the meetings, the doctor pointed and turned to her, saying:

—You'll be in charge of keeping watch.

As if it were a matter of preparing herself adequately, Rosa exchanged her nightly work for a rest, which was already overdue; from then on, she was only occasionally seen with a client, to avoid all possible suspicion at such a sudden absence. Yet even at those inevitable moments, imposed on her by the demands of her disguise, she acted distant, transfigured, as if living in another world, untouched by the music, the alcoholic stench, or her companion's clumsy words of love.

Fortunately, the designated day soon arrived, as Rosa's stomach filled with so many butterflies that she appeared to tremble along with her secret. At the crack of dawn they arrived at the place and immediately began to discharge their duties. The men ran from place to place like insects about to disturb the grayish sleeping monster. Some, attaching themselves to the railing with one hand by way of minimal support, swung their bodies in space. Others cleared the undergrowth of weeds at the other end in order to uncover the base of the structure. From her place behind an improvised wall of stones, Rosa kept vigil over every visible patch of the road: The little whitish strip rose up from the valley, zigzagged through the mountains, got lost for a few feet, and finally died away in the mouth of the silvery structure.

When everything was ready, everyone returned to his place of hiding. Spaced out and submerged in the thick vegetation or sea of rocks along the sides, they were united only by the minute synchronized upon their wrists. They all looked at their watches almost at the same instant. At that moment, Rosa, the only one able to cover the entire view, observed something like a woman and a child appearing at the other end of the bridge and beginning to slowly cross it. A ray of light penetrated her eyes in a strange way until it hurt her brain. The doctor's words began to echo again with anguish. From the wall she watched her own body running across the structure, slowly, stopping at each moment, decomposing itself into a thousand small undulations, dilating in leaps, expanding each advancing step as if pretending to reach the infinite. During the ascent, the picture of the dance hall with its interlaced couples stayed fixed like a star in her hand. Through the right foot, as it rose, were filtered the music and the voice of Luis Antonio saying no, no to the child, no to her, no to the hemorrhage, no to her father, the other arm began a new ascent, copied the maps, don't forget to mark the X's in their right places, head bent backwards, what noise from the city, so many men in one night, this liquor is making me nauseated, the other one smelled so bad what damp disgust how much blood is coming out and more blood without stopping the bus runs without stopping your body has the perfume of a woman I probably opened a hole in her head the poor little one I didn't know I would be a heap of tacks and nails that soaked sheet the brute goes away and doesn't realize red light thousands of red lights red sky everything red lights and sparks popping out of lights and sparks red everything red going up up up....

Translated by Sabina Lask-Spinac

From: Macaya, Emilia. *La sombra en el espejo*. San José: Editorial Costa Rica, 1986.

ANDRÉS CEJUDO, READER

Rosibel Morera

It was one of those nights on which Lázaro Fuentes, the poet, would go for a walk and would lose himself in places where family and friends would not find him. As he entered the Harbor Café, his most faithful reader was about to take the floor. The sharp "memory" of what this reader was going to say came from a certain book of Lázaro's which dealt with the subject of reincarnation. Lázaro did not discover this until later. Evidently they did not know each other.

When he related this extraordinary event to me, I had to tell him that this kind of character harmonized very well with the kind of material Lázaro wrote. "It's just like you," I told him.

I still wonder if he lied or told the truth, or if it was just a short story that he was too lazy to write down and preferred to deliver orally at my home, hidden behind the steam of a cup of coffee.

*   *   *

I came across Andrés Cejudo (that's what he said his name was) in a bar, café, soda fountain, dockside restaurant, whose doors never closed, according to the information presented on its street posters. It must have been close to ten o'clock at night when he defined his memory as the succession of several remembered lives. He claimed he knew about four of his births.

"I had slept very late," he said, "something I don't do very often because at the time I wake up I have very unpleasant sensations, at times even a headache, and always because I am not unaware that the sun feeds consciousness in those who are awake and the unconscious in those who are asleep. I arose with great difficulty. The sound of dead leaves in my head had never been so strong. Two entire lives came to me. It was myself, you see, but a strange self that I myself had forgotten."

He spoke with great parsimony, concentrating as though he were telling the truth. I questioned him, concealing the duplicity of irony.

"If I'm not too indiscreet, could you tell us something about those memories, tell us who you are, who you have been? We would like to know if there is some meaning to existence. The succession of bodies visited by the soul does not resolve much of the mystery of being alive. Could you, being the traveler from world to world that you say you are, explain to us if becoming incarnate here today and there tomorrow adds a different sense to existence? Or if remembering it—if there is some order to it, or a plan at least—adds anything. Or if it is just chance alone that brings us to one place or another, if, as you affirm, we actually are brought...?"

"That is a very interesting question, doctor. Don't think I don't know you all take me for a charlatan. But who is not, doctor? Who, whenever he opens his mouth to say something, anything at all, in principle, does not run the risk of passing for an idiot?"

We laughed. He was witty. He apparently knew what he was talking about. I took a chance on a promising conversation. It was cold outside.

"The first thing I saw was a woman: My sister. And faces superimposed on hers, or rather, contemporaneous with hers. Although time does not exist there, you see, in the sense that there is no succession, everything is simultaneous. I had a sensation of detachment, of distance, as though nothing belonged to us, or better yet, as though everything belonged to us and we could suddenly be the parents and children of everyone."

He laughed. He showed his grimy teeth which were tobacco-blackened. I thought about his lungs. They must have been just like his teeth: phlegmy and filthy. He salivated a bit and continued.

"As a youth I was what is called a religious fanatic. I had the enormous vanity of believing I was one of the chosen. I followed one single line in my reading and in my opinions, in my absolute truths. I had several rules. I would always get around them whenever I could. For the saint, everything is holy. You know, the old excuse. Later I would fall into the temptation of depression, that black water of consciousness, and I would think of myself as an absolute nobody. From pride to humiliation there is but one step. You see?"

He spoke for close to fifteen minutes without interruption. We uttered no sounds save those indispensable to encouraging him.

"I clearly recall, as one example, doctor, having been a suicide, as well as my previous incarnation in a deformed body. Does this frighten you? To all the consciousness already weighing on me I added the shame of being ugly, lame, cross-eyed and bow-legged. If anyone were to search for a proof of reincarnation, gentlemen, he would have to seek it in that timidity felt by a deformed creature. In some way the feeling persists that it is itself to blame, that God has directed His wrath toward it for good reason."

Until then he had said nothing I did not already know. In order to write *Resurrections*, I had had to study the subject, even suicide. Now, however, for the first time, I knew someone who claimed that he remembered his previous lives. Naturally, I did not believe him, you understand; it was his ability to weave falsehoods that fascinated me. His bad habit was a quality of inestimable value in literature.

"I attended the school for exceptional children. They provided rehabilitation and some manual skills. And there was reading, writing, general preparation. Mother, that is, my sister, would wait at the entrance to the house for my return. Father was a young man, good looking, whom I would occasionally see pass by across the street from the house or standing on the corner. We had never spoken. One day he decided to change sidewalks and provoke an encounter."

"We continued to see each other. He oscillated between acting like a father to me and behaving like a not-very-close-friend who had assumed certain kinds of responsibilities. He soon revealed to me that he was my father. He spoke with mother. He asked to be a part of my life. He argued that I had to be well prepared for the time they might die. At that time mother already knew that dying is not something that happens only to 'others.' 'He'll be able to take jobs without leaving the house,' father explained. They argued, but he won. I studied accounting. I earned good money..."

"That old mansion is still there. After 'remembering,' I visited it several times. It is completely overgrown with weeds and grass. Within three months the State will be able to claim it. In this country fifty years must pass before the State can expropriate real estate not left to heirs. If I say anything more you will take me for a fake."

The sudden transition brought us back to the Café. We begged him to continue, subtly assuring him we were prepared to put up with any exaggeration on his part. Any at all.

He laughed, and looked at us out of the corner of his eye. He lit an unfiltered cigarette. The flame made him look like the stereotype of an old salt, a sea dog, with a worn pipe deforming his lips. I left the question of his possible incarnation as a sailor for later. No liar would forego the chance to extemporize an adventure story, I thought.

For the first time I noticed his clothing. It smelled of old rags, of rot caused by drops of water falling over and over on an infrequently washed article of clothing. I carefully noted his unsmiling rotten teeth. His thick eyebrows, his eye, terrible when he leaned over, always on the same side, to look at something. A man prematurely aged by alcohol.

I screwed up the courage to ask, "And who are you, where do you come from?"

For someone who said he came from here and there, who gave as a frame of reference so many places, so many people, and always the same loves, my question was proper: Who was this man who hid behind that supposed, and so skillfully defended, wandering?

"One of my names is Andrés," he said, sucking on his teeth. "Andrés Cejudo, the son of Carlos and Ana Cejudo."

Now, a writer—always in search of different twists, always easily impressed—is greedy for subject matter. But never until that day did this greed make me feel so ridiculous. The spinner of yarns was a fraud! He was not weaving his own stories, but mine, already published in a book. Reincarnations! Andrés, Carlos Cejudo, Ana... I admired his cleverness at inventing details and his histrionic capacity for identifying with the characters. I meditated for some seconds on how to unmask him. "You faker," I thought. "Faker! Robber of other people's stories, thief!..."

But I still had one doubt. What if everything he said was the truth? Had he stolen my stories, or had I stolen his life? He returned from the terrible shadows which had smothered him for some seconds.

"My sister and I had loved each other very much, you see. Very much. This time everything was different. We won."

He smiled. He paused for a long while. Someone bought him a drink, offered him a cigarette. One man, perspiring profusely, asked for a glass of cold water. The night had reached its zenith. He left before that. He said he did not want to enter his house backwards, nor did he want the ghosts of the night to follow him in.

"If you find yourself on the street at midnight, doctor," he said, staggering, "turn around and greet the spirits, lest they stick to your body and want to come in. Go in backwards. That's what the witches teach."

I pardoned him or, perhaps on the contrary, I was pardoned. "Andrés Cejudo" was a terminal character, like the old sea dog: a character on his way to extinction. I bade him a literary farewell.

*   *   *

Before leaving, Lázaro wrote a message for his companions:

His entire story is false. According to my studies, one becomes incarnate no less than three times, but not more than seven in the same sex. Furthermore he was never named Andrés Cejudo. I knew the real Andrés Cejudo.

I asked him why he had written the statement instead of saying it.

"He was an extremely inventive speculator of subterfuges for avoiding death," he said, "of suppositions either true or false, imagined by me or by him. I didn't want to take away his credibility, his authorship, to his face, or to go into detailed explanations. The old fellow was a good character...."

Lázaro was too. It's astonishing how someone can lie so.

Translated by Clark M. Zlotchew

From: Morera, Rosibel. *Las resurrecciones y reencarnaciones de Lázaro Fuentes*. Heredia, CR: Departamento de Publicaciones de la Universidad Nacional, 1988.

LAURA

Rosibel Morera

She reacted only to punishment: then she would come out of her self-absorption to re-enter the real world. "You hit me," he would hear her complain, her resentful little face set in a pout. He would then recover from his fit of rancor, to say nice things to her, to listen to her plan impossible marriages and even to captivate her with some kind of love game. She was his sweet thing, his little pet, a part of himself. A little creature of nature that knew how to track him down in space and in time.

He saw her coming, her eyes flashing, stopping every few paces, lost, tormented. He would have to strike her. He was annoyed. Hadn't they spoken all afternoon yesterday beneath the trees, the big trees, the ones by the river? Then, why was she going around today as though she were in heat, as though she were jealous of everything, as though she were angry with the world, only fearing that he would be snatched away from the privileged position in which she kept him among all her things? He felt put upon. He felt like swatting the golden hornet that continually buzzed around his head. He kicked a stone.

She spotted him. She walked toward him. He began to walk off hurriedly, taking evasive action among the trees, the stones and the high grass. He headed for the mill. She followed him along the path. Furious, he picked up speed as he went through the thicket, leaving clumps of hair on the branches.

They kept an eye on each other, he in the brush, she on the path. She would stop to look when he did, but her little face had a look of embarrassment on it, her hands were clutching each other as though she were in anguish, as though she were asking a question, as though she were begging. Obsessed, older than anyone, aged by much love, hidden inside her own head, watching the air so that no one who might know how to read it could listen to the very secret voices that tell her that he belongs to her even though he does not understand this.

Almost on purpose, impelled by an irresistible wickedness, he walked as though he were following someone's trail, getting closer and closer to the danger, looking out of the corner of his eye to see if he was being followed. He climbed up to the shed. He walked along the plank that was used to throw hay into the barges. He stopped at the end. He maintained a dangerous balance. The mill wheel was banging loudly.

She too climbed up to the plank. What was she trying to do? Perhaps she wanted to stand there, right under his nose, as usual, standing on tiptoe to look for him behind those accusing hiding places, wailing furies, in rancorous sadness.

The narrow plank swaying. The river below. He wanted to hit her again.

"Stupid girl!" he said, and pushed her aside to pass. Laura tottered, fell with her legs straddling the plank, held on, hung for some moments by her little pink dress and fell headlong into the river.

He saw her floating, without many warlike gestures, motionless, silent within. He sat down upon the plank in order not to fall. The current turned her over. She stared at him.

He was afraid to remember. What will happen when some time in the future we talk about this and she interprets everything I thought or said that time as indifference or hatred? Nothing is going to convince her, because behind this crime must lie another, probably older, crime, one that is archaic, the archetype of an original crime I have never heard of, by which she judges me and asks for justice, like an old sin of abandonment in which I took part without being aware of it. Yesterday, today and tomorrow. It's as though she were making me pay in advance for a future absence or disloyalty. With her one is always at fault.

"I must remember," he insisted. Miguel was angry, dirty, in some way, like all of his frayed clothing. A coarse cotton undershirt, always the same one, old earth-colored pants which came to his knees, held up by suspenders, the big black shoes from his Sunday best, stiff, without socks, occasionally that straw hat, for the summer, which most of the time he couldn't find. As a rule he went around barefoot, and when his mother forced him to wear shoes—she never stopped calling "Miguel, your shoes" to him—he would hang them by their knotted shoelaces from some tree or from the belt loops of his pants.

"We were hunting birds." She heard Manolo's voice emerging from some atemporal conversation. He was violent, the leader, the boss. No one dared to touch anything that belonged to him. Laura belonged to him. He would hit her for no reason, sometimes when she would arrive in her fancy little dress, one for the morning, another for the afternoon, as though just for him, so he could see her freshly washed and combed. She always forgave him. She would turn her back to him, feeling resentful or afraid. Only on very few occasions did he seek her out. Then it was different. They would sit by the river bank, in the shade of the trees, and he would crumble leaves in his hand. On one occasion he gave her a flower.

Manolo's voice was languid, drowsy, summer-like. "She once showed me her scrapbook. She had the little flower in it, and lots of poems, and stories, sad stories in which Miguel was always hitting her. In one of them he even killed her. He threw her into the water from the river bank. She was floating face down, her dress full of air on the surface. Afterward he would go there to cry for her, without anyone's seeing him. And she wanted to tell me, without reading it to me, that at night, already dead, she would rise up out of the water and the two of them would stay together until the dawn."

"Laura was very strange..." Now it was Pajarito's voice that came to mind. Pajarito disappeared one day with his father, a buyer and seller of everything, and a sharpener of scissors and knives. He used to call himself a professional wanderer. And he fulfilled that calling. When his second wife left him, he gathered up his belongings and took them with him to see the world.

She was in love with him. She would follow him everywhere. Nobody knows what they would talk about, but he became annoyed just seeing her arrive. He was a silent type, too. Sometimes he would talk about when he would go away. He kept a book on one of the roof beams of the sawmill. That's where we used to have long talks. He told me that Laura was his girl, but that was a lie.

"Laura was *my* girl, secretly, so nobody could think so, or talk about it, or do anything against it," he said out loud, remembering, now that no one was opposed to it.

"You would say things that hurt." He spoke differently. "You hardly ever laughed. It was always serious stuff: about your mother and school, about books and about our getting out of there or you and me getting married. But I never would have hurt you, never. I would have killed anyone for you."

"Laaau-ra!" It was Doña Luisa calling. She ran over to the house. Before going in, she stood in the doorway and turned around. Between these two, the air did not represent distance. They listened to each other think, wordlessly, by desires, by knowing each other, nothing more.

She embraced her mother's smell of nest and of smoky cave—half her own, half something distant and beyond—lost in her obsession with times long past, in her absent thought.

*   *   *

He saw the door to the house on the left side of the place in his mind. In dreams it was especially dark. Instead of his mother, a Halloween witch was inside. From time to time he would turn around and

Laura would gesture, beckoning for him to enter. It was cold. The colors were white and light blue, and the house that he did not wish to enter was black.

"Wake up, you lazy thing!" She fanned her face with an empty bottle. She had been recuperating for scarcely two days, and she was at it again. She threw it at him. She did not include the money. He would have to take care of that too. He was the man of the house, as she had once said.

"Please. I'm burning up."

He hurriedly went out. He wiped his eyes to get the eyelashes out. He forded the river. He picked up a small branch. He walked energetically. Among lichens and stones he counted ten odors he liked. He came to the fence, and whistled for Gypsy, who came wagging his tail. He threw the branch to make Gypsy run. He removed the bottom rail of the fence, which was loose, and slipped under it.

Gypsy was following him, and caught up to him in seconds. The dog was his friend, but wouldn't allow him to force the fence. This was an attack against his canine sense of self-esteem. He touched his head and was given the branch. He threw it into the henhouse again. Gypsy continued playing the game. He took three eggs carefully, to avoid upsetting the hens, and went out hurriedly. He threw the stick once more and ran off toward the river. He heard Gypsy bark twice, as though saying goodbye.

He left the bottle on the table. He thought of cleaning something. There was too much to do. He found the notebook under the bed. He had just unknotted his shoelaces.

He saw him arrive. He felt himself becoming red in the face. He sat down in the back, with the older children. He heard the low sound, reproof in some, respect in others. He also heard the "Barefoot Sisters" giggling. His blush became a conflagration and he clapped his hands over his ears. No one noticed this. Miguel was too obvious, and everyone walked on eggs around him in order not to disturb him.

The teacher continued to speak about the Civil War. Miguel drew a blue-uniformed soldier, but in black and white.

At recess Manolo gave him some of his bread with lard. The Discalced Sisters stayed with him, jumping up and down. He kept his back turned, as though Laura were a black sun. On the way out she sent Manolo with her cake. He pretended he didn't know where the cake came from. Manolo did not make the effort to lie. Laura, seeing him eat it eagerly, went away satisfied.

...He dove into the river, and swam vigorously. The water was calm, although the noise of the falls, of water moved by the mill, feigned an anger that did not exist. He seized her by the dress. He inhaled her scent of a baby with wings, diluted by the water. He put his arms around her neck. In this way, his cheek against hers, he once more perceived how tiny she was against his body, in strength and stature.

He understood that this was the closing ceremony. That from now on they belonged to each other, because she had agreed not to die, and because he had refused to let her die. On the threshold of the unknown he had taken her, and she had wanted to come. On the threshold, where children and love and farewells are conceived.

Her arms firmly around his neck, she sometimes held her face against him, fearful of angering him. He floated slowly with her to the shore and pulled her out.

She looked at him with resentment and pouting. He smiled. He kissed her forehead. He straightened her hair a bit. He adjusted her sock inside her shoe. He brushed the dried grass from her, after the sun had dried her dress. Finally, he readjusted her bow. It was as though he had bought a little doll. There was no more resistance.

That night he dreamed that Laura was inside the house. That the left-hand door was open and that he was walking rapidly down the hallways. Laura's and other voices were asking him to come in. He was afraid of the witch.

...He pushed the little boy. He forced him to go inside. There was no witch.

Two months after the death of his mother, Miguel went to live with Doña Luisa and with Laura—the echoes of Manolo's tired little voice still spoke. He changed a great deal. The clean clothes did him good; anyone could tell. Three years later they were married.

*   *   *

He awakened from his catnap. On the sofa, to the side, his wife embroidered some tablecloths. He enveloped her in his gaze. She raised her eyes. She smiled. She confirmed that they still mutually perceived each other's thoughts.

Translated by Clark M. Zlotchew

From: Morera, Rosibel. *Las resurrecciones y reencarnaciones de Lázaro Fuentes*. Heredia, CR: Departamento de Publicaciones de la Universidad Nacional, 1988.

MY BYZANTINE GRANDMOTHER'S TWO MEDIEVAL SAINTS

Carmen Naranjo

I went along saying farewell little by little, like poets, or men who know of a slow death that will bring back old memories, old faces, the sensation of a new encounter with infancy, the somber note of approaching senility.

I will never be able to say a final farewell to that old house, with all the dampness in its corners and in the cold of its bricks, because it was the best of my possessions, with never any insolence, never saying or thinking that its owner never forgot the rents or that the pleasure of sleeping the way you sleep when you believe that tomorrow will never return. That kind of dog-tired sleep that hits you when you're worn out from trying to keep your eyes open to watch the time and looking over the faces of Don Cleto and Don Ricardo, wanting to speak to them like you'd talk to just anyone and to tell them impertinently what they did to the Costa Rica that is disappearing, just like the two medieval saints of my Byzantine grandmother went away.

I am the son of a washerwoman, of the poor woman who washed others' miseries and took pride in herself for bringing them back white with pure cleanliness, scented with dawn and care. Son of the common people, who knows the value of bread and eats it up slowly so that he can taste how much it costs in pennies and effort, so that it will last a long time and not warm his belly for only a short while. Son of an honorable woman and of a father who could be almost just like Don Ricardo and Don Cleto; perhaps he was, or perhaps unfortunately he was never more than a common drunk and really what does it matter anyway. I never met him and neither did he get to see me growing up nor now all grown up and somehow patched together. Poverty is a state of mind, and even now that I'm given to squandering and to throwing away half-smoked cigarettes for some ragamuffin like me to finish smoking, I remain poor, simply and sadly poor.

How sad is the destiny of those who arrive late. My farewell was always a farewell. When I first arrived at the house, they told me my stay would be very short, as short as the encounter of the one who left me at the door, already plenty old enough to understand, to have it engraved on my soul that she, the washerwoman, the ill-fated one of the neighborhood, the one who doesn't talk because she is mute but she thinks and she's gone off with who knows what poor devil, *she* says no but it's really yes because only she does those things and this isn't the first child she's cast out. Thus I entered the world, all alone as if mine were a birth without moans, without stained sheets, without any hope that the baby would be blond and blue-eyed. They looked at me suspiciously, since he's not of my race or my blood, and so in a hidden corner by the fire with no prying eyes, I began to warm my cold feet, the melancholy residual of orphanhood.

When I came across a mirror I already looked like the skinny aunts who were stuck all over the walls like mildew. On hot afternoons, they would all attack each other with a flurry of insults and I was the child of the streets, of sidelong glances, of violent names, that Dulce muttered to Triana, that Manuela would spread to Antonia, that Renata repeated, irately, to Josefa. In the calm the mute washerwoman would again appear, totally shameless, and that was that.

I bid farewell, yes I bid farewell to all of them, who touched me really as much for their pleasure as for mine; when I found myself next to one who was becoming tender, she confessed her sins to me and, touching me with a sweaty hand, said that I was the Moses of her guilt because prayer can't keep the flowers from blooming and penance doesn't stop desire, perhaps it is the wind's fault, perhaps it is because of the night that seems interminable and murmurs strange things or perhaps it is due to the cold that expands like an uncomfortable bone that will not fit into your chair nor allow proper young ladies to walk as they should.

I met the washerwoman. I wanted her to be pretty but she was ugly and she couldn't hear a thing, not even if you shouted. From behind she was a wall of indifference. I reached for her hands that were like stone slabs, and her humble look crucified me with more devotion than the Way of the Cross. Mother, mother, and she smiled at all the children of the world as if she had none.

I learned the things you want to learn when you feel like living and you know life is short. Grandmother showed them to me without teaching me, the frightening grandmother, the one with the medieval saints, the one who was Byzantine because that was what her dried up little husband was, with a moustache like a curtain that hid his nasal cavities and mouth. Byzantine the spirit and the body, Byzantine the left eye that wasn't aligned with the right, Byzantine the veneration of Saint Nepomuk, the unjustly drowned one who should be invoked when one faces the perils of the waters and of unfair verdicts, and of Saint Norbert, he who without being one-eyed was still wise and good.

The grandmother who never loved me, because she wasn't mine nor did she learn how to be mine, except during her candle orgies, when she put her fingers into the candlewax to make white catacombs, and except because of that way she had of stopping her eyes before the saints and telling them that the world was lost and fervently asking for a flood, an earthquake or the severe cleansing by fire. Whenever she entered into her great raging trance and clamored for the end of the world, then she was my grandmother, the magical, the Byzantine, the one with the medieval saints, who happily paid no attention to her, because she lost control whenever she felt like it, and she never even had any control to lose. She never said goodbye to me and I felt that she didn't take even one good memory with her when she died. She was on her deathbed time and again and then woke up as if nothing had happened. She was like one of those long wax candles that is snuffed out when the door opens and the wind silences it, after a tremble of singing while it plays, disfiguring the shadows. Once she was really snuffed out and she didn't leave us time for a lot of prayers. With death inside her for so long, very soon she rotted all the way through. Along with the aunts, I accompanied her to the cemetery and I didn't tell her goodbye nor did I cry, and therefore I carry her inside me and perhaps never, never will I leave her completely behind. She lived for a long time, and it was only an instant.

The aunts became very affectionate. Dulce called me son many times, but Triana said that it was a lie, because there is only one mother and she was it. Manuela began with the alphabet because her son will be intelligent, the pride of the family, while Antonia made me repeat verses about roses, or Bethlehem with its shepherds, because her son will be an artist, a poet. Antonia took charge of my cleanliness so that I would be like her, clean inside and out, because flesh doesn't deny flesh nor can spirit flee from the spirit. Renata worried whether I was eating right, because your strength is extracted from what goes in and there isn't man nor beast that can triumph if blood is as stingy as the earth, and as she measured me every day she confessed to me that he, my father, was tall and hard like a great horse. Josefa saw to it that I laughed like happy children do, happiness, my son, is everything in life, it is the substance that makes the seeds grow, if not, what makes chicks break out of the egg, if not, what makes flowers and also children, if not, my son, if not, my son, if not, my little prince.

I say farewell to all that and to my washerwoman. The one I looked for at the river and I asked about her, about my father, about myself, about the night when I was conceived, about those hands that weren't like hands that cut my umbilical cord, washed me and gave me a name. Which name?

I say farewell to that, the name. Because Dulce called me Claudio, Trina named me Francisco, Manuela whispered Alfonso, Antonia proclaimed me Eduardo Arturo, Josefa knew me as Alberto, Renata recognized me as Napoleon. Only the washerwoman never named me at all. And I, afraid of birth and death, like the candles of the Byzantine grandmother, she who belonged to some child with curls and damask robe, I called myself Norbert, just like that, the best one of the medieval saints of my long goodbye, or at least the best-looking.

And I don't want to say farewell completely because I was born of a short encounter of love, I know that for certain without anyone having to tell me. And of all the wombs from which I could have come into the world, I prefer the simplest, the humblest, to be the son of a washerwoman, because that short encounter with love, she was the one who most needed it. She, deaf to the noises and to words both stupid and wise, to the ones that come on the wind and from the moment, she was the one who most needed an encounter with what is called love and echoes of many things, those things that I will never be able to leave behind because I carry with me, pierced into me, her eyes and the eyes of the medieval saints, that Byzantine grandmother with a grandson of curls and damask, who isn't me. I am the son of a washerwoman, without more history than that of remembering the "so be it" of those times.

Translated by Linda Britt

From: Naranjo, Carmen. *Ondina*. San José: EDUCA, 1985.

WHEN NEW FLOWERS BLOOMED

Carmen Naranjo

It was and still is a round village making a circle in the hollow. The houses face the mountains, and seeing them one can predict the weather: it will be hot; it will rain; the wind tonight will be terrible; a calm day, perhaps sultry, around four o'clock the rain will start to fall; it will dawn drizzling; there may be a tremor today.

A town that grew and shrank according to the unsteadiness of the country, sometimes the leaders would think about agriculture, at others about industry, always about commerce, most of them about seeing that everything went along as it should, calmly, without worsening the poverty of so many poor. A town with eucalyptus, orange trees, cypresses, dusty streets, orchards, chayote plants, happy shouts from everyone who meets and greets you with jubilation, loquaciousness, nonsense, and a sky with convulsed clouds. The houses were built with whatever was at hand, some wood, a little brick, some zinc, unsheltered, wind, cold, heat, some decorated flower pot and primitive disorderly gardens where the chickens wander among the marigolds and the ducks among the lilies.

A tranquil town in which an old man dies between the details of the agony and the inventory of what he left: a yoke of century beginnings, a mortar in disuse, a rare sewing machine for sewing who knows what, some open-toed shoes, a shaving razor completely rusted through. A peaceful town in which the birth of a child is communicated in a very loud voice from hallway to hallway, from alley to alley. It was a girl. Another one. Poor things, what's to become of so many? And the illness is combatted with medicine prescribed by the doctor and with herbs recommended by those who know about those things.

A town that always faces towards the mountain and admires, loves and respects it, please God don't send it down on top of us, because then we wouldn't even be able to tell what happened. And the mountain, ever-changing, brings them news of events that their timid minds of shut-ins don't dare to consider. A new priest will arrive, don't take him too seriously, he is obsessed with sin, poor sinner, everything frightens him, don't be frightened. And in the summer two very young and ingenuous young people will come, however, you'll never have such an incredible opportunity to rely on such excellent teachers, who will teach you what had been forgotten a long time ago and it's necessary to remember so that new flowers can bloom.

It was an age in which the town almost became a village. The young people emigrated in search of work and a different life. They were drowning in the ravine and the slimness of the mountain. Some had stayed: the old ones, old grandparents and great-grandparents, a couple of great-great-grandmothers totally committed to God, and the parents who were aged prematurely and disconnectedly by the accelerated changes of the telegraph, the telephone, radio and television.

She arrived first, one Sunday on the last of the four buses, she was going to take charge of the school and teach first to sixth grades of the diminished school-age population, which approached thirty children, ages seven to twelve years. Her name preceded her. Eugenia Maria de los Angeles Rivera Mancilla, born in a place known as the Cumbres de lo Alto for the Perfection of the Holy Birth. She looked very pale, too young for that rabble of sparrow-hawks, but the mountain told them it is she, the awaited, the one who manipulates the winds and knows her letters, and behind those blue eyes resides the wisdom of life.

Eugenia Maria de los Angeles stopped on a corner, and ran her eyes over the row of houses that only required a few seconds of investigation for her to know that she was at the ends of the earth. She raised her eyes to the majesty of the mountain to rapidly verify that she was at the beginning of the exposed beautiful things, that she knew were not given gratuitously or by chance but for legitimate merit, earned through will and that stubborn tenacity for overcoming any adverse situation.

Her first lesson was brilliant. She kept the kids awake, in spite of the fact that they had arisen before the mountain could become a profile, a black and threatening shadow, much less a grid of stray trees and weeds in the disorder of God, who was quite disorderly when it came to spontaneous natural growth. She simply showed maps and contrived to stimulate curiosity about the flat vision of the everyday.

The announced priest didn't arrive, as the decision to transfer father Toño had been changed. With a certain inertia he had been doing good work; at least he hadn't provoked any complaints or unnecessary intrigues or problems with the tranquil and patient community.

The young man arrived eight days later, carrying his youth on his back and his enthusiasm for beginning his first professional job in the administration of a farm that had everything and was going to cultivate even more.

They met in front of the school with burning glances. He couldn't stand it and approached, reaching out his hand. José Luis Villacencio, at your service. She smiled in the most natural way imaginable, a smile that couldn't be extinguished or terminated.

From then on they were inseparable during their free time, they went to the plaza, walking tirelessly down all the paths of the town. For them the birds were singing, the flowers open, the eucalyptus perfumed, and the day and the night began, the clouds turned a chalky white, the twilights lengthened.

No one in the village made any comment; it seemed very natural to them, they were so perfectly matched, so together.

One day the little old lady Refugio, one of the oldest of the village, watched them at length. But what was this. That way of slowly passing his finger down her arm, from her shoulder to her fingertip, tirelessly. Then that touching of heads, and how they petted each other, just like puppies. Then she associated the scene with an old rose bush that had begun to bloom with true passion, after years and years of dormancy. Something strange is happening, she thought, because her blood circulation had accelerated and her rheumatism pains had vanished. Then from so much contemplation, she caused others to contemplate too and she saw they were emotional, enthusiastic, absorbed in that torrent of true caresses.

That night the old woman didn't sleep, the hours passed as she remembered the exact movements and searching in vain for happiness. The following morning she had made up her mind and at dusk she passed again through the plaza and the whole village was there watching and watching. She saw what she could as long as the light permitted it, and then went down river looking for Don Miguel, who was almost as old as she was. That night she slept like a log.

The couple became the number one spectacle of the village, now no one read, even the newspaper, in the general store the television stopped glowing, in the houses the radios were turned off, no one was interested in the soccer game, not even the players wanted to wear themselves out with their running and kicking. The priest and the sexton, together with the altar boys, joined the contemplation. It was a lovely spectacle, so pure and innocent that the priest dedicated Sunday's sermon to the art of loving, loving each other without end and without rest.

Strange things began to happen in the village. The potatoes tasted like yams, the yams like papaya, the papaya like turnips, the turnips like tomatoes, the coffee bean while it was still green smelled of orange blossoms, daisies bloomed from rose bushes, gladiolus from tulips and bougainvilleas from lilies. Everyone realized that the summer was staying around too long and it wasn't raining, there wasn't even a hint of rain in the sky, only chalky white clouds. But they didn't worry, because the river brought more water than ever and it was as soothing as the sea, it caressed them to sleep with caresses that were every day more creative, more imaginative as it slowly carried out its journey.

When the old woman confessed that she was pregnant, they thought it must be her senility or maybe nostalgia for times past, she had given birth to nine children, she had almost seventy-five grandchildren and her eighth great-grandchild was about to be born. They began to believe it when they noted that all the women, old ones and young ones, some of them almost children, were in the same state, along with the sacristan's wife, the girlfriends of the altar boys and the priest's blessed servant.

The odor of the flowers truly intoxicated the village, they were blooming everywhere, even among the stones; the plaza was filled with them, and the paths, and the sidewalks, to the point where it was hard to walk and calmly find a place to step, without a guilty conscience for causing harm to some generous plant.

Perhaps that was why the people stopped going out, and they didn't realize that the couple wasn't there any more. They had gone, each one their separate way, as they had arrived, on different days.

He left first. In that village, filled with flowers, of tranquil, good people, a smiling priest who always put good before evil, he arrived at the conclusion that he had made a mistake in his calling. He wanted to be a sailor, instead of a farmer. She left afterwards, perhaps a few weeks later. By then the smile had dissipated and her eyes were filling with solitude, the solitude of an island in an unruly sea where someone was shipwrecked.

Neither she nor he perceived anything different in that village, so quiet and so covered with flowers. She left as if shutting a door, he as if opening one.

When the village realized that they had gone, busy as everyone was with babies being born, almost all of them around the same date, and with the care of that enormous quantity of children, because there were many twins and triplets, another teacher was already there, and she arrived obviously pregnant, and another farm administrator, with his wife and five rather grown children.

Now in this epoch it rained day and night, the flowers had disappeared, the river ran with less music and less water, things tasted like what they were, plants produced what they were supposed to. Everyone confessed his confusion to the priest and the priest sought out his superior to do the same. He counseled him to say solemnly what he had repeated in the confessional: one swallow doesn't make summer come faster, nor does the bird song bring the rains. Fleeting things have no transcendence and if the disorderliness were ordered, it wouldn't contain the gravity of the sin.

The couple appeared in some dreams but without doing much damage, everyone had rediscovered that one sleeps better and more profoundly in one's own solitude and with the expectations of the era.

Translated by Linda Britt

From: Naranjo, Carmen. *Otro rumbo para la rumba.* San José: EDUCA, 1989.

THE VESTIGE
OF THE BUTTERFLY*

Eunice Odio

To Rodolfo Zanabria, whose butterfly,
on the bed of the world, gave me this
story.

The Author

"It is theoretically possible," said Hans as he crossed the room, trembling. There was a loud hissing sound. Rafael looked at the tube, in the form of an inverted umbrella, connected to the other bubbling glass shapes.

Hans adjusted the belt of his immaculate lab coat. He approached the laboratory, regulated the valve from which the steam was escaping in minute quantities; he went towards a corner illuminated by a light that appeared to have no source; he opened the little door of the cupboard built into the wall, took out a glass bottle and served two glasses of a violet liquid.

"Your black elixir," murmured Hans in the tone of a true-believer at his devotions, and handed the glass to the artist.

Instead of taking it, Rafael stood up and looked intensely at the liquid which Hans was offering him and which, on being exposed to the light, was turning to the color of black olives. He brought his eyes up close to the surface of the full glass, covered in undulating flames of silver mercury which flickered, inexplicably yet visibly, in dimensions larger than their strange sphere of operation. Unintentionally, his glance moved from the waves of flaming mercury to the hand holding the glass. He felt dizzy as he saw that the hand was infused with the same gaseous, undulating flame of mercury...or was it all a delusion? Was the mercury not burning in the cells of that hand? Despite himself, he raised his eyes and met those of Hans. Their feverishness was more intense than usual. And, too,...or was it another delusion?...the urge to

*Mexico: Finisterre Impresor Editor, Inc., 31pp. This text is from the book. A comparison of this version with the first one, published in *Zona Franca* (Venezuela) LVIII (June, 1968): 6-13, shows minor variations.

supply answers. But Rafael never asked any questions. He took the glass avidly, while the cold blaze on the surface grew and the flames receded, took on the form of a spiral, and dissolved on contact with the outside air.

Although he had often witnessed what he called the human scene, he never failed to experience an indescribable state when faced with it. And despite the fact that he had received that unique gift innumerable times, he had never before noticed that, when close to the wave of mercury, the savant's hands transcended physical limits. In whose presence was he, in what presence? How often had he asked himself the same question?

A spark of silver remained in the bottom of the glass. After a few seconds, it disappeared. It was then that he took the first sip. Once again, he experienced the taste that seemed to delight all of his cells, as if they had each become bodies with a sense of taste, linked in a single sensory attraction. He savored it, little by little, and became intoxicated with an intoxication that had nothing in common with the one produced by wine, but rather with what could be called the supreme energy of consciousness. But he was not alone, not even with Hans. Together with him, felt by him, feeling him as a content and not a mere container, his cells became intoxicated in that great lucid delirium of consciousness. And suddenly it ceased, as suddenly as one comes out of a hypnotic trance, without leaving the slightest trace. How long had it lasted? He had never found out the length of this indescribable state, although it would have been easy for him to measure it (Would it really have been?) by merely looking at his wrist watch. But he did not want to know anything...."I hate knowing. It would slow down my senses if I were to think about the durability of a flower instead of looking at it."

"It is possible, theoretically, " repeated Hans.

"It's an *idée fixe*," said Rafael to himself, irritated and fascinated at the same time.

He raised his eyes from the large topaz which shone on the little finger of Hans' left hand. Hans was staring at him with those tiger's eyes, like those of an unconscious predator.

"Others tried it long before you," said Rafael. "Numerous people have dreamed of creating a living organism in all its prodigious complexity, from the simplest cell to one of the greatest complexity. But all they have done is to break their wings...."

"Until now," interrupted Hans raising his voice "they have been unable to reach their goal because they worked with instruments that were both complicated and crude...and because their knowledge is fragmentary. To discover the secret of the ritual dance which the chromatics carry out, you need more than a super-electronic microscope; their theoretical bases and rough dyes are insufficient. For all of this and other things you need dyes that have gone through a continuous ultrarefining process."

"Are you talking about the alchemistic refinement process?"

"And what else would I be talking about? Of course! The difference between me and the others is that they are working with substances, and I am working with *the substance.* Ultraelectronic microscope! And to think that the existence of this useless gadget puffs them up with pride! Poor Dr. Nirenberg! Believe me, I almost feel pity for the 'achievements' of poor old Dr. Pelo! No, no, my dear friend. In order to be able to see the intrinsic subtlety and, more importantly, the secret power of a molecule of DNA, it is necessary to have an apparatus which functions with enormously subtle forces. Do you understand? Let us look for things with the appropriate instruments. In order to examine the minute stamp on a silver spoon, you use a powerful magnifying glass, don't you, and not the eyeglasses belonging to an astigmatic person? But the fact is that they're looking for the essence and even its cause with long distance glasses."

"I agree. Or with toothpicks," agreed Rafael, and he added, "But what are you planning to do now? I'm asking because you seem intent on telling me. Whether I want you to or not."

"Don't you want to hear what I have to say?"

"I prefer not to."

"You have to listen to me...and you will listen to me because you are less out of touch than I am...because you have ties to something ...because today...precisely today, I need to find a link at all costs... because I have to show my pride, not as an act of contrition but of humility...."

Hans' voice was hoarse, as always when he was filled with emotion. Rafael, startled, straightened up to listen to him.

"What do I intend to do now? Now...hm...now. To say now means that you know nothing about me....But it's not your fault. I myself have lived so many centuries...that I've forgotten a great deal.... There is so much I no longer know about myself. Yes, you don't know, you'll never know how much, because even for me, that falls into the category of the most profound mystery. But no one is interested in that, not even I. The important thing is that I wouldn't know what I know if...one needs time...yes, yes, time, my dear fellow, a lot of time...."

Rafael looked at Hans' pale but fresh skin; his pitch-black, shiny hair; his eyes like those of a young man of forty, tiger-like and changing, as if he were inspired. For the first time, he was surprised to find himself taking seriously a frequent utterance of Hans': "I have lived many centuries!" He asked himself once again when this man could have accumulated so much and such complex knowledge. It seemed miraculous. How could anyone be so learned by the age of forty? Was

Hans forty, four hundred, a thousand years old? He felt the need to ask questions, something rare in him, but he suppressed it. He was conscious of Hans following his inner turmoil with penetrating eyes.

"There's another reason why you have the honor and obligation to listen to me. Because you don't ask questions...because you are able to live in silence and joy....That is why you are one of the few living beings whom I almost love...and admire."

Hans smiled. That smile, which Rafael saw for the first time (he had not realized that he had never seen Dr. Hans Arnim smile, much less laugh) caused something unwanted, indefinable, to invade his being. Hans Arnim became transfigured. That smile changed him into a fallen angel, profoundly seductive and questing, with something reminiscent of the angels who persevered. It was a stunning revolution because it concealed another: this man must have loved at one time....

"Yes, listen carefully," Hans was saying. "For many, many years, I have been looking for the secret of the butterfly....I want to construct one, from its very foundation to the top of its wings. Are you amazed that I don't aspire to construct a man, cell by cell? Are you surprised that I am concentrating my power and my efforts on a being apparently inferior to 'the great king of creation'?"

"There are no inferior or superior creatures. There are only different ones. The difference between them lies only in degrees of beauty."

"Exactly. Stated more precisely: in the beauty of their essence."

"You want to be God's equal."

"And what about you?" As he often did, Hans answered with another question.

There was a time I looked for enlightenment," murmured Rafael.

"What's the difference?"

"You crave power. I wanted to integrate my infinitely tiny being into the All, which is infinitely great. I once searched for the same thing as you, in alchemy. But you will not find what you are looking for by your means. I found what I was looking for in my way."

"You're not listening to me. That's why you're challenging an artist who neither wants nor is able to accept the challenge."

"Allow me to be childish. Everyone is childish at times."

"That isn't childishness, it's alienation. Something is wrong with you, something not just strange but extraordinary, for you to monologize to the extent of not noticing that I was using the verb in the past tense."

"Haven't you resolved your Koan?"

"No," said Rafael.

"Do you think you will?"

"I don't think I will ever resolve it. I am not, nor will I ever be a Zen artist. I shall always be simply a painter, inevitably a painter above all. Whatever I do, I can't manage to free myself from aesthetic pleasure. Neither my mind nor my spirit, attracted by manifestations of beauty, can manage to become aroused by the exaltation of the Koan."

"Have you given up?"

"Yes," said Rafael, without bitterness.

"Are you sorry?"

"No, I have my painting. I shall get somewhere along that path. Finally, a door will open for me, or perhaps several, or none; but that is my way, the one I ought to follow. My mistake was to go down a road not meant for me. But perhaps it was not a mistake but rather a necessary move, one that was foreseen."

"What do you mean?"

"For two years, I noticed that the more I advanced along the path of the Koan, the more I felt drawn to aesthetic pleasure, rather than detaching myself from it...until I became so united with it that we are now one and the same...I...a state of the soul, while I am causing endless life to be born on canvas. There is nothing more that I want or to which I could aspire. The mystery of the Koan didn't give me Nirvana, but it did give me the center of my equilibrium on Earth...and I foresee that I shall perhaps never know more than this....The designs of the Almighty are inscrutable."

"So now you're *only* a painter," observed Hans, stressing the adverbs.

"Only a painter," said Rafael, smiling with his entire strong and virginal face, in a manner that seemed mocking to Hans.

"Don't you long for more?" insisted Hans, choosing to ignore the mocking smile.

"No. I'm satisfied with more modest pleasures. I think I have become extremely wise....I should like to be the fellow creature of a dragonfly...or, at the most, its equal, but never to be its material and spiritual father. I'm out of danger."

"Out of danger of what?"

"I'm no longer in danger of making up one of the legion of the desperate who burned their wings."

Hans hurled himself forward. His immense, long hand seized the painter's wrist. They looked at each other. They were two powerful forces that simultaneously attracted and repelled each other. Hans continued squeezing the wrist of the man who was now more than ever his enemy.

"Listen," said Hans, "Don't you know that there are still many undiscovered molecules, and that I know some of these undiscovered molecules? And that is not all....For years, scientists have been probing how genes multiply billions of times in order to populate billions of our cells. And I have the answer to that extraordinary question. Yes, yes, dear fellow...I have the answer...to that and many others...for example, to a fundamental one for the making of the butterfly."

Rafael shook free of the fingers that circled his wrist like a tourniquet; Hans unbuttoned the neck of his tunic, while the perspiration ran down his forehead.

"I'm going to tell you what follows in a few words," said Hans, standing facing the painter with his arms crossed on his chest; his eyes slightly narrowed as if he wished to concentrate his power on Rafael.

"What follows, is this:" he continued, "as you know, it is the master molecule DNA that knows how to make the nails, the heart, the skin and, in short, all the parts of the living organism; and another protein molecule, RNA, is the one which transmits the information provided it by DNA to the ribosomes so that they can produce the proteins of which living organisms are made up. You also know that up to now, the molecular mechanism of the transfer of information from the DNA to the RNA and from this to the ribosomes has not been discovered. So, would you be surprised to know that I have discovered it? Do you realize that the person who knows this has a lot of power? With this key in hand, everything is child's play....Yes, it's pure child's play to read the code of the amino acids of a butterfly whose species became extinct 5,000 years ago. What a delightful creature! I found it in a glacier, embedded near the surface. I was alone, looking for something else, when I found it. I did not find what I was looking for. Transparent, white, elongated wings...that's what it's all about...about ...no, don't assume that I simply want to revive it. It's a matter of making a copy of this animal that lived thousands of years ago. To make a copy of one still alive would be senseless...at least for me...this isn't everything I know, but let it be enough for now. I shall add just one last lesson: you know that a special enzyme produces the light of the firefly. You also know that man has been asking himself for centuries why and how certain animals fly....I have discovered that this phenomenon, like that of the cold light of certain insects, is also due to a special enzyme, and that the difference between the wings of a bird and those of a butterfly, for example, are due to variations in the placement of ultrapure substances....If you place them in a certain way, you have an animal of a determined species as a result. In addition... this is not only the key to the wings, but to the totality of living creatures. Each of their parts also owes its form and function to certain geometric placement of the material. The so-called "genetic code: by means of which DNA, RNA, and the ribosomes communicate and operate is simply numbers and pure geometry....I abandoned alchemy when I had arrived at the penultimate step because I was not interested in its final conclusion, but rather its means...and because I had become interested in the movement of every being creature...the multiplicity of movements that occur in every living being...the interplay of atoms, the movement of molecules...the cell capable of carrying out two thousand different acts per minute and in which, therefore, time is disintegrated by the velocity and simultaneity of the motion which occurs within us, and of which we are totally unaware....This is my obsession... movement taken to mathematical reaches which you can only dream about, because the numbers that govern them are a supreme equation. Do you understand now why I went to biochemistry, to physical chemistry, to molecular biology, and to other, equally seductive things? The rest was natural and came by itself. I don't mind the years of suffering, because now I know...."

Hans suddenly leaned over, bringing his lips close to Rafael's ear and said in a low voice, as if someone else might overhear: "I'm going to show you something. It wouldn't matter if you were to talk about what you're about to see, because no one would believe you. Come with me."

They reached an immense iron door. In the great vaulted room, lined with a metal that Rafael was unable to identify, there was only a large apparatus in the center, which looked like...what did it look like? Perhaps an enormous camera?

Rafael was unable to determine what the object looked like, because Hans pressed a button and everything came into view. What absorbed Rafael's attention was not the vitreous material in which some discs of a nebulous consistency were submerged, swaying as if stirred by a breeze, on structures similar to high tension towers. Something even more noteworthy caused him to fix his eyes in one place: the round, vertical mirror with a liquid appearance, held up by two spheres; and a ray of light reflected within the mirror. Hans pressed another button and the scene changed....Illuminated by the ray, there appeared a geometric form which moved symmetrically from one spot to the other on the mirror, while intermittently, with a pulsating rhythm, flashes of bluish-white light surged from it.

"The carbon atom," explained Hans. "The life surging from the electrodes that form its valence....You're looking at the most powerful atom of the Earth...the form from which the spark of life is born...to see it is to contemplate the first day of creation. Beyond the mirror is a laboratory where several atoms of carbon are really operating...."

Rafael felt vertiginous when he suddenly noticed that everything he was looking at had grown to enormous proportions and filled a space many times greater than the room in which they were...and that all the forms they could see were illuminated by their own light, within a black, palpitating atmosphere. Shaking, he fixed his eyes once again on the flashing atom that moved within the mirror.

When they returned to the laboratory, Rafael felt himself trembling inside, assailed by a feeling of nausea.

He took his leave without a word and went out into the cool dusk as if he were penetrating the outward world in which men move about for the first time. He experienced everything around him as strange, hardly recognizing the almond tree that had always been to the right of Hans' house....He identified it moments later, but did not understand its meaning. It was hard for him to realize that the street light was not an hallucination; neither was the large-eared, long-tailed dog, lying in the middle of the sidewalk with his front legs placed parallel, like a sphinx. Objects and beings had become submerged in the unreality of the other world. He decided to walk home. Perhaps in that way, he would find something to grasp hold of...something that would return him to the beautiful and simple world to which he belonged; the world with a lowered veil which does not permit the arcanum to be seen. It was necessary for him to find it before turning the key in the door of his house....He felt that if he were to fall asleep in this state of knowledge of the profound unreality of reality, he would not wake up as himself. He turned in the opposite direction from his home. He stopped in front of the window of an antique shop. From the center of the window, a personage from Byzantium, framed in gold, was looking at him; a King of Hearts who, on his right palm, was supporting an orb with a triangle in the center from which an eye looked out, and who, on his left, supported another, transparent orb in which a scepter gleamed. At the very top of the sphere was a shining crown. The King of Hearts extended both hands while the two orbs whirled vertiginously. The King of Hearts lowered one of his eyelids; then he lowered the other. His two eyelids reached the ground. Rafael looked into the store. The antiquarian was observing him with kindly and somewhat clouded eyes. Rafael retreated, walking slowly; then he ran without stopping.

Exhausted, he rested under a tree of the great avenue, almost deserted because of the lateness of the hour. He leaned against the enormous trunk and glanced around; he was afraid to be seen in his present state; but he soon calmed down; the tree gave a lot of cover and the closest passer-by was a newsboy who did not seem interested in selling his newspapers. "*The Evening News,*" the child was saying in a low voice, as if talking to himself, "*The Evening News*, with the latest news of the expedition to...."

Rafael saw that the child was pulling a string behind him. What was that wriggling along the ground tied to the end of the string? A bundle of string. The child interrupted his almost inaudible cry and murmured, addressing the bundle of string: "You'll soon see, horsey, when we get to the magic island, with the singing tree, the bird that talks like we do and the great fruits of pearl that...."

Rafael looked in fascination at the child who was moving away with his horse—a bundle of string. He felt a return to earth; to the joy of not openly participating in the unknown. Almost overwhelmed with pleasure, he headed for the park. There, several men were discussing the forthcoming elections. To his surprise, he realized that he was listening with interest to the political debate, something which had never interested him before. That day, for the first time, he felt that he was a man like any other. The sudden feeling of joy took his breath away. He wanted to kiss and embrace all those men in the park.

"Buy these tropical fish from me," said a little voice. The voice dropped a hoop on the ground and picked up a fish bowl.

"Tell me they don't shine," said the child, lifting up the glass bowl so they would shine in the lights of the park.

"They shine a lot and are very beautiful. Where are they from?"

"From rivers and from a place called India...which doesn't exist," replied the child, his face brightening at the thought of a place that did not exist.

"It doesn't exist, and that's why it's marvelous...and produces shining fish and enormous flowers."

"About what size?"

"The size of your mother's sunshade."

"My mother doesn't have a sunshade. The only person who has one is the lady in the flower shop."

"Well, then, the size of the lady in the flower shop's sunshade." Rafael took out a large, new bill.

"Give me the tropical fish."

Rafael watched him leave, skipping and rolling the hoop. He dreamed that he had dreampt that Hans was taking him into a black and palpitating atmosphere. He awoke, startled; he felt ill again, without knowing...but no...there, on the drawing board, he saw the fish, swimming to and fro in the fish bowl. He had not been dreaming.

He felt something in his heart...as if it had grown and was weighing him down. He stretched out his arm for his dressing gown. He felt the bones in his arm from the humerus to the tip of his little finger. How strange! How was it possible to feel your bones in this way?...In what way? Rafael tried to analyze the sensation. Did his bones hurt? No, they did not hurt. Did they feel good? No, not that either. They were simply there. And it was not pain or pleasure that made him conscious of them. What was it then? He remembered that, "...as far as I know, it's Wednesday...I haven't eaten since Monday... I'm hypersensitive because of the lack of food...that's all. How stupid I am!"

In the park restaurant, almost deserted at this hour, old couple sat at their usual table. She was very sweet, with a large beauty spot painted on her cheek and a big-brimmed hat to protect her from the sun. Or why else?

He was cold. He asked for hot red wine. He noticed that he no longer felt his bones. As he savored the innocent and cheerful local wine which had nothing to say to his cells, it seemed the best in the world to him. "Dr. Hans Arnim...I'll never drink your wine again. Never again will I desire that ephemeral benefit reserved for the very few. You can drink it with the demons who surround you, not with me." He raised his glass and toasted nobody, or the air, and said: "Cheers!" He noticed that the old lady was looking at him quizzically, surreptitiously. She must think I'm crazy...so what? I think she's crazy, too.

The waiter was standing over him. He was not really hungry.

"Bring me anything, and the newspaper."

A blue butterfly moved through the park. Rafael looked away.... "Hans once again!" he said in irritation; but an instant later, he looked for it again, despite himself, and followed it with his eyes, absorbed. Suddenly, it seemed to him that the birds and flowers were visions of birds and flowers...that the trees were not trees, but metaphors of trees that lived far away. The park...the park was not real in its usual way. The jets of the nearby fountain...why did they sound distinctly and separately, like syncopated notes?

He fixed his eyes on the newspaper. The words had the effect of lightning. There, in large print, "HANS." He unfolded the paper. He read: "STRANGE DISAPPEARANCE." The notice was short. It said: "Today, at about 3 a.m., the sound of an explosion awoke the neighbors of Dr. Hans Arnim. The more than fifty people who left their homes to find out the cause were startled by another explosion, which seemed to have occurred in the house of the mysterious doctor."

"While one of the observers went to call the police, the others approached the house cautiously. They subsequently heard the crackling of a fire and noticed that the rooms facing the street were brightly illuminated."

Rafael perspired, riveted to his chair, hardly able to understand what he read. He continued laboriously: "The firemen lost no time and broke down the front door, carrying their hoses. Nevertheless, when they entered the completely deserted 'burning' rooms, they discovered no sign of a blaze, even though the temperatures there were excessively high."

"Certain that Dr. Arnim had been the victim of an accident, they looked for him throughout the house and the small garden in the back, without finding a sign of him."

"On the other hand, with the exception of a few broken windows, there was no damage."

"It is possible that Dr. Arnim was away at the moment of the strange explosion and the even stranger 'fire'; but, if that was the case, why has he not returned home by now? All the morning papers reported the incident. At press time for the evening edition—5:30 p.m.—Dr. Hans Arnim has still shown no signs of life. On the other hand, if the accident caught him at home—the most probable version because, according to his neighbors, he never went out at night—why was not even the slightest trace of the scholar found?"

"The professor lived alone. He is not known to have relatives, nor has any indication of them been found in his papers. His neighbors have declared that he seldom received visitors."

"What is behind this mysterious disappearance? The police are actively working on the case."

The park had receded. It was a park seen through binoculars. Or had his eyes sunk into the depths of his brain? Who, other than himself were Hans Arnim's friends? Who was Hans Arnim? Where was he? Rafael thought he knew.

The park had indeed receded. There, in the center of the lenses, he located all its inhabitants. The animals and vegetables were in his eyes simultaneously, as if they were gathered in his pupils or as if he were everywhere in the park at the same time. He remained still while the overwhelming consciousness of all his bones gradually invaded him. He looked for something that would place him in the material center of the park, which had become the center of the universe. As if through a fog, he saw a plate containing something. With surprise, he discovered that he could pick up the fork. He put it aside with disgust. "If I can pick up the fork, then..." He did not dare claim: "I could leave." He simply said: "I should leave."

He placed a foot on the floor with all his might. He stood up completely. He began to walk along the path, while the park receded, along with him, as if both were being observed through a telescope by a third party. He saw his house receding with every step he took. It was receding like the park and like him. How long would it take him to reach it? Nevertheless, he went forward, stepping firmly, choosing carefully where he placed his foot. He saw an ant there, on the distant ground, but not his own foot...."Where is my left foot?" He noticed that he could not see his own silhouette clearly. He realized that his bones were becoming lighter. With a bound, he crossed the street.

Who was putting the key in the lock of his door? It was he! Finally!

He entered. His hip bone had become as light and thin as a wafer. Moments later, it dissolved, together with his whole skeleton, which scattered around the room. Now he felt as light as day, caressed within his flesh. His suit, now empty, fell to the floor. He tried to see himself from outside....There was nothing to be seen. He looked inside himself. He saw that he was a luminous hole.

There was the paper on its easel and a flexible paintbrush. He rose from the floor and supported himself in the air on one finger. With a hand which did not feel the effort, he took up the brush, moistened it, and began to sketch "the summary of the most beautiful memories of life." He concentrated on the apex of a flower and added the crystalline yellow that made all animals happy. He thought of the winds that carry the odors of everything and the forms of everything they touch, and the songs of wanderers under the sun. And the tree instilled in the spirit began to be created, resounding with and lost among the flying animals. And that tree was contained in a flamelike flute that amazed travelers.

And suddenly, the heavens appeared to him in body and soul. His brush flew ahead of his illuminated hand, his hand flew, followed by a spirit which welled up from the air and the fire and the earth and water and covered the walls with the butterfly and its great suspended bareness. White, mobile, extended over the bed of the world, the butterfly began to come out, variegated like the sun, flashing invisibly between the songs, in every way similar to a palace of bubbles. It was followed by a troop of mirrored beings that its wings reflected.

It was done. The brush fell from his hand.

He was awakened by the light of the sun that came in through the closed windows and by the profound joy of the day following creation. He looked, enraptured, at the sheet of paper. Startled, he sat up. There was the tree and the yellow that looked like it would end quickly, just like the light of day. The butterfly had disappeared. Disturbed, he looked away from his work. Had he dreamed that he was painting a butterfly worthy of the sun? Was it all an illusion of his own overwrought spirit?

He fixed his eyes on the picture once again, and saw...yes, there was no doubt. On the yellow, which was like a brief moment, there was a space identical to the form of the chosen one. It was its outline. Where its wings had been, one could still see a luminous mark. He held his head in his hands. "I'm sick. You poor devil, wretchedly inferior to your dreams. How could I believe that this material in motion, this step from nothing to the perpetual motion of the air, was real! God, someday make me identical to one of my dreams!"

He got up dejectedly and approached the table to look more closely. On it, on its stand, the tree, lost among the flying animals, was looking at him. He approached more closely. The table top seemed to have an unusual glow. But, since he was absorbed in the contemplation of his work, he did not look for a reason...I'll just look at the tree and the empty space...where I thought I was giving it life...I'll never look at anything else again."

The glow became concentrated in one iridescent and transparent spot. It was then that he noticed and bent down to look with the eyes of someone possessed. There was only this: an iridescent, transparent chrysalis, broken open only seconds before, still damp.

He opened the large window and cast down his eyes, because he realized that he would not be able to look at it and continue living.

At that instant, the painter saw his body again. He, like the vestige of his chosen one, had reappeared on the earth.

Translated by Birgitta Vance

From: Valbona, Rima de. *La obra en prosa de Eunice Odio*. San José: Editorial Costa Rica, 1980.

URBAN WAKE

Yolanda Oreamuno

I arrived early. Death may be the only thing you come round to too early. The house was already full of people. Unfortunately, I have to cross the hall and make a series of hellos. That strange and uncertain agitation that rises in me like something hammering in my throat when I have to say hello is already starting. Legitimately, the hello should be accompanied by a smile, but I try it and it turns out that when I've already turned my face and the person can't take note of my good will, that tight and difficult smile explodes.

The poor little thing has come rising from my stomach, through my throat, climbing a laborious stairway through my mouth, onto my tongue, ending up at the tip of my nose. With the momentum it has, it can't stay in my mouth and it goes on up to my cheekbones and then I see it, the foolish, fictitious, slow-witted thing. I think the smile was made for the eyes and the mouth, never for the cheekbones and the nose; but there it desperately clings, like a rag, awkward and ashamed, it stays hanging there like a fool, and I find no way to make it go away. I almost feel like running my hand across my face to wipe away the splotch.

The gentleman to whom I was directing the splotch was an acquaintance, someone you give a familiar smile, on an everyday basis, but it came when I was in front of a lady who never liked me and it didn't want to come off before I had said hello to a gentleman with whom you have to be serious. That fat lady who is standing next to the victrola always creates a shameful inner conflict for me. I don't call to her because I don't know which name I'm permitted to use, nor do I kiss her. Should I kiss her? She waits smiling broadly, with her face split by a toothless grimace, a little too good natured. I have the feeling that she's going to pinch me. I doubt it. No, I don't doubt it. I'm convinced. But on which side do you kiss a lady with such aggressive cheeks. I've decided against the intimate approach. But she has decided yes, and suddenly she becomes serious. Her seriousness has made her cheeks fall a little, now she's more sympathetic. Nevertheless, I insist against it. But what am I going to say to her? I'm going to shake hands with her. She won't expect this move and she would grab me around the waist for sure. An embrace is still more difficult. In a burst of courage I close my eyes and stretch out my face. Is this a kiss? Sticking out your tongue is more of a kiss *and* this one tasted like corn silk.

I'm sad. What became of my smile? The poor and ridiculous smile that cost me so many contractions of my esophagus. Now I have to start over again...

There, in that chair in the dining room, I think I'll be in better condition for this interminable night. I touch it and I'm convinced that it's quite acceptable. I take permanent possession of it. I'm near the door and in direct contact with a draft.

In the next room, beyond the entryway, there are three beds and a chair and many, many people. The ones who are crying are there. I'm not in the mood for crying and prefer to stay in the dining room. There's not enough room for the people who are in the beds. Charitably, they have given them to the closest relatives and several women are fiercely defending the position, very correctly thinking it's quite uncomfortable to sleep in a chair. No one takes pity on that little girl who is crying desperately next to a little boy who's wet. They murmur phrases to her and stroke her head and they wrap her legs with a towel. The smiling lady is seated at the head of the bed. The little girl snuggles up to her and insistently asks why her mama died.

Now she is softly maternal. If she said nothing her compassion would be perfect. Her face has become smooth and there is static electricity in her hand as she caresses the blond and tearful little head. The little girl has almost fallen asleep. The lady has many children, surely this is the reason her compassion is gently, affectionate and real.

The others cry and cry...

I've gone back to the dining room and I start my tenth cigarette. It's nine o'clock at night and they're starting to serve rounds of strong black coffee to keep us awake. In the kitchen, coffee is all that's being prepared. No, they're doing something more. There are industrious women who are filling sacks, serving cookies and ordering servants around. They will probably spend the night on this. They've never entered this kitchen before but now they're bustling housewives. With agility and ease they expand inside a halo of responsibility. They must feel horribly responsible and maternal. They are insistently, tenaciously taking care of everyone. Some think they deserve a rest and sit around the kitchen table, with coffee and cookies of course, to tell stories of shocks and sadnesses and to arrange, with conscious self importance, the situation of the family that is upstairs crying. They feel terribly comfortable with their job in the kitchen, this job which they desperately snatch from one another. Certainly they have to make a good impression.

I have decided, with a profound sense of ethics, not to have coffee.

I sit down again. In front there's one of those unpleasant wall clocks that strike the hour and play a little tune. A fourth of it every fifteen minutes; it plays and you hang waiting for the rest. It's as if it had been cut off with an abrupt slash. You have to wait another quarter of an hour...What a long time! The little tune continues by stages towards completion. Now...No. It still doesn't end and my waiting has turned into anxiety. Never has waiting been such a great annoyance as this. The hand travels slowly, slowly. My heart wants to pick up the beat of the tick-tock. I feel something moving my legs and almost tickling me. I was trembling. Even though I was quite comfortable, I'm going to have to get out of here. But no. This pulse in my legs is too rhythmic. Now I feel it in my arms and my back. My heart is wild because it can't catch up with the clock. Now another quarter of an hour and the tune is almost compete, only a tiny piece is missing. But it's enough to make me desperate. Damned clock and damned tune and damned time! And it won't pass. It must be making fun of me. The more excited I get, the more ground I lose in this struggle with the clock, the more out of rhythm I get. Or, my heart gets our of rhythm, shaking me like a fool. I'm upset, I've lost the beat again like sometimes when dancing. I try to find some absurd excuse to have it out with the clock, which isn't laughing out loud any more, but rather laughing between its teeth, between the filthy false teeth of its pendulum. What a shame. I don't know how to get out of this mess. I look again at the clock. But if I'm not to blame, it was your fault for insisting on singing the same song. Who says that everything has to be in four movements. I haven't done this in years. I must be out of practice. Or rather, I'd never done it before.

These excuses only manage to increase my confusion. I think I'm blushing.

Perhaps the clock feels sorry for me because at that moment it plays the tune. It's a somewhat martial little air. I thought this was going to relieve me of this burden but no. What stupidity! The best thing is not to think about the clock. It's made a fool of me and the tune is as unfinished as it was in the first quarter hour.

I'm not alone in the dining room. There are two or three people seated here. No one is fond of this room. I suspect it must be because the coffin is in the facing room. Almost in the same room. This dining room is joined to the other by an arch and there across it is the coffin. Gray. With an enormous red crown at the foot. It would almost seem to be an offering of love. But crowns also have the shape of a heart. It's terribly beautiful against the background of the sitting room.

But this evening I've seen something greater and more beautiful. So great that I felt microscopic next to this girl. She too is a daughter. She is seated here with me. There's a surprising serenity in her face. She stands up at times, too often, gently. At that moment she has an almost happy expression; maybe not completely so, but straightforward and clear. She hasn't cried nor will she cry. She crosses the dining room. Now I know what she's about to do and it nearly gives me a chill, like the ones you have when you're in a very high place. She walks elegantly. She's on good terms with the peace and serenity of this room. She's not in any hurry but she goes straight there. When she arrives, her smile is almost satisfied. She opens the wooden lid of the coffin and she caresses the dead woman with her smile and her hand and her eyes. This blond girl has a great sadness. You feel infected by such peace, such serenity, such calm.

When someone at her side, looking at the dead woman, said poor thing, she, with an ingenuous surprise on her face replied: "Why?" And as a conclusive explanation: "She's better off now." And there she remains one, two hours, until someone begging her not to overdo it, tears her away from her place. If she's not overdoing it, her torment wouldn't be in tune with her magnificent attitude. In lowered voices, people say that she has no feelings. And I would say out loud that I'd like to have such a vast and clean love.

When she sits down she talks to us about anything and everything. Her brain is as transparent as her soul. Embarrassment doesn't exist in her. She comments, she reasons. She is the only one who clearly sees how to straighten things out.

My admiration is almost a knot in my throat. They go on talking and I go on smoking. After a while, she gets up again.

One of the girls there is a portrait of depression and distress and weakness. She is so thin and pale and upset. I feel the same charitable compassion as the women in the kitchen when they're handing out coffee.

I go to the room with the beds and ask for a place for her. I have to mobilize a lady. That one, the one who's been sleeping since eight. She breathes deeply with great satisfaction, full length on the bed. She breathes from her head to her feet. The pillow (because she's even got a pillow) must be soft and warm. She sleeps so well! She turns over. From time to time she opens an eye. She scrutinizes the horizon to see what she ought to say. She opens the other eye. She tries to make a desperate effort so that we'll think that she's been awake. That's why as soon as she wakes she speaks, trying to thread a phrase into the conversation that will seem to be a continuation of a previous one. She wipes away time with one stroke and rushes to catch up with the others. She must feel somewhat lost, ashamed, maybe she'll even have some doubts about what she did while she was sleeping. She'll look again at everything around her. She'll ask herself if maybe that one doesn't have an ironic expression. She'll escape from her confusion only by talking hurriedly. Then, with a renewal of optimism she cries (at that moment she thinks it appropriate to cry) and beginning with suspension points or with "and" so that her phrase won't seem to be dislocated from the general conversation, she says between one blink and another "...and as much as I asked God for her to die on Monday (her daughter was getting married on Saturday), he didn't want to grant it to me." A tear, a sigh and she turns around to the corner. She's already asleep again.

I leave my work of charity finished and return to the dining room.

It's two o'clock in the morning. When the hours are lived with nothing to do, time is pure life. My hands are in my lap, my soul is racing. Each minute is valuable not for what you can do in it but rather in itself. Everything in the organism becomes a clock at this hour. I go from one room to another. He who doesn't sleep lying down nods on a chair. The decorum of posture was lost a long while ago. The idea of sleeping is an obsession in every head. The night throbs like an immense heart.

No one can be on the street, it must be dark and black, the pavement has to have withdrawn its white finger from in front of the house. The two pines can't exist in this solitude and silence. More than beauty the pines are melodiousness; a pine without wind wouldn't be a pine. Since there is no wind tonight, I don't know what strange duct is bringing us this intense, wet, almost tearful cold. The air must have frozen in indifference over the house and the pines. I go to the corridor. Yes there's a moon, a small and cowardly moon. When I arrived it went into the mouth of two clouds but now it's come out again. You almost don't think at a time like this. It's a strange situation and I don't know if I'm thinking. Perhaps I'm thinking that I don't think. The street, the houses don't have any meaning for me. Inside and out, everything is dissolved in an anonymous vagueness. You almost don't feel life. Is death like this? This not feeling. Am I seated or standing? I don't have any question to ask myself nor the outside. Everything is densely heavy. I haven't moved in a long time; I think I probably wouldn't be able to. I can only think about possible movement. My leg is rigid against the floor, my arms on the corridor railing, my hands...I don't know where. If I wanted to move would I be able to do it? Would my sleeping muscles respond to my will? Do I have a will? Do I have a desire to move? I don't think so. Has my body died? My hand moved and I didn't need a will to make this movement. I think this isn't my hand. It must belong to someone I don't know, because mine, the one I had, is resting there on the railing. I'm certain. If I looked again, its ever so familiar silhouette would take shape against the wood. But I won't look again.

My head is fine like this over my shoulders in this position which I don't and can't remember.

Suddenly I see my hand in front of my eyes, against the moon. How did it come back here without my noticing it? There's no doubt. It's my hand. It's almost skeletal against the background of the night, I would almost think some fine and blue veins are there. But I prefer not to see anything. My hand goes away again because certainly it didn't want to feel the crude light of dawn that is beginning.

I go inside. Contrary to what I thought, this total movement of my body hasn't cost me anything. I think a very cold wind pushed me.

I sit down again in the dining room. It's no longer so lonely. There are several ladies trying to get an audience for a rosary that never was prayed and struggling still more vainly with sleep. I look at them and I almost don't recognize them. Are they the same ones from last night? Now I almost don't see them. I have morning mist in my eyes. I probably picked it up in the corridor. I clear my optical powers. I don't see them. Or do I see them? Are they really there, sleepy and dressed in mourning? Haven't I probably gone to sleep too?

I haven't slept and I know that I haven't drunk coffee all night.

Translated by Don Sanders

From: Oreamuno, Yolanda. *A lo largo del corto camino*. San José: Editorial Costa Rica, 1961.

OF THEIR OBSCURE FAMILY

Yolanda Oreamuno

He had the soul of windless moorlands. There was nothing more desolate than those eyes where there was no drama, devoid of tears, smiles, fear. He had come to earth to sleep a long dream from which he would wake with surprise only when he died. If peace was a state of inertia, he was at peace with everything, even with those who breaking into his routine had now marooned him in the unknown. But peace is not a state of inertia; it is a state of cautious combat, of active anonymous gestation, of postponed fertility. That's why, seeing his passive gestures, you couldn't speak of peace, nor of calm, observing his open and sleeping eyes.

He took up the customary habits, unfamiliar with any others; the gentleman's ways, just for lack of fertile inspiration. River without a channel, he lived the life of a lake that had neither beaches, nor echo, nor mirage, nor reflection, nor wave. He stood before things in a moment of edenic ignorance as if the creator's hand had left off without giving the divine spark to his form. He was there because circumstances had put him there. Now he was a creedless political exile, earlier, a vocationless judicial official. He became a magistrate because his father made him study law, his relatives installed him as mayor, circumstances produced a vacancy, and finally, two superior court chief justices died and turned over to him his inevitable appointment. His birth didn't open any paragraph with a capital letter and his death wouldn't place the final period after anything. He was only a comma, accidental, fortuitous. With the same lack of tragedy and glory, he was converted through the agency of a revolution in which he didn't participate, into the anonymous political exile who was now setting foot on the magnetized soil of Mexico. His wife and three children were with him. He had married and procreated without love or passion, almost without choosing his companion or wanting children. He had married. Why? Probably because men get married. That was all.

In the airplane he felt no fear, at most a little surprise. At each tremor his wife anxiously took him by the shoulder, squeezed his lifeless arm and said:

"It's falling Raul...it's falling!"

"It's not falling," the man answered unhurriedly.

During the several hours she passed repeatedly from terror to delight and from premature homesickness to venomous memory.

"Look below there, Raul. It's wonderful!"

He looked. But already what she saw wasn't below. Next to her face, a mad curtain rose up vertically: a piece of the sea made rosy by the dusk, strange watery barbs of an open delta, four islands boiling restlessly, a small boat clambering frenetically along the abrupt slope of the landscape.

"We're falling, we're falling!"

"We're changing course," he said.

Horizontality restored his wife's tranquility. "Right now," she said, "Mamma is probably setting the table for dinner and we aren't there....All because of those...Pigs! They're pigs!"

"Who?"

"Now you ask me who? The filthy gang who stole everything we had and sent us off to Mexico. Those pigs."

"The revolutionaries?"

"Well of course the revolutionaries! They threw us out and now you don't even know what we're going to do."

"I suppose we're going to live in Mexico City."

"Mexico City," she said bitterly. "I've heard it's a dirty place where they steal everything you have. Why did it have to be Mexico City, especially Mexico City, that I dislike so much..."

"I don't know. They're giving us asylum; we ought to be grateful."

They flew awhile in silence. A long and short while because time boards an airplane like one more passenger and you never know if a minute or an hour is going by. And as the woman was furiously repeating, "Mexico City that I detest so much!" she cut herself short to observe vehemently:

"Look Raul, what a marvel!"

"That's Mexico City which you detest so much," he said without irony; and he looked.

Innocent, parallel stars, offering a warm hand in the darkness to declare the way; dizzying trajectories of shadow; red and green and yellow lights. White lights in a milky group; vague, dissolving, blinking lights. Fleeting, hermetic, rectangular lights; high, challenging, spread out lights. Closer every moment, slow twin car lights and lights in a bundle; travelers giving friendly winks in the night air, their paths intertwining, becoming one, opening into angles, triangles, rectangles,

sharp, obtuse. Airport lights and city lights and vehicle lights spread
out over throbbing Mexico City.

*   *   *

He had never had urgent economic problems. He didn't have them
now. He had a room for himself and his wife, another for the children.
In this boarding house they were served a curious mixture of *gringo*
breakfasts with fruit juices, waffles and coffee; and odd chililess Yucatecan meals, with cheese, *tortillas* and thin strips of pale frozen meat.
It was strange that with this diet nothing happened to their stomachs but
absolutely nothing did happen, neither indigestion or nutrition. The
house did not give off any definite aura and when things ought to have
openly clashed, the color of the afternoon, the song of a bird, the or-
namental tree on the balcony or the voice of Chona the maid would
reestablish the dangerous harmony. Dangerous because on the walls
and ceiling of every room, the old Porfirian mansion had garlands of
pastel painted roses; there where the ceiling becomes a corner, Cupids
with bows; on the capital of the columns, overflowing cornucopias;
ribbons interlaced with leaves forming a circle in the place where
resplendent chandeliers of cut glass might have hung in the old days
and now the squalid cord of an electric bulb dangled; and below, as
furnishings, *sarapes* from Saltillo and Toluca serving as carpets; loud,
cracked carvings with pretensions towards 'colonial' style and Lagunilla
trademarks; American couches with huge springs, big *charro* sombreros
on the wall, fragile, blown glass trinkets every place and, in the most
unexpected places, huge straw dolls mounted on straw horses, and dry
straw Indians along with dry straw children.

As you lay on the couch, frayed edges of a Strauss waltz would
come loose from the ceiling, and when you sat up, the violent shout of
a Veracruzan *tapatio* or the nasal echo of an Huastecan *sol* would
explode from the loud colors. Through the intermediate neutral zone a
clean, very pure air came in, and in the niche of the balcony the or-
namental tree trembled and the high violet sky of Mexico trembled, as
sensitive to the light as skin. Those palpable, sedative elements restored
the harmony between the architecture and the decoration. Nothing
would ever happen there.

Chona, the Mayan Indian, did the cleaning; Doña Mercedes, a
calm Yucatecan landlady, did the cooking. Between these two domestic
poles, Raul's wife paraded her plaintive, purring maladjustment. His
wife's mental state was so prickly that Raul, accustomed to fitting
comfortably in the midst of something; his work, his home, his
microscopic joys, his orderly hardships; began to swing towards
another frontier, however hostile and unsociable it might be, so long as

he didn't have to hear her constant whining monologues and didn't have to watch the spectacle of an idle Isabel, negative, refusing to even look at the city, as if it were just an overnight stop.

*   *   *

He lived on the corner of San Luis Potosi and Medellin, a block from Insurgentes, the broad white way that divides Mexico the way a handkerchief waving farewell divides the afternoon. Fleeting but unforgettable. There he would take a bus and few minutes later he would enter the vital anthill of the city's center via the streets of Articulo 123, or Hidalgo or Juarez.

The center of Mexico City doesn't have a purely commercial activity and this is what distinguishes it from any other city. The activity there overflows all boundaries. It's rhythmic and off-tempo, muted and noisy, elegant and common, noble and sordid. The Mexican moves in this chaos with a sort of secret accuracy and the foreigner doesn't explode, he melts. That hidden mobility of the human mass that blocks Madero, San Juan de Letran, Gante, el Caballito, Cinco de Mayo or the Zocalo at all hours, is the mobility of an aquatic plant, floating in the waverings of the current, but attached by a flexible line to something secluded and fertile.

Time in Mexico is marked by the yellow note of its mid-day, the sour note of its dawn or the violet note of its twilight. Time doesn't depend on the clock that presides over the corner of San Juan and Madero, but rather on the urgency of an appointment that's postponable at any moment, or on the pleasant and inevitable stop for a *taco* eaten at any food stand, or for a conversation begun at any moment. Mexico City is always ready to walk, to stop, to run, to lie down; it is only not ready to die. There is a life there that has nothing to do with urgency nor with time; it's a life sometimes moribund, sometimes vigorous, but always in a state of acute contagion.

Raul liked to stop at the Nieto Building and contemplate with greedy delight the two incredibly disparate currents that met there: the elegant humanity of Madero, inhabited by gloved women with beautiful legs, perfumed and distant; men in dark overcoats, with voracious male-animal faces and gestures of attentive diplomats; children with uniformed governesses, luxurious buses, luxurious automobiles, luxurious stores. And meeting them transversely at this point, the virulent human river that travels through San Juan de Letran: men in *sarapes*, women in *rebozos*, ragged children, insolent boot blacks, effeminate punks, coarse shouting vendors, gray clerks, loud, brown and nudelike women, *taco* stands, beer joints, everything laid out for sale on the ground, cheap restaurants, cheap merchandise, cheap women. On the corner of Nieto, in front of the clock, the two humanities intertwine; the punk makes way for the lady, the diplomat flirts with the girl, the rich governess shoves a poor child who is just about to get on a bus, the village woman envies the lady's suit, and the lady envies the village woman's breasts. Afterwards, the two currents go off, the light has changed and the warm human channel loses itself from San Juan to Santa Maria la Redonda and Cuahutemotzin, while the frozen human channel loses itself from Madero to Juarez and Reforma, from Madero to the Zocalo.

Raul was watching and his eyes were beginning to see. With the slowness of a blind man, who learns little by little, but whose pupil already held something human. Clandestinely a fleeting instinctual appetite, or a transitory greed, or also, often, a till-then-unknown warm pity was awakening there. Raul's eyes, still mute, were participating in the chaos. His eyes belonged, although not all the rest of him did.

Later, he would go to the boardinghouse again, to his moaning wife, to the bittersweet silence of Chona, to the cornucopias and the straw dolls. And then he felt that he didn't belong.

At first he wanted to drag Isabel along on his travels:

"Let's go out to Guadalupe."

"No," she would say. "It's dirty, they'll rob me, there's smallpox."

And Raul would go alone. He began to get up early, so early that he was almost starting out at the night watchman's final call. Without hesitation, sometimes without bathing, trembling and urgent.

"But where are you going?" Isabel would ask.

"I'm just going out," he would answer, drily.

"Where?" his wife would insist.

"There's a fair at the Merced Market. I want to see it."

"They'll rob you."

"...steal the socks off my feet without taking off my shoes?" and he smiled as he repeated the saying that Mexicans invented to make fun of their own larceny. And Raul, yes, Raul was smiling.

*   *   *

And he liked—oh how much!—to mingle with the market's multitudes. At that early hour, the fish would arrive from Acapulco, Tampico, and Veracruz. There was still a final shudder left in those silvered bodies, and as the sticky mass rolled from the cargo wagons to the stevedores' baskets, something like an imploring glance could be seen in the millions of fixed, opaque eyes. Raul examined it, sadistic, delighted. A rebellious fish traced a delirious trajectory and, striking someone's face along the way, fell in the filthy torrent of the gutter.

"Son of a bitch!" and a hand as active as the voice put the dead animal back into the basket.

Lobsters, shrimp and prawns waved their thousands of legs without losing, even in death, their grotesque tendency. Raul felt a shudder of disgust and fear run down his back. He felt claws all over him. He was feeling. Yes, he was feeling.

At that early hour the vendor tries out his shout. Making its debut in the morning air, his howl splits the instant in two. The horizontal sun vibrates, the odors are still asleep, the soaking wet janitors who have already cleaned the market are going home to sleep, the Indians rehearse their language, which in the course of the day and use, will show a masterful skill for flattery, suggestion, and insult.

At that early hour they call out to him haltingly:

"Whitey..."

And he vainly awaits the offer that doesn't arrive. It's so early! It begins to smell like stew. Not having eaten breakfast, Raul's hunger is growing. At an Indian's stand, they're selling blood pudding. He's about to buy some but...

"Have you got something to put it in...?"

And there with the pig blood soup in front of him, he doubts if he can hold it in his hands or his mouth. The Indian woman suggests...

"Go buy yourself a little cup, sir...."

And sir buys a little cup. At the first mouthful a reactive salivation floods his mouth, the chili half closes his eyes, then his ears ring, then a frightening heat takes hold of him, then the heat becomes lukewarm, comforting, friendly, and with the following mouthfuls of blood pudding and tortilla, a blissful, abdominal placidity overcomes him. He feels like laughing, like embracing the Indian woman and eating more chili. Why do they say that chili burns? Okay...it burns but it burns deliciously. He tastes and everything he tastes has a delightful flavor, as if it had turned into fruit.

Dirty women graze against him and leave threads of hair on his jacket, the stevedores push him and insult him; he lets them insult him. He is happy. A man soaked with sweat passes against him, leaving his hand wet. He, who has never sweated, now welcomes another's sweat. There's something so vital in that salty liquid, that if it weren't absurd, he would taste it. He puts his hand in the sun and the drops shine there as if they were his. Warm liqueur, the color of the sunbeam that pierces its authentic product custom made by human effort, so authentic that it always has a positive value, even there on a strange hand. He doesn't dry it, he watches it dry up on his skin in the wonderful heat of the sun. When it's gone, it still leaves a salty crust, a frosty architecture on his white skin, the fleeting rough branch of a sea coral, a volume of filaments; meanwhile he feels infected, stricken, and a delirious euphoria motivates his step and livens up his glance. He is so happy!

The jungle of shouts stretches out over him, his solitude protects him, and at every moment a solicitation shatters his previous glassy indifference.

"A suit? Try it on?"

"Buy something Whitey..."

"Like it's made to order, very cute, buy it Whitey..."

Fruits, vegetables, suits, shoes, colored ribbons, pots, baskets, women, dogs, cars, buses, everything. Between the streetcar rails a man placidly and carefully spreads out his load of oranges. He negotiates with a woman and when the streetcar arrives, he has calculated so well, that the vehicle passes over the merchandise without touching it or moving it. Impassive, the merchant and the buyer reunite, and resume their shouted bargaining over the tower of oranges. An infectious impulse possesses him: he has to buy something. He has to somehow share the surrounding activity, he can't be just a passive spectator. And he sees so many things that he doesn't know what to choose, and finally selects a straw doll.

* * *

If not for his eyes and the retrospective weight of his apathy, Raul would have had energetic features. The hard chin, the thick beard, the long and straight nose, the high forehead. He dressed with uncommon correctness; something of the immaculate and abstract dominated his expression. But a touch of weakness detracted from the gravity, and especially the profundity of his bearing.

His wife was made of aged elements: her skin sallow, her eyes earth colored, her teeth calcareous, her hair thick, her lips fleshy. She wasn't ugly. It was just that the breath of spring had never blown over her. He was evanescent, she was stone-like.

And so, with the tenacity of ivy, she clung to the past. She repeated the domestic rituals with discipline and would venture out only if the event was capable of producing retrospective images in her. She went to the church, to whatever little store, to some neighborhood movie, because these places reminded her of her land. But nothing else. Decidedly hostile to everything new, she hated Mexico City, so new and so different.

She also began to hate her husband's surprising attitude. She was accustomed to predicting his movements, foretelling his ideas, regulating his habits. And now, all of the foresights weren't enough to control the internal disorder in which he was living. A kind of intoxication, a state of critical awareness, a secret eagerness was shaping him. And then she was jealous. For whom was Raul dressing with this breathless tediousness? Why had he bought soft woven and odd-colored neckties? What friends, or what lady friends was he with all the time? Sometimes he would telephone from town:

"Isabel, I'm calling to let you know that I won't be coming to dinner. I have an appointment."

"With whom?"

"With a friend."

"Someone from there, or from here?"

"A Mexican."

"A Mexican woman?"

"Isabel, I've never liked anyone to question me. You never used to do that."

"Maybe because there was nothing to ask you."

"Maybe," he said and hung up without saying goodbye.

He was experiencing the urgent call of new places, and of those to which he went, in his turn finding his rightful place. He would sit in the Restaurant Prendes, where the dining room has such a transitory aspect that later he could only remember the white tablecloths, the neither greedy nor conniving air of the head waiters, the floral appearance of the little carved radishes and the suspect whiteness of the celery stalks. He watched the customers being seated and, with solemn seriousness, discussing the menu. He felt suddenly included in an amiable wholeness by the familiar expression with which the waiter welcomed him. He chose the table with delight, calculating the light, the proximity of a Frenchman who was always discussing wines, or the sparkling warmth of a group of expatriate Andalusians. And he would open his eyes with delight, his ears with surprise, his palate with pleasure. He was learning to eat with the savage liturgy of an authentic Mexican, who permits himself the luxury of betraying his own stomach in order to sample a duck in orange sauce, a T-bone steak or a bunch of repulsive yet delicious goose barnacles. He had succeeded in mastering Mexico's gastronomic itinerary and his previously silent palate harassed him with unpredictable demands that he satisfied the way one caters to the whims of a favorite child.

Later, joyously, he would go out to meet the city. Its monuments, its climate and its humanity. And like a dazzled ascetic discovering patterns, he would split the street's crowd until he came upon the harmony of a girl with innocent, frozen, transparent eyes; or the multiplication of a building's architecture. Like exotic women in the night or the wind, he contented himself in caressing with his glance, or sometimes with his hand, the rough and brown, light and solid skin of the volcanic stone masonry. Softer than granite, nobler than wood, more plastic than marble the volcanic stone also embraces the entire warm range of ochres and reds, from light Alizarin red, light rosewood and burnt umber, to earthen red and wild saffron. And when the dust storms from Texcoco tint their surface with yellow, it looks like a spurious vegetation, that through an excess of luxury, has formed on the petal of a rose in order to give it a more unusual appearance. Now, in winter, the volcanic stone is vibrant, in summer the volcanic stone was fresh. Raul passed the back of his hand over the skin of the building and admired the august age of the doors, the windows distorted by the sinking of the monstrous shell in the unstable soil of Mexico. Volcanic stone, dust, wind, light and rain were his friends.

He went out early to find her and returned late from their encounters. Once, dawn surprised him in Tacuba, beneath the Tree of the Sad Night. Painfully sipping the pain of that real man, Cortés, who spent his bitterest insomnia there, without discovering that he wasn't keeping vigil alone. Mexico was with him, keeping him company, and now, Mexico would always be with him.

He saw couples going openly into the hotels, he saw them surrendering themselves to long, transitory kisses in the parks, and he was beginning to comprehend the profound skin of the women, their obscure intimacy, their geometric bones, surrendering and taking each time as if were the last time. The women made trips for passion; the men remorselessly set aside their hope, that way neither betraying their inmost being nor their first vow. That's not where the human being is betrayed; not in what is similar to it but rather in what is dissimilar to it. One hurts oneself with what's lifeless; what's lifeless is always strangely alive and you must kill what's lifeless before being able to make what's living sprout up. Until then, he had vegetated in all his deaths and only now, with these men who resembled each other in what's essential, with these women who surrendered to what's alive, he was experiencing the greenness of a new harvest. He was ready to be infected by everything, just for the prodigious joy of taking part.

Now he was living extravagantly and excessively, but something serene, something eternal like the precarious equilibrium of a pier in the afternoon, always docked his dreams in the tepid water of a final discovery. He was ready for it, standing on the earth where fertility reigns, where the mother word takes possession, from the blessing to the insult, and the father is nothing, can be anybody, because Mexico is woman, female and lady.

*   *   *

"It's a real embarrassment for you to be getting in at such hours. Does three or four o'clock in the morning at least twice a week seem like nothing to you? You've never done this before. And now you refuse to spend time with me."

"I refuse," said Raul, like an echo.

Isabel tried the imploring touch:

"Raul, those people can help us go back...they're issuing isolated permits to people who didn't actively take part. You're one of those."

"Unfortunately," he confirmed.

"What would you want then? To have taken a rifle and gone out to shoot? To have killed someone?"

"To have participated, participate..."

"Okay...Let's drop that. Are you going to go with me?"

"No."

Isabel stiffened up, furiously.

"Well, I'll have to drag you out of this damned city! We're going back! I'm sick of this boarding house, of the people, of the food. I want to go back and I'm going to do it. I'm not going to spend the rest of my life stuck inside these four walls with the kids getting skinny and pale and sick. I'm sick of it!"

"You never take them out....How do you expect them to be healthy?"

"There's smallpox, typhus, Maltese fever. And you say to take them out..."

"I didn't know that all the Mexican children were sick."

"They are, there isn't any milk here, or cheese or butter. We're leaving this city full of women...and men..." she added in order to hide her secret jealousy.

"A city full of women and men..." he ratified in order to verbalize her last thought. "Of men and women. You're right."

"Then you're going to go back with me?"

"I'm not going with you."

Crying, Isabel flung herself on the couch. He felt only infinite indifference. He watched her trembling without being able to tremble for her. Isabel was there in memory; he, who had no memories, felt incapable of sharing that sadness. After a while, the woman got up, disillusioned and bitter. Now she wasn't crying...She was challenging:

"Okay. I'll have to do it alone, but I'll do it. We're getting out of here. After all they don't have anything against you. I'll bring you the permit and then you'll come with me."

She tidied herself in front of the mirror. She combed her mat of thick hair. She smoothed her clothes. She went to give Chona instructions about the children and returned, bringing out a letter which she held out towards Raul:

"Since you're going out. Because I suppose you're going out..."

"I'm going right now."

"...put this letter in the mail. Not here in the neighborhood, but at the central post-office, airmail special delivery. I want to have a reply this week. I'll inquire by cable too, and then..."

Meanwhile, Raul was putting on his best tie. He also combed his hair, but with slow tediousness. He took his overcoat because it was cold; it was November. When he closed the door of the room, she opened it again behind her husband to challenge him at the top of her lungs:

"Then we're getting out of here! You'll leave that woman you have!"

Now, as he stepped into the street, Raul was touching the belly of that fertile woman.

San Juan de Letran at seven in the evening! San Juan of the magic and bewitchment! Miracles for sale, to be invented by the buyer. The cold wind he saw entering geometrically by the narrow streets on the 16th of September, Madero, Cinco de Mayo and Tacuba, enchantingly let down its hair upon reaching San Juan. It flung itself from one side to the other, putting its hand beneath a garment, combing a head of hair as if it were a pine, circling a waist as if it were an arm, picking up the vendors' merchandise from the ground as if it were a child. Raul surrendered to the game. Buying useless things, eating without being hungry, looking at the risque postcards, listening to a sales pitch, reading all the posters, watching a furtive transaction. Advancing so little that when he arrived in front of the Palacio de Bellas Artes the transparent night had already fallen over all of Mexico City. Mexico City, sleepless, was watching over the pleasure of her men, the pain of her men, the dream of her men.

He stopped again to contemplate a street miracle. On a black rag, a man was making three disjointed skeletons dance. The marionettes would straighten up, they would jump while the man, without moving his hands, directed their leaps with a resonant command. Then he offered his picturesque merchandise for sale. Raul bought a pair of puppets. "You'll make them dance," said the man. He knew that afterwards, in his hands, they wouldn't move again. But he had bought a miracle, and miracles must be invented in order to happen. He was not buying the miracle of the marionettes, but rather his own miracle.

He put his hand inside his jacket and touched the letter. Airmail, special delivery, we're going away, you'll leave that woman you have... he took out the envelope and carried it in his hand; he was close now. The Palacio de Bellas Artes, in its nocturnal nakedness, almost seemed beautiful. All of the ignobility of its imitation French architecture, all of the ostentation of its colored marble, all of its grotesque robustness disappeared with the night. Over the gilded cupolas, a ray of moonlight and a ray of sunlight were competing to produce unstable sparks. He let himself be hurriedly dragged along by the fevered traffic of the avenue. They were pushing him. They were forcing him to advance. He surrendered. Suddenly, the torrent pulled up alongside the building.

And there anguish anchored him. In a side entrance, on the luxurious stairway, illuminated by a small gaslight, twenty-five or thirty human shapes that could either be male or female, were lying every which way. Some stretched out full length, others seated, others crumpled up on themselves. Most, like those Mexican figures that commerce has made commonplace, were seated, their arms fastened around their legs beneath a black or gray *sarape*, their enormous *sombreros* hiding head and knees; immobile, silent, tragic. A cordon of police kept the questioning public from the Indians. He had to wait his turn to ask. They told him:

"They're strikers from Aguascalientes. They've been on a hunger strike for twelve hours."

The man who told him this was looking at the group as if electrified, with a menacing sparkle in his eyes, to a certain extent delighted or hostile. He made an energetic gesture with his hands and said:

"That's the way to do it. They're very tough. A man shouldn't give up. You'll see, they'll keep it up till they die; an Indian doesn't quit."

"But why are they striking? What do they want?"

"I don't know. I just saw them. But you can be sure that they'll drop dead before they'll quit. And there are women with them. That's the way to do it!"

He wanted to ask, "That's the way to do what?" but he didn't dare. He went to the next corner, mailed the letter, and his action seemed terribly useless to him.

He returned the next day in the morning. And the next day, and the next. The strikers were always there, immobile, recumbent, silent. The same cluster of spectators surrounded them and the police were maintaining a tight silence. It seemed like they might be with them, not against them. Each time, Raul stood watching them a long time. Afterwards he would slowly go down San Juan de Letran without being able to look at the vendors, or the women's legs, or the display windows, or anything.

He was ashamed of his futility, of his satiety, of his meaningless life, without human contact. 'You don't have to sell yourself,' he thought, 'and I've sold myself. I've sold myself out of fondness for luxury, out of inertia, to a government I didn't believe in, to a job that brought me no benefit but money.'

'I,' he said to himself, 'was the man who administered justice.' And he was more ashamed.

*   *   *

That afternoon his wife greeted him from the balcony, jubilantly waving a blue paper in her hand. "It's the cable," she shouted, "they gave you a permit."

Then when Raul came in, she leapt about her husband, carrying on a monologue:

"I've got everything ready, the reserved seats for tomorrow, the passports, visas, everything, everything. I've already packed the bags. We're going by train because I don't want to risk an airplane again. By train to Guatemala. Then we'll see. No more sour milk, or rancid butter or typhoid fever, or smallpox...or that woman!"

She paused before the strange passivity of her husband.

"Aren't you glad?"

"Yes, I'm glad," he said mechanically. Then he added: "They've gone fifty-six hours now."

"Gone fifty-six hours?"

"Without eating. The strikers from Aguascalientes...at Bellas Artes."

"What do I care about the strikers. Come on. It's time to eat."

*   *   *

Then, suddenly, everything before seemed like a lie. Till here, till now, he hadn't shared anything. Neither his land, nor his marriage, nor his work, nor the revolt that set him to flight and placed him in Mexico. Nothing. All of his life had been a succession of repetitious little deaths. He had only been dying. And today he was finally going to kill his death. His lie.

They were right, those men who didn't turn their faces to heaven, begging blessings, but rather to the earth, sinking the fertile roots of their knees into her. What did it matter why they were fighting? The important thing was to share something real. And the man who stands on his own two feet is real. Mexico had incorporated him in her pleasures, in the flesh of her women, and today in the tears of her man. To refrain from words was to be with this great silence. The first attitude of total surrender that he had enjoyed, had been given to him by this strange land with its rebellious men and its throbbing women. There in the little city where they knew his name, he was just that: a name. Here, anonymous, he was some part of what was surrounding; an atom, whatever, but he was, he belonged.

He walked, always returning from time to time to the stubborn strikers. He heard midnight tolling high above from the bells of the

Cathedral. He felt hungry and he smiled. Afterwards he went home to bed.

*   *   *

In the euphoria of the trip, his wife didn't reproach him and said nothing about the delay. They got up early and she amicably offered him a quick breakfast; the train was leaving at eight.

"I'm not eating," he said.

"You'll get sick, it's not good to travel on an empty stomach." But Raul didn't answer nor did he eat. Docilely he took the bags, carried one of the children in his arms to the automobile; on the way he kissed the three of them several times. Then they arrived.

He made his wife comfortable, he worried over all the details. "He's happy," she thought. Now, when the train was leaving, he stood up, the last whistles were sounding and the employees were rapidly checking through the cars.

"You go on," he said. "I'm staying. Goodbye."

Isabel looked at him, stupefied. It was too late to do anything. Later, perhaps later...

"Is it that woman?"

"Yes, that woman," he said.

And smiling from below as the train began to move, he waved a white handkerchief.

He slowly walked back to Bellas Artes. The Indians were still immobile. They still had the same position of stony waiting. Raul seated himself in front and he knew he was one of them, a member of their obscure family. He had gone sixteen hours now without eating.

He was questioned by another spectator and he answered mildly:

"They're strikers from Aguascalientes. They've gone seventy-three hours without eating."

"But why are they striking? What do they want?"

"I don't know," he said. "But that's not important. You can be sure they won't give up. They are men who are close to this land, fighting."

Translated by Don Sanders

From: Oreamuno, Yolanda. *A lo largo del corto camino*. San José: Editorial Costa Rica, 1961.

THE COUNTRY
SCHOOLMASTER

Julieta Pinto

The horse was so thin that the saddle rested upon the very crest of its spine, with areas of light showing through on each side. The short stirrups cramped his legs and when the trail was not very steep he took them out to stretch them. One, two, three hours through that heavy jungle which in places devoured the narrow path that the cowhand guide only found again by instinct. Trees so tall they nearly hid the sun or else transformed it into droplets of light as it filtered through their crowns; strange sounds, sometimes very deep, at others strident: the noise of rushing streams, footsteps running through the underbrush, the rustle of dry leaves, bees buzzing, and the snapping of a branch crashing through a world of grasses and insects—these sounds broke through the majestic silence of the prolonged spaces.

Isidro rode a horse even skinnier than his own and he used a heavy piece of sacking instead of a saddle. Himself thin and shrivelled, his body joined with that of his mount so that they moved in harmony. He answered questions in monosyllables as if the effort to speak might weaken him.

They got down off the horses to stretch their aching bodies and eat the sandwiches his mother had prepared. Made clumsy with the constant movement, they looked in pretty bad shape, but that did not affect their hunger. The guide ate in silence and a few minutes later they went on.

The light fell straight down on his head, adding to the heat and that heavy odor given off by the forest: a mixture of flowers and musk, dry leaves and new shoots, rotting wood and young sap. The horse's gait became quicker but the sound of its hooves more muffled. The sunlight was slowly sliding over his shoulders.

Finally the guide came to a halt and in a clearing he saw several huts and the gaze of children and adults in the doors of their homes. No one made the slightest movement to come forward. He dismounted and looked around him. The hermetic faces without smiles made a bad impression on him. He was so tired that he would have liked a cordial welcome, a shaking of hands, timid smiles—not this silence that seemed so menacing.

"Over here." The guide led him to the far end of the clearing and pointed to a hut.

"You can live here while you build the school room."

"I'm to build the school?"

"We've already got some wood cut, but we don't know how to put it together."

He was unable to answer. His fatigue was so great that he could barely eat the plate of beans with green bananas the guide offered him, and he threw himself down on the pallet in his clothing. Dreaming, the long trail on which he had been traveled for six hours went on and on, together with the disappointment of having to teach students in a village without a school building.

The confused hubbub of the children playing about near his hut awakened him and with great effort he got up. His whole body hurt, and his cramped legs hardly allowed him to walk.

"They're saying how if you tell us the way to do it, we can start building the school." The guide offered him a cup of coffee along with some tortillas while he spoke.

How could he tell them he didn't have the slightest idea of the way a school room was built. How to explain to them that the Ministry should have sent out a builder before it sent him? "It's in a very remote place," they had said, "and no one has dared start classes there. But there are so many children now that it's past time for some one to give them some education." "I still don't have my degree," he had responded, "I've got another year." "That doesn't matter, you're a candidate, and you can finish your studies during vacations. The important thing is to get someone in that teaching post." He had felt somewhat heroic to be going out among those smiling children and grateful adults. Now he was afraid he had accepted too large a responsibility. But several men were waiting outside the hut for him with hammers and nails in their hands. "Good thing they sent tools. I don't know what we would have done."

He invoked the spirit of his carpenter grandfather whom he had helped once when he was a boy to choose the boards for building a chicken coop, and he set to work.

"Pity we don't have have any cement to make the foundation, so it won't rot."

"*Pochote* wood's like iron. The rains never touch it, and several pieces are cut already. We got a couple hatchets dull just smoothing 'em off."

He sensed the man's eagerness despite the lack of expressiveness in his voice, and he felt calmer. The kids watched everything with eyes wide open, but half a smile showed on their lips if anyone asked them to hand up a nail or to hold a board in place.

They labored two weeks straight, sunup to sundown. His hands formed calluses and wore them off several times, and his arms and face turned the same color as those of his companions. Although words did not fill the air with their vibrations, there was a solidarity that made him feel good. He wasn't a stranger any longer but someone who shared their work, their food, and their interest in seeing the school become a reality. He was deeply frustrated when he found there was no corrugated iron to interweave with the palm thatch and the school ended up with a roof just like the ones on the huts. Rough benches with table tops were sanded off with *chumico* leaves for the children to write on.

The first day of classes forty children were packed into a room that could hardly hold them all. A simple room where, as the years passed, he would eventually have to provide for all the different school grades at once. Years? He was only committed to stay for one year. With his teacher's certificate he could aspire to a better position, near the city, with access to the movies, the library, perhaps more studying, and also to live with his mother, alone now in that room her sister had lent.

Meanwhile, he had to draw the letters very painstakingly for the children to imitate him, had to explain very patiently how those letters went together and made words, had to hear the satisfaction in their laughter as they wrote their own names.

With the adults the task was tougher. Clumsier hands, eyes more impatient, greater desperation when they couldn't manage to puzzle out what was written.

The copious rainfall brought new difficulties. The rivers became swollen and nearly wiped out the village. The schoolroom had nearly three feet of water in it, and for three days straight he had to work beside the men, under torrents of rain, attempting to deepen the river's bed.

He had almost no contact with the outer world. He received no help in the way of advice or textbooks. Only a letter from the Inspector of Schools arrived, scolding him for not having attended a meeting held in his district. He responded respectfully that the swollen rivers had not permitted him to cross and that no horse could get through the jungle swamps in six hours. The reply was a renewed threat that he had to obey orders if he wanted to keep his post. It seemed to him as if they had determined to put obstacles in the way of his work, or perhaps worse, to totally ignore what that work meant.

The constant rains penetrated the thatch of palm leaves, and the leaks dripped on the notebooks. Shivering, their clothing damp, the children suffered through their classes, and he couldn't even light a fire for them to warm themselves. There were nights when he considered abandoning them. To get a job as salesman in some shop. It wouldn't take a great deal of money to maintain his mother and himself. But the shouting and uproar when he greeted them every morning made him ashamed of his night thoughts, and the trust of the men who saw in him something akin to a magician who would resolve their problems obliged him to remain in his post. He had taken on the role of schoolmaster, counsellor, adviser, priest, nurse, and all the rest.

He who had had such a horror of blood was forced to bandage an arm left dangling by a swipe from a machete, had to cure infections so full of pus that he wasn't able to eat for the rest of the day, had to be the mediator in matrimonial difficulties. "Lola wants to get her fingers into my marriage and take my husband away from me. She lives alone and goes around like a bitch in heat trying to pick up any man she can." "But Paco was my sweetheart before he married Mercedes. She was the one that took him away from me." And his voice, counselling: "But they did marry, Lola, and they have four children." "OK, you've convinced me—but only because of the children."

To interrupt the lessons when the rice harvest ripened and help the whole village collect it because in one night the insects could swarm in and leave the fields devastated. To hear Guido's threats that if his son didn't pass into the next grade he would make him pay for it. And to realize that the son was as slow-witted as the father.

Classes were over, and he was able to pass half of the students into the second grade. With great effort. The adults had laboriously learned to decipher words. The final day, fathers and sons met at the schoolroom to hear his last words, and it was difficult for him to pronounce them, to bid good-bye to those faces who looked at him without daring to ask for anything.

Isidro waited for him with the same horse at the edge of the forest. "To go back to the city, listen to different words, live in a room where the noise of the gutters or the river out of its banks would not awaken him, to walk on sidewalks where there was no mud, read without the constant trembling of the candle flame, hear the autos, the blare of their horns, the joyfulness of the voices in the night, teach in a school with glass in the windows so the wind and rain could not come in, with varnished desks and kids who would know how to hold their pencils from the very first day..."

The horse moved along listlessly. It knew the journey was a long one and was saving its strength for trotting around the pasture, still green because summer was just beginning. The jungle was more humid than the first time he had gone through it, and the dripping from the trees got his clothes wet.

The voice of Isidro surprised him.

"Naturally..." His voice was quite firm.

"We didn't have a teacher for so many years, it's such an out-of-the-way place..."

"But it's different now."

"Ah..."

The monosyllable held a nuance so special that he turned to look at him in surprise. The man maintained his gaze without saying anything.

"You weren't expecting me to stay, were you?"

"I don't know..."

An uneasiness began to shoot through him. How did they ever imagine he might bury himself in that God-forsaken spot? He had a right to live a different life, to establish a home of his own in some civilized place. The sorrowful faces of the children appeared before him, one by one. "Adios, teacher, I hope you get along OK." "We're gonna miss you..." The horse did not hasten its step although he was beating it with his *guayaba* branch, and the time stretched out so long that it seemed as though they were going around in circles in the forest. It was a curious thing how he had come to love that people who were so reserved, so little demonstrative of their emotions. And what if a teacher came who wouldn't understand them, who would just do the teaching without having any interest in their problems? And worse, what if no teacher came at all? What a frightful disappointment for them, after they had built the schoolroom. Of course, teaching both first and second grade in the same classroom wouldn't be easy at all. Perhaps he might have been able to get another room built during the summer.

Why didn't he think to tell them to get the wood cut now so it would be dry enough in March? Maybe they could even build a room for the teacher, and life would be less uncomfortable. And the water? Why hadn't he told them to build a channel from the spring they had discovered so close to the village? They might even manage to have some pipe sent in. What a different village it would be, with clean drinking water. The kids wouldn't be so bothered by parasites, and their faces wouldn't always be so pale.

The voice drew him out of his meditation and it was a shock that to see the bus waiting for him.

"We didn't think you'd make it. We were about to leave."

He looked at them with his eyes wide open, and without saying a word he turned his mount half around. The horse started trotting happily, having recognized the return path.

This time Isidro allowed him to lead the way.

Translated by Leland H. Chambers

From: Pinto, Julieta. *Los marginados*. San José: Editorial Costa Rica, 1984.

THE MEETING

Julieta Pinto

One by one they were entering the little store. It had not rained, and sunbeams fell that the branches of the cedars and the *guanacaste* trees turned aside toward the leaves, tinting them with gold. Step by step the men came forward. The words from the previous week were sounding in their ears: "Starting tomorrow there will be no work. The boss is being sued in town, and we don't have enough money to settle accounts." "What are we going to do now?" one of the laborers' voices had sounded hoarsely against the silence. "I don't know, it's not my affair. They told me to let you know, and so I've done my duty." The overseer had called these last words over his shoulder to them while walking back toward the house.

Some were sitting on the benches in the store, others squatted on the floor.

"Mario, what did they tell you in the city?" asked a heavy man with hunched shoulders and a face covered with wrinkles.

The man spoken to spit out a wad of tobacco and wiped his mouth with the back of his hand.

"They're all a bunch of bastards. They just laughed and came out with "the boss this" and "the lawsuit that" and I didn't know what it was all about, except it was just to say for us to calm down, that they were going to pay us some day."

"But did you tell them we don't have anything to eat?"

"Of course I did, what did you expect me to say? They just said they would send us something to tide us over until they paid us."

"What we want is work," the old man said with an arrogant air that gave a new shine to his deeply wrinkled eyes.

"Oh yeah, when your kids keep asking you for food all the time, you don't care who it is as long as they give you something to eat. I could stick around the yard and survive on a stick of sugar cane and some bananas, but the family won't go along with that."

"Not only the kids, *compadre*, I'd like to see you nibbling on sugar cane and bananas for a whole month straight; the first time a chicken got in front of you you'd stuff it down feathers and all."

"The storekeeper already said he wouldn't give us another day of credit," a redheaded man with blue eyes said as he approached the group. "Fact is, we're just stupid. A lawyer in the city told me we should have complained way last year, when they made us accept the money instead of our benefits."

"Complained? who to?" asked the old man.

"I don't know. To someone. The thing is, now we're not doing anything at all."

"And what do you want us to do? The boss warned us if we didn't accept what he gave us he'd take away our houses. And after living so many years here you can't just go out looking for another job. You love the land, you get to know it, your old lady's gotten attached to the house, and the kids to the yard...And what good is it to look for something else if it's going to be the same everywhere you go?"

"Elias is right," another one of the group joined in. "I went down to the Zone year before last, I wanted to get out of this God-forsaken place and make some money, but I got the fever and almost died. And now I don't even have the strength to work. The thing about being poor is that no matter where we go we're always in a bad way."

"Isn't that what I'm telling you? We're just being lazy," the redhead insisted. "It's been days since they told us there wasn't any more work, and we haven't done a thing. The most we did was we sent Mario to the city instead of going ourselves all together so they would pay attention to us. When there's only one person alone they just wave him aside with a flick of their hand and tell him, Just be patient, the law will take care of everything. We ought to go all of us together to the city right now and make them give us work and pay us what they owe us. We're too accustomed to giving in, we can't even ask for what belongs to us any more."

"Juan is right, by myself I couldn't do anything. And when they begin to talk about laws and regulations they get me all mixed up and I can't even answer. That's what happened to me last year when I gave up my social security benefits for just two hundred pesos. You know: the law says this, the law says that, and the boss would be so grateful he'd give me a chance for a better job, and I was so tired I just said "yes" and signed the lousy piece of paper."

The old man had been listening with his head bent over, outlining a strange figure in the dust with his big toe. He straightened up and his phlegmatic voice reached all the listeners.

"Juan is right, Mario is right, but I tell you the devil knows more because of his age than because he's the devil. I've got a lot of years of experience on my back. We've got all these governments, we've got all these laws, these political campaigns where they offer us everything and the only thing we get out of it is a swig of brandy and ten pesos for our vote. You notice that we always come out just the same or maybe worse off than before. That's why I'm telling you that the best thing to do is stay here quietly or go and speak with the boss to see if by chance he'll let us work. You old guys here must remember what happened to Victor. He sued the boss for his wages, with the help of some jailhouse lawyer in the city; the boss didn't want to pay him because he was so young. I told him, 'Wait another year and you'll get paid, and stop all this nonsense about lawsuits."

"This blockhead didn't pay any attention to me. That lawyer had just gotten his law degree and was simply waiting for a good case to fall in his lap, and he'd already got Victor's hopes up. So Victor spent two months going back and forth to the city twice a week, with his ticket paid for on credit because he didn't have a job. It's true he won the suit, but do you know who got all the money? The lawyer, of course. And he still claimed Victor owed him money. Victor got screwed, he didn't have a job, he had to haul himself down to the Zone, and he died years ago, wiped out by the fevers."

The men remained silent after the old man's words. The whole sky had become tinted with color, and the reddish light put a grave look on all their faces. The children were playing ball in the street, and one could hear their shouts together with the complaints of the blackbirds begging the cloudless sky for water.

Juan rose to his feet to make his point clear to the cluster of men. As he spoke, he got red in the face.

"We can't let Elias make cowards of us. Times have changed, and we have to be strong. We have to go to the city and speak with whoever is there. If they talk to us about the laws we'll just tell them we don't understand anything but that the kids are hungry and have to eat. So the boss'll fire us? You just heard the man say there isn't any work because the farm is shut down, so we don't have anything to lose."

The men began to react to Juan's final words.

"Well, it's true that they've already let us go."

"Yeah, so we don't have anything to lose now."

"I've got a sick kid, there's no money for medicine."

"Don't tell me about it, my wife is due any day now, and we don't even have enough for a blanket."

"Yesterday the milkman told me he couldn't give me even one more bottle of milk on credit, and the baby needs it because my wife is so worried she can't nurse him."

Their words became whispers. With the last light of day they began to toy with dreams. "Maybe the farm will start up again soon." "At least they could pay us for the week they owe us and we could get out of debt." "If we all went down there together they'd have to listen to us."

The sun was hidden now and only a few lilac-colored clouds could be glimpsed in the sky and around the mountain peaks. The men got to their feet and step by step headed home.

Translated by Leland H. Chambers

From: Pinto, Julieta. *Los marginados*. San José: Editorial Costa Rica, 1984.

DEATH IN MALLORCA

Victoria Urbano

I don't know what made me get up in such a foul mood. Maybe I slept and dreamed longer than I should have. When I awoke it was so dark I thought it must be about five o'clock. I bunched up the pillow and rolled over, trying to fall asleep again; it was cold and I didn't want to lose the warmth surrounding my body. When I stretched I noticed that my feet were bare although I couldn't remember having taken off my wool socks. This little detail was enough to keep me from getting back to sleep. Then I noticed the time. It couldn't be as early as I thought; the trash cart donkey had already passed the house. Every morning at eight its strange braying wakened me. It was very punctual with its laments. When the trash cart stopped on the corner, the donkey brayed in a hoarse, mournful voice. The first time I heard it I thought someone was being murdered and I rushed out to the terrace to see what was going on. The poor donkey wore a funny little hat between its ears. While the trash collector and her daughter, dirty and ragged, went up to the houses for the trash, the animal impatiently lifted a hoof, shook its ears, wrinkled its velvety muzzle, bared its teeth and let out its strange wail, just once on each corner. The same thing happened every day. It was a perfect alarm clock until I became so accustomed to hearing it that it no longer disturbed my sleep. I had already heard it this morning. I turned on the light and looked at the time. It was eleven. I opened the blinds on the wide window leading to the terrace and a harsh, grayish light flooded the whole room. It had rained, and a breeze stirred the potted geraniums at the window. I lay down again and was engulfed by an intolerably bad mood. It was Good Friday, and there wasn't a sound from the street. My mouth felt dry; I took two sips of water that sent a disagreeable shudder through me. As soon as I pressed the bell to call the maid, I remembered that I'd given her the weekend off and, since my husband was in Mallorca, I was completely alone in the house. Friday has never been my favorite day, and this one was worse than usual. The gray sky was beginning to make me sad, but not with that romantic, melancholy sadness we sometimes feel. It was more like a dull inertia, a spiritual dejection, a capitulation, an overwhelming indifference to everything around me, complete oblivion toward all the things that usually interest me. In a word, the sadness was like a minus sign of myself that burst out into my cranky mood. As I pulled off the blankets, I destroyed the pleasant warmth my body had been relishing stealthily, quietly, as if it feared that I would deprive myself of that heat. My skin crawled when the cold touched it. The heat had been in our building since April 1st, and although it was a modern building accessible only to powerful wallets, most of the apartment owners refused to pay for another month's fuel, although the weather was still terribly wintry. They preferred to save their *pesetas* at the expense of their own discomfort. They were tightwads, maintaining their provincial thriftiness although they could afford not to. The cold made me even more grouchy. In the bathroom I let the hot water run while I brushed my teeth; steam fogged the mirror and I could no longer see myself, but I knew myself well: black eyes and well-defined lips. I didn't need a mirror to see myself. Over the living room fireplace hung an enormous portrait done by a famous painter. According to my friends, he had captured me masterfully. I was pleased with it too. I liked to look at the hands and the eyes because they were, perhaps, most like me. My hands could be languid or lively, independent or submissive. They seemed to possess a kind of mind of their own. They were like two living beings, versatile and eloquent, that recognized no obstacle to communication. At other times they were quiet and decorative like two lovely plants in an aristocratic garden. My eyes were dark, as I've said. But that in itself would not distinguish them from other eyes if it weren't because they were mine. What was personal was the look, the internal fire, the hatred, the love, the scorn or the indifference that projected me through them. There are plenty of dark eyes. What varies is the intensity, the sharpness of the pupil, the art of their expressive mechanism. Mine were frightening when they showed me what was hidden to others: that deep, intimate truth that can't be seen in a portrait or a mirror or by anyone else, but that shows itself to me in private in a strange process of self-inspection. Today my eyes were enemies because they made me see myself as I felt I was. Suddenly I became uneasy as if someone were staring at me impertinently, trying to penetrate my deepest thoughts. I stepped nude onto the scale. I hadn't gained any weight, but still I felt a crushing heaviness in my slender body. I entered the shower, and hot water streamed across my shoulders and back in a sensual caress. Then I decided to fill the tub, spilled in some aromatic bath salts I had bought in Paris and, as I sank into the water, I closed my eyes and forgot about time. The troublesome lie of the clock vanished. The scent of roses expanded in the water, rose on the steam, and filled that little tiled world I no longer saw. The fragrance and the heat made me drowsy. My body became weightless; it floated as if it were made of plastic. Gone was the troublesome lie of time. My outstretched hands, floating on the water, reminded me of that day in Mallorca...the day I met Juan. It was a splendid morning of sun and sea. I had swum a long way; when I felt tired, I started to float. As the waves held me up in their foam arms, I looked at the blue sky through my lashes and I felt happy, forgetting everything—even myself. Then I walked up to the beach, put on my dark glasses and, dropping onto a beach chair, prepared to enjoy the Mallorcan sun. A French couple sat nearby listening to a transistor radio. The music lulled me and suddenly, opening my eyes, I discovered a man staring at me. At first I saw only his unattractively hairy dark legs, firmly planted a short distance from my chair; then I met his eyes and his smile. His teeth were very white and his arms were crossed over an extremely hairy chest. He watched me without blinking, enjoying the sight of my complete relaxation. Thinking he might be a mirage, I pulled the glasses down to the tip of my nose, and he laughed aloud.

"Life's a dream here, isn't it, Miss Cardona?"

"I'm sorry, but I don't think I know you..."

"The bathing suit probably makes me look different. But I recognized you instantly. You've been in the sun too long. Your nose'll get red."

"I still don't know you." I pushed the sunglasses up again and tried to ignore him.

"I'm Juan Azagra...from the hotel. I wished you a good morning at breakfast. Don't you remember?"

"That's right.... Someone did speak to me this morning...but how do you know my name?"

"I saw your passport at the desk."

"Are you an inspector?"

"No, I'm co-owner of the hotel. Once in a while I fill out the guests' registration slips."

With this explanation, Juan Azagra sat down on the sand, his back to the French couple. I opened my beach bag and took out a pack of cigarettes.

"How do you like Mallorca?"

"It's nice. I enjoy the scenery here very much."

"Will you be staying long?"

"I have no idea."

"Terrific! That's the best way to travel—without a schedule. There are some wonderful places on the island you ought to see."

"For the time being I just want to enjoy being lazy, with no obligations of any kind."

"Your only obligation is to write, and you can find enough material here for ten books."

"Aha, so you also know what I do?"

"Of course. I told you I've seen your passport."

"You must have a remarkable memory to learn the personal details about all your guests."

"When I'm interested in them, I do."

"And might I ask what was so interesting about my passport?"

"Not your passport, but you. I like intelligent writers."

"Have you read my books?"

"No, but I've read your eyes. They're very beautiful. Tell me, are you famous?"

"Not exactly."

"What do you mean?"

"It's really very simple. The only books that have made me any money are rather bad mysteries published under a pseudonym with a foreign flavor: Nora Blake. But the other books, the ones I'm proud of—well, those don't seem to appeal to the publishers."

"That's the way it often happens. But what's important is to make a name for yourself; once you're well known, you can bring out all the other books."

"Impossible! I loathe the name Nora Blake."

Professional envy?"

"Yes. For me, Nora Blake represents the readers' stupidity."

"Don't be angry with them. Remember that if your books didn't sell, Emilia Cardona might not have been able to come to Mallorca!"

"You're right. Being able to afford to travel makes it worthwhile. I love the sun and the sea, and I just want to forget about everything and everyone."

"If you get too much sun you'll get dusky like me."

"Do you come to the beach every day?"

"Without fail when I'm in Mallorca—and that's two months a year."

"Oh, then you don't live here."

"No."

"What about the hotel?"

"My brother runs it year-round. I come only during the season. I live in Madrid."

"We might even turn out to be neighbors who've never met."

"We might. May I call you Emilia?"

"Yes, of course."

"Tell me then, Emilia, what plans do you have this afternoon?"

"Not to go anywhere with a stranger," I replied with a smile.

"That's very wise, but I don't consider myself a stranger, so I'd like to invite you to Soller for lunch with my niece and me. I'd better warn you that lunch here at the hotel is going to be awful today."

"In that case, I'd be delighted."

Juan rose with startling agility and held out a hand to help me up. I gathered my things and he threw my beach bag over his shoulder. When we reached the hotel, he said:

"I'll meet you here in an hour. Don't be late."

"I won't keep you waiting."

*   *   *

I took a last look in the mirror before going downstairs, and I was surprised to see how dark my face and arms looked against my white dress. My skin felt smooth and soft. When I got out of the elevator I saw Juan standing in the lobby beside a slender, graceful adolescent. He looked very different in street clothes. He was wearing a sport shirt and nicely tailored summer slacks. It was then that I calculated his age. He'd be about forty.

Juan introduced his niece; her name was Mariángeles. Her coming along with us made me feel more comfortable, so I prepared to enjoy my unexpected outing.

We rode in a small Seat, and I turned my attention to the splendid scenery. Mountains and sea, almond trees and windmills—perfect combinations to inspire anyone with a poetic imagination. Mariángeles hummed incessantly in the back seat, and Juan smiled.

"Today you're going to taste the best *paella* in Mallorca!" I've phoned Manoli and asked her to make it for us."

"Who's Manoli?"

"An extraordinary woman. I'm anxious for you to meet her. I'm sure you could write a book about her and make a million."

"What a nice idea! What kind of a book?"

"A mystery."

"In that case, Nora Blake would have to write it."

"Who's Nora Blake?" asked Mariángeles, interrupting her song.

"Nora Blake is Emilia's rival," said Juan, and we laughed.

It was hot, but a salty breeze entered through the window and created a sensual impression of the seaside that has remained in my memory ever since. I felt like a stranger, distant from myself, forgetting all my thirty years, all my discipline as a young writer determined to succeed.... What nonsense! I didn't think about the romantic disappointment that had made me decide to take a trip or about coming to Mallorca quite by chance, since I let my travel agent make all plans and reservations with no suggestion or objection on my part. And now, here I was riding along with a stranger whose company I found enjoyable.

"Here we are!"

"That was fast," exclaimed Mariángeles. "You drive faster every day."

"And your father is always criticizing my little car, and it never gives me any trouble."

"My father, poor thing, doesn't know how to drive like you do. He's so nervous he makes you afraid to ride with him."

Juan parked under an arbor in front of Casa Manoli. The brilliance of beach, sea, and whitewashed walls blinded me. I felt intoxicated by the light, happy, and terribly hungry. I was looking forward to tasting the Mallorcan *paella*, to meeting the woman named Manoli and, above all, I was dying to enter Juan's unknown world and learn his true story. I wondered if he had one.

We went in. It was a large house with old wooden ceiling beams, brick floors, and tile-bordered walls. Gleaming copper pots hung in the rear of the bar, alternating with garlands of garlics, peppers, and sausages. The dining room was filled with tourist, all dressed in shorts. Germans, Frenchmen and Americans enjoyed seafood and wine, and their red noses seemed to shout loudly that they were having a fabulous vacation. One of the waiters led us through a private door to the interior of the house. We came to a charming terrace filled with flowers. Manoli was waiting for us there. Very different from what I had imagined. She wasn't fat, aging, or vulgar, but an extremely attractive women. Her hair was jet black, so black that under the sun it seemed to send off blue sparkles. She wore it pulled back in a bun, showing off her beautiful Spanish forehead. Her skin was pale, her eyes almond-shaped, and her mouth very beautiful and serious. It was the kind of mouth that rarely smiles. Her classic serenity reminded me of the Dama de Elche.

"Hi, mother," said Mariángeles, with a sort of natural indifference, and my surprise grew with the unexpected revelation.

Manoli held out her hand in greeting.

"Welcome to Soller, Emilia."

"Thank you. What a beautiful place you have here."

"I'm sorry Juan didn't give me more advance warning..."

"You don't need any apologies, Manoli," he interrupted. "Your *paella* is always the best in the world." He came closer and kissed her hand ceremoniously.

Manoli invited us to sit down. Mariángeles settled in a hammock, where she sat stroking a cat. While we had cocktails, my imagination began to weave a mysterious plot around Manoli. Were she and her husband separated? Was Juan in love with her? My conjectures were interrupted by a sensation that I was being steadily observed, and I looked up to meet Manoli's scrutiny. Suddenly I felt strangely self-conscious. I think I blinked and said something foolish to disguise how affected I'd been by her penetrating eyes. Then, for the first time, Manoli smiled.

Juan told her as much as he knew about me and spoke highly of my literary talents and the success I'd achieved under a foreign pseudonym.

"Perhaps some interesting experience awaits you here, and it may become your best book," said Manoli. "Your future will be brilliant."

"You say that with such assurance, it gives me chills. Do you know how to read the future in a person's eyes?"

Manoli wrapped Juan and me in an expressive gaze and, so softly that she seemed to be talking to herself, said:

"Yes, of course I do." Then, in a completely different tone, she added, "Well, here's our lunch."

Mariángeles dropped the cat and got up to wash her hands in a lovely little fountain on the terrace.

"I have to talk to you about Dad," said Mariángeles, taking a seat at the table beside her mother. "He's furious with me because I went to the movies with Fernando."

"You have to be patient with him."

"My father is all nerves. He finds something wrong with all my friends. He doesn't want me to ever get married."

"When you're really in love, we'll find a way to convince him."

"You're the only one he listens to...you and Juan."

Manoli looked at me and, by way of explanation of that exchange she must have realized I'd find puzzling, said:

"My husband and I are good friends. We get along well at a distance, don't we, Juan?"

"Well, he doesn't like the idea of being separated from you, but he couldn't stand losing you altogether."

Understanding the discussion of family matters was keeping me out of the conversation, Manoli came to my rescue.

"Don't be embarrassed, Emilia. Everyone knows that my husband and I are separated. In a situation like our, the best course seemed to be to keep our distance."

"How do you like *paella*?" Mariángeles asked, and I was grateful that her spontaneous remark changed the conversation.

"It's delicious. I've really never tasted any better."

"Don't you have *paella* at home?"

"Not like this!"

"I'll give you the recipe."

"Don't you keep it a secret, Manoli?"

"Of course not! There are some things I like to share with others."

"In that case, I'd like you to teach me to foretell the future."

"Oh, that's funny. I see you were intrigued by what I said earlier. That's a good sign my prophecy will be fulfilled."

"What was your prophecy?"

"That you'll never forget us or this place..."

Manoli smiled somewhat mysteriously, offered me a cigarette, and then, rising, suggested:

"While Juan and Mariángeles take a little rest, I'll show you my castle. Would you like that?"

"Oh yes, I'd love it."

"I hope you like it as much as I do. I adore this place."

"Are you going up to the tower?" asked Mariángeles.

"Not today."

"Don't be too long," said Juan, dropping into a lounge. "I'll miss you."

"Well then, why don't you come with us?"

"No. I already know the history of your house and don't care to hear it again."

Manoli smiled and invited me to follow her. We went down a staircase at the back of the terrace and before continuing along a flower-bordered path, she told me:

"What you're about to see is the oldest castle in Soller. The whole area of the restaurant and kitchen, the terrace where we had lunch, and the bedrooms you haven't seen yet are new, although we used old materials and the panelling is authentic. But everything you'll see from here on is part of a castle that dates back to the days of the Moors. The walls and tower had to be restored, but the inside was remarkably well preserved because the doors were sealed for several centuries."

Manoli opened a door and a strange emotion swept over me. I was about to walk on ancient stone floors and enter a place that had witnessed many centuries and many lives whose secrets I could never know. Manoli's voice brought me out of my thoughts.

"The property has belonged to my family since the time of James the Conqueror, but it was in ruins for centuries. My father was the first to become interested in restoring it, and then, a long time ago, just after I was married, I got the idea of turning it into a tourist attraction. That way I'd be able to carry on the excavations; I'd had to stop them because I'd run out of money."

"It must be wonderful to own a castle like this!"

Manoli flicked a switch, and a flood of light revealed an enormous stone stairway with heavy chains hung like garlands on both sides. We went down fifteen steps and reached a somber, austere chamber boxed in by thick window-less walls. There was a line of engaged columns with intertwined arches along three sides. It looked like a dead end, but Manoli pressed against one of the columns and, to my amazement, a small rectangle opened in the wall, leading to a tunnel.

"What a mysterious place!" I exclaimed. "How did you ever discover the door?"

"I found it by accident. This room didn't make any sense all by itself and so far away from the castle, and it occurred to me that it might have been an escape route. My father had made a careful study of all the historical documents that mention Soller castle, and he told me that this room was used as a cell for some important prisoners."

"I'd like to hear the whole history of this place."

"I've been studying every inch of it for years and I'm still discovering fantastic things. My husband is convinced the place has me bewitched. He doesn't have patience for all this."

"It would be the perfect setting for a historical novel."

"If you're really interested, why don't you spend some time with me? There's enough material here for many novels."

"Are you serious, Manoli?"

"So serious that I won't hear of you leaving tonight. Tomorrow we'll have your luggage sent up from Palma, and you can move into my house as if it were your own."

"It's an exciting idea. But go on, please. Tell me how you happened to find the secret passage."

"Well, when we were installing the electricity, I noticed how beautiful the capitals of the columns were, and I decided to photograph them for illustrations of my father's work. When I rested a ladder against one of the columns, it yielded a little under my weight; then the stone block that forms the entrance opened. It was quite a discovery because we had no idea this tunnel leading to the castle even existed."

"Incredible! Weren't you afraid to go in?"

"No. I've always had the feeling that I lived here centuries ago. And every new place we discover seems to confirm it. Come on, Emilia, don't be afraid."

Manoli turned on a light that revealed a narrow gallery. An underground chill made my skin crawl. We advanced some distance and, on the lefthand side, I noticed an archway leading to a ramp.

"That section hasn't been worked on yet," nodded Manoli. "I'll show it to you some other time."

"Doesn't it scare you to walk around in here alone?"

"No. On the contrary, I find it fascinating, because I seem to hear the voices of all the people who ever walked here in ancient times. If you lived here, you'd come to love every stone in this fortress as much as I do. It's a wonderful place for anyone with a vivid imagination."

"I can believe that; I don't think I'd be at all surprised if a Moor suddenly came through the wall!"

"I've seen more than one," Manoli assured me seriously.

I stopped and looked into her face. In that vaulted light her eyes looked larger, deeper, more mysterious.

"You're joking, and I'm getting the creeps," I said, half-smiling.

"No, I'm not, I'm being perfectly serious, Emilia. I really am. But don't be alarmed. I'm not crazy, if that's what you're thinking. You're a writer with a good mind, and you understand many things that escape mediocre people. From the moment I laid eyes on you, I knew you were different. Don't think I could talk to just anyone as frankly as I'm talking to you. Most people are stupid, like my husband. Nobody understands me except Juan."

We came to another flight of stairs with twenty-seven steps and emerged onto an enormous yard surrounded by protective walls and watchtowers. In the rear, imposing and sober, rose the castle. Manoli closed the door.

"Some other day we'll come earlier to see the fortress and the baths. There's no electricity there yet, and it would be too dark now. We can go back to the house across the field. All right?"

"Yes, of course; it's a lovely afternoon."

For a while we walked in silence. The sea breeze wrapped me in its warm caress while my mind worked feverishly to understand Manoli's strange personality. She was a very attractive woman and somewhat mysterious, although she appeared to be very open and frank. Against the reddish setting sun, her classic profile seemed to accentuate her magnetism. I started to think about a book. I was prepared to discover all the hiding places of her soul. I was more interested in her personality than I was in the castle, although the castle provided a wonderful springboard for my imagination. And what about Juan? Why had he invited me to Soller? Why hadn't he told me about Manoli? And Mariángeles. She was a strange youngster too, remote and indifferent. What was going on between mother and daughter? And Manoli's husband? Why was he separated from her if, as Juan said, he couldn't bear to lose her altogether? And what about me? Why had I come to Mallorca? What made me accept invitations from perfect strangers? Why had Manoli said I'd never forget this place? What mysterious web was fate weaving for me? Why did she say she didn't mind sharing some things? What were the others, the ones she wouldn't share with anyone? Why did she sometimes look at me as if she could really penetrate my deepest intimacy and probe my most hidden secrets?

Manoli's voice interrupted my thoughts.

"Do you know Alfonso, my husband?"

"Only by sight."

"We were very young when we married. It was a ghastly mistake."

"Have you been separated very long?"

"Since Mariángeles was born but, as they say, we're good friends. We started both our businesses together, and we never disagree about financial matters. Mariángeles is his great love."

I was tempted to ask her who hers was, but decided the question would be too presumptuous. But Manoli seemed to guess what I was thinking.

"It must seem strange to you that my daughter doesn't live with me. Doesn't it?"

"Frankly, I haven't had time to think about it one way or the other."

"You're very tactful and diplomatic, Emilia, but I don't mind telling you. I've never felt any maternal love. The birth of my daughter Mariángeles was a catastrophe for me."

"Were you in love with another man?" I heard myself ask, and immediately felt like biting my tongue, but Manoli seemed to expect the question because she replied without hesitation.

"Yes, I've been in love with Juan all my life."

We reached the house. Juan and Mariángeles came out to meet us.

"You've been gone so long!" the girl exclaimed.

Juan added, "Well? Was it worth the trip, Emilia?"

"You bet it was! It's a fascinating place. Manoli has asked me to stay a few days and I've brazenly accepted her invitation. What do you think of that?"

"Manoli always has brilliant ideas. Are you going to invite me too?"

"Of course, Juan. You can stay too," Manoli said with a bright expression in her eyes.

*   *   *

An enormous moon over the shore. The sea dragged its lace of waves toward the beach. Some tourists were swimming, and their floating silhouettes took on a strange, inhuman aspect under the moonlight.

The night was warm and cool at the same time. The breeze wafted through my hair and moved down over my bare shoulders and curled around my arms like an invisible filigreed bracelet. Juan suggested we sit on some rocks facing the sea. We had walked a long time, visiting the most delightful corners of Soller. Juan took out a pack of cigarettes and offered me one. I noticed the brand.

Smiling, he said, "I stole them from Manoli. I think they're quite mild."

"They are. I tried one this afternoon. I'd never heard of the brand before."

"An Englishman who lives here gives them to Manoli. He's been in love with her for years." Juan laughed. "Poor fellow!"

"It's not surprising that men fall in love with Manoli. She's a very beautiful woman."

"You should have seen her when she was younger. When she was twenty, she was stunning. My brother fell madly in love with her at first sight. It happened right here on this beach. Manoli had her hair loose, and she looked like a mermaid that had escaped from the bottom of the sea. Three months later, they were married."

"Then why..." I didn't dare finish the question, but Juan continued.

"It was an absurd match. Manoli is an extraordinary woman while my brother is a very common man. Soon the castle came between them like a wall. Manoli set herself, body and soul, to the study of the fortress. She's had some strange experiences that my brother, who's not very imaginative, interprets as witchcraft. Soon after Mariángeles was born, my brother tried to make Manoli leave here, and he took the baby to my parents' house, thinking that Manoli would follow, but he was mistaken. Since then, as she says, they've been good friends."

"I don't understand how your brother can be so arbitrary."

"That's how men are; we're arbitrary."

"Don't joke. I'm very interested in Manoli's story; to tell the truth, I'm dying of curiosity, I find it all so strange."

"You have to be careful of curiosity; it can be risky."

"Why did you invite me to Soller?"

"Because you could write your best book here, make a fortune, and get rid of the name Nora Blake."

"Stop talking nonsense, Juan. You had some very definite purpose in bringing me to Manoli's house. What was it? Why? For what?"

"I see you have the mind of a detective, Emilia. Or is it Nora Blake asking all these questions?"

"Come on, tell me. You can be frank."

"Well, since you insist...first of all, I'll tell you that I was in love..."

Juan paused and looked into my eyes. I'll confess that my heart gave a leap, but he didn't finish the sentence as I'd expected.

"...I was in love with a girl who looks like you. That's why, when I saw you at the hotel, I looked at your passport and then arranged to meet you."

I remained silent. I was beginning to be suspicious of Juan. Was he sincere? I was convinced that Juan was in love with Manoli.

"What does one thing have to do with the other?" I asked.

"A great deal and nothing. It's very complicated. I brought you here to meet Manoli. I was sure you'd be impressed by her story, her castle, and her beauty; and I knew that once you'd met her, the novelist in you would persuade you to stay on in Soller, and that way I'd have a chance to spend more time with you."

"What a fibber you are!"

"No, Emilia, I'm perfectly serious. As soon as I saw you at the hotel I told myself I'd marry you."

"Oh, nonsense!"

"Why? Ask Manoli if you don't believe me."

"Manoli?"

"Yes, don't be surprised. When I phoned to ask her to prepare the *paella*, I told her that I'd finally found the woman of my dreams—you."

"You can't be serious!"

"Does the idea of marrying me sound so outrageous?"

"I've known you for less than twenty-four hours, Juan, and even if it were longer, I'd still think all this was some kind of a bad joke."

"I'm forty years old, Emilia. I don't want to be a bachelor for the rest of my life. What's wrong with that?"

Juan looked into my eyes and I felt a tug at my heartstrings. For a brief instant I thought that perhaps he was serious, but how could he be?

"It's not my fault you haven't married," I smiled, "but I have no intention of complicating my life for your sake. You know I came to Mallorca for a vacation, not to find a husband."

"You came to forget a love, and I'll help you do that."

"Oh? So you're clairvoyant too?"

"The end of a romance can always be detected in the eyes. You can't hide it. Manoli saw it in you."

"Manoli! Manoli!" I exclaimed in annoyance, "I'll end up thinking you're all witches!"

"Don't be upset," said Juan, taking my hand. "I can be patient; I'll wait for you to learn to love me."

"But why me, Juan?"

"The whims of Fate."

"That's enough talk about Fate! Let's go, please. It's getting late."

"As you wish, Emilia."

I had never in my life seen the moon so large. It was like something out of a Japanese painting. Never before had a man disturbed me as had this Spanish Don Juan at my side. We walked in silence, holding hands, and although I didn't want to admit it, even to myself, I sensed that I would never again be free of him. Under the immense moon, the idea was intimidating, but, at the same time, pleasant.

In the distance we could make out Manoli's castle. It was like some medieval specter trying to eat the moon. I thought of it as a strange monster burdened by centuries and secrets.

"It's imposing, isn't it?"

"Yes, very."

"My poor brother detests it."

"Is he jealous of the castle?"

Juan smiled. "He's not very bright, but the poor man has suffered a great deal."

We arrived at the house, and Manoli received us with the most natural happiness.

* * *

My room had a small balcony that overlooked a delightful garden. It was furnished in Moorish style, with tooled leather cushions and a table with a lovely carved glass chess board. On the dressing table stood crystal jars filled with delicate perfumes and covered with metal cut in geometric designs. A small lute inlaid with gold and mother of pearl hung on the wall beside the low bed, and several antique musical instruments surrounded it. A silver basin stood on the nightstand. Manoli smiled as she showed me into the room and, throwing open the shutters of the closet, she revealed the richest clothing imaginable, all in Moslem style. To my surprise, Manoli offered:

"Make your choice, Emilia. You can wear whatever you like and feel a little bit like the Arab princesses who once lived in our castle."

"What rich fabrics! It's like a dream!"

"Or absolute nonsense, as my husband insists."

"Where did you get these robes, Manoli? In Morocco?"

"Oh, no! I made them myself; I followed descriptions I've come across in some Arabic documents and poems. I'm going to show you a very curious robe."

Manoli spread a white tunic on the bed. A poem was embroidered on it in gold thread:

> "By God, no greater beauty than mine need you seek!
> I go my way; in vanity I find my bliss;
> But to the man who loves me I surrender my cheek,
> And I never refuse one who begs for a kiss."

After reading the verse aloud I exclaimed:

"I know those lines! I think they were written by the poet Ben Zaidun's mistress, in the year 1025. Wasn't she Princess Walada?"

"That's remarkable, Emilia. Not many people are able to recognize the verse. Just for that, I'm going to make you a gift of the robe."

"Oh, no, Manoli. Your generosity is embarrassing me. I couldn't possibly accept it."

"Why not?"

"Because it's very beautiful, and you must have spent a long time embroidering it."

"I'll have plenty of time to make another. I keep myself amused with these things during the slack season. Take it, please. I'll be offended if you don't."

"It's really very lovely, but don't you think it might be a little risky to wear it?"

Manoli laughed and exclaimed:

"I'm sure Juan will be the first to 'beg for a kiss'."

"And you wouldn't mind if I gave it to him?" I asked, looking into her eyes. It wasn't a challenge; I was simply curious to see her reaction.

Manoli sat on the bed, took some cigarettes from the nightstand, offered me one and, after lighting hers with all the deliberation of an important ritual, she answered.

"No. Because Juan's happiness matters to me more than my own."

"But why me, Manoli? There's some mystery in all this I don't understand. On one hand, your frankness confuses me. On the other, Juan...well, I don't know, everything seems to have been plotted step by step. The only thing I really don't understand is why I'm here."

"You're here because we've been waiting for you for a long time. And it was today a hundred years ago."

"What are you talking about, Manoli?"

"Don't look at me so bewildered, Emilia. A hundred years ago it was today. Juan and I love each other. We have loved each other for centuries and centuries here, in this castle. For centuries and centuries, the ring of love shone on our fingers. For centuries and centuries, passion, in its red tunic, blessed us with the fullness of its beauty. Until one day, a hundred years ago today, I died in Mallorca, and my pain at leaving Juan was so great that my soul was torn in two, and then *we* were born...."

"What are you saying, Manoli?"

"That you and I were born, Emilia. Don't you understand now?"

"Yes, we were born. You of one mother and I of another, with an enormous distance between us. Don't you see how different we are?"

"My soul suffered the torture of duplication: a hundred years ago I was born, reincarnated in two bodies, and ever since then I have been looking for myself frantically. At last I have found myself. Only you can return what is mine."

I began to worry. There wasn't the slightest doubt in my mind that Manoli was mad, but there was no hint of her insanity in her expression. Quite the contrary. Her face was beautifully tranquil, and a faint smile played on her lips. Then I looked at her eyes and there, in the deep black pupil, I sank into a hundred years of forgotten memories. Manoli stubbed out her cigarette, stretched out on the bed, folded her arms across her chest, and closed her eyes. Death had just come to her, but her soul, unbroken and whole, smiled within me.

I put on the gold-embroidered robe and went out into the garden. Juan was there, waiting for me at the fountain. And it was today again, a hundred years ago.

Translated by Irene del Corral

From: Urbano, Victoria. *Y era otra vez hoy*. San José: Editorial Costa Rica, 1978.

THE GOOD GUYS

Rima de Vallbona

The whole atmosphere was tense and everyone was arguing about the elections, young and old alike. At home that's all we could talk about. Even Pura, the maid, an active member of the Popular Front, dared to bet me two *reales* that her party would win. I told her I was betting my two *reales* on the good guys. Pura asked me if they belonged to the Popular Front, because if so, we were betting on the same guys. I said, "No, they're not, Pura, because those guys starve people to death."

"And what about the Rightists? Have you forgotten, Lola? They shot up my boyfriend when he tried to make his land claim. And my brother...we'd better not even bring that up!"

I always had the habit of noticing anything that was new. My eyes discover things and try to figure them out. Now my eyes are constantly bombarded by nothing but posters and political propaganda. Aggressive, defensive signs, plastered all over the city walls, publicize the misdeeds of one faction or the good deeds of another. Amid the film advertisements, in the hubbub of the market, in the sadness of the jail, at the stone fountain, political posters: the same woman, her head bowed, on every wall in the city asks her duplicated husband, "What are you thinking about, Antón?"

"If the Popular Front wins, we'll be hungry again," answers the poster husband, who is pasted onto stone walls, concrete, a tree, is tattered, or floats on the wind like a hopeless good-bye.

How could anybody bet on somebody who starves people to death? They couldn't ever be the good guys. I imagined a thousand-headed hunger monster devouring all the people in Nograles. Until then the monster's victims were only in the slums, where money couldn't buy muzzles for his thousands of insatiable mouths. I understood that hunger was an evil as gruesome as the plague, because of the face on that duplicated husband: "If the Popular Front wins we will be hungry again...we will be hungry again."

Then I said to Pura, "Dumb bunny, how can you even think that the Popular Front is the good guys. Sometimes you're dumber than the dumbest. Now, I'm betting on the good guys, the real good guys, you know; not on somebody who starves people to death."

"Yes, yes, you're smart, all right! You're blowing hot air, Lola! The ones you call good have the jails full of—you know who? Of a lot of people they've starved to death with miserable little salaries that won't even buy bread. So, I'm betting on the good guys too, the ones who ended up in jail for fighting about the few *centavos* they earn with a pick-ax, a hoe, a miserable saw or a hammer. Like you, I'm betting on the good guys."

My brother was laughing at us both, "Yes, yes! Everybody is betting on the good guys. A beaut of a bet! Well, we'll see tomorrow who wins."

The day was filled with that stupendous, on-going bet of two *reales*. That little bit of money to me represented an entire week of nothing but studies, errands, hard work and obedience. I was convinced that my bet was worth more than Pura's. Hers was just another coin jingling in the pocket of her apron fragrant with kitchen aromas. On the other hand I had bet the fun of a ride on the merry-go-round, the thrill of a roller coaster, a Roy Rogers or Tarzan movie, the dark flavor of a Nestle chocolate, a refreshing Coca Cola, or a kite flipping its tale in the wind. Mine was an expensive gamble; it threatened to cancel all my possibilities for fun during an interminable week.

"If the Rightist Party wins," my older brother said, breaking into my monetary considerations, "let the politicians look out; not a single puppet will keep his head."

I was sad when I thought of Ramon, who sometimes brought fresh vegetables to the house. While he ate a bite in the kitchen, he used to spout off about the army brass, the factory owners and the priests. He was in jail now and he must be missing his grain and corn fields, all green and full of chirping birds. If he's dead, Ramon won't be able to pamper his crops, or protest or talk in the kitchen about agrarian reform. I supposed, from what he said, that wanting agrarian reform must be something like wanting to pee during class: if you left the room, even if you really had to go, the teacher made you kneel on the floor where the edges of the rough hewn stones cut your knees and you had to stay there until class was over, even if you couldn't hold the peeing and you wet your pants, like I did once. Everybody laughed and the teacher fussed at me and punished me for another hour.

I knew they were going to kill anyone who was for agrarian reform. Then, was Pura right? The ones in the Popular Front...were they the good guys, and I...what about hunger?

*   *   *

Election Sunday. It was an early daybreak, an excited, expectant day, clear and bright. Early Mass was a must because the lines to vote at the library were so long. Father came home at noon, happy because the Rightist Party had the election in the bag; victory was a sure thing. The Popular Front only had a few big cats and our dumb cousin Jaime, the plumber.

"God forgive little Jaime his stupidity," Grandmother often says.

Whenever Grandmother talks about cousin Jaime the plumber she shakes her head, looking very solemn. It's because cousin Jaime relishes asking her if she, being so righteous, is going to pray for him when he dies since he doesn't even believe in God.

"How many souls do you get out of hell every day, Grandmother, with all that praying?" he asks.

And she replies without losing her ancient dignity, her voice firm, "I get out every last one you send there to be consumed by fire with your curses, you outcast atheist, you heretic, you disgrace to the family. And how is it you decided to show up here in shirt sleeves and without a tie? Is it the fashion in the country of the atheists? You are a Cretin, Jaimito...the day will come when all will be tears and gnashing of teeth. Just wait." "That boy will come to a bad end, a very bad end. It's a miracle he's not already in jail," she mutters.

Brother says, "It's a good thing to have family members in the other party. You never know what might happen."

Grandmother shakes her head. Whenever she talks about Jaime, grandmother obstinately shakes her head.

It's pointless to argue. It's time to drink champagne, to toast the victory of the good guys, our side; everything will be the same and better still. Friends who drop by say victory is ours. Father paces back and forth restlessly, listens to the radio, goes out to the street, returns gloating. Now there's no doubt, ours will win. Tomorrow will be special, because I will have in my hand my two *reales* and Pura's two, money for pleasure, fun, laughter. I drop happily off to sleep. Tomorrow...tomorrow...

The biggest merry-go-round in the world, all skyblue and garlanded in fresh azaleas that perfume the Nograles air—they put it right in the middle of the town square. I ran to climb up on a high-spirited, chestnut steed. The little man dressed in dirty clothes took the money I won from Pura from my hand. It was a coin the size of a saucer with large letters spelling "victory to the good guys". I climbed on happily, very happily and the merry-go-round started. Up and down, around and around and around. The shabby little old man, tied to the gears by a cord around his waist, made the little horses speed around and around and up and down. The little man was running, running, running; he tripped and fell, got up, went on, and on and on as if he would never stop. I was dizzy, nauseated, felt like crying and screaming that it doesn't matter whether the good or the bad guys win (don't know which is which anyway) because it's all the same, going around and around and always with someone tied to the wheel. Finally, the little man in the shabby clothes lost his footing and fell into a heap, his flesh torn to shreds and at the same time the skyblue merry-go-round tumbled down at my feet.

Monday went by with no election news. Nograles was on edge. Was it Tuesday? I don't know when the news hit us about the betrayal and my two *reales* ended up in Purita's pocket. Victory for the Leftist Party! And the proud possessor of my two *reales*, Pura, donned the uniform of the militia and left to serve the Popular Party.

My father walked around the house scattering a litany of "It can't be," "It must be a lie," "I don't believe it," "Can I be dreaming?" "But, we had victory in the palm of our hands! My God! now what?"

Now the public, who own the power and the weapons, ravage sacred vestments, votive offerings, the sacramental wine, Stations of the Cross, altars, chalices, prayers, baptisms, Masses, blessings...burn churches, convents; massacre priests, nuns, friars, and never again will there be Sundays or holidays with bells, or words in Latin or incense. And there is hunger, a lot of hunger. I'm hungry now and not a crumb of bread is left or a drop of that quart of milk I walk a kilometer to get every day, under a continual bombardment and the incessant machine-gun fire that echoes through all of Nograles.

It's true then; hunger is a monster that devours us. The guys in the Popular Front aren't the good guys. Are the others the good guys, I wonder? What if they are all bad guys? If they are...famines, massacres, assassinations, rapes, imprisonments, bombings have taught me now that...does it matter? Now all I know is I'm hungry, very hungry ...starving to death.

Translated by Elizabeth Gamble Miller

From: Vallbona, Rima de. *Cosecha de Pecadores*. San José: Editorial Costa Rica, 1986.

THE WALL

Rima de Vallbona

When the fragrant stewpot no longer bubbles with its meat and full-bodied stock, the truth is it's no longer a stewpot. If it is copper and is burnished with generations and years, it may have the good fortune to grace an antique shop, with a little card hanging from it that says "circa 1710," or "from the estate of the great magistrate of Mexico and Guatemala Don Juan de Maldonado y Paz," or "from the Pericholi. family." Just being in an antique shop won't be enough to qualify it as a stewpot, but from that moment on it will become something else.... Never again will it experience the excitement of being water that announces with its bubbling the break of a new day, offering aromas of daily nutrition and lively sounds that fill the home with soul. From that moment on it will fail to fulfill the role its maker designed into its shape.

Sitting here, behind this enormous, cold window glass that views a lengthy succession of structures of cement and brick, with no green foliage or tiny remnant of sky, I am that stewpot. Ancient and worn with the years, with no life bubbling within me, in a monotonous routine of hours and hours, little by little, repeated and repeated, to my horror I gradually discover that this interminable repetition is a boring eternity in hell. There was a time many, many years ago—so many that they're lost now in the mist of memory—when I contemplated the silent stillness of things, I never imagined the eternal damnation inherent to this kind of existence, being left, discarded, locked into a single place. Have you ever given a thought to—think no—to the tragedy of being a thing and not being able to act—like me as I face these structures of cement and brick?

Now I'm just another bauble in a world full of trinkets...I have no value even as an antique; the only historical event I ever experienced was seeing Major Blanco's troops pass on their way to Nicaragua to overthrow the dictator, William Walker and his *gringo* henchmen; I was only a spectator, not a protagonist; but...if there were no spectators, would there be any historic events? Why kid myself? I'm a nobody, just another bauble in a world full of trinkets. That's all.

A nothing with only an illusion that once, ages ago, I was like an aviary bustling with sounds and hubbub. Just an illusion that once I had an aura of a warm, delicate feather and my years were passing in an intensity of kaleidoscopic emotion that would cut them short and turn them into a puff of time, a wisp of existence, a fleeting Eden. And now this infernal eternity of being a immobile bauble facing structures of cement and brick with no green foliage or little patches of sky!

As I face the wall and contemplate the endless extension of cement, I count one, two, three, four, forty, four hundred, four thousand, thousands of millions of bricks, and it lightens my burden as a thing-condemned-to-silence. And I pour memories into my inner being, now starkly bare though blanketed with desolation. They are memories that creak inside me like joints and muscles stretching when awakened in the morning, when getting out of bed—and to think—never to get up again for I have only a faint memory of what it was like to put my feet on the ground and walk! It would be so wonderful to be able to walk! But at that time I never suspected it was a valuable gift...

Once—I remember well—I did have the illusion that I was human, not a thing, like now, old, forgotten and abandoned here facing a brick wall. At that time I was filled with my sense of self. It was then we decided to marry. The tenderness of a warm little feather was flooding my entire body and he desired it for himself. Then I had the illusion that those were the happy days of newlyweds: we used to spend them together busily inventing love each day, shaping it with our hands, our eyes, our words, our kisses, our caresses, everything, everything, even our movements and our breaths. Later, love became two children, two beautiful, healthy sons. But then, I don't even know when —centuries later, perhaps—existence carried them away one by one: marriage, better opportunities abroad, who knows! They had their own lives to make and mine was already done. Letters, a long distance call at the beginning; then, silence.

Sometimes I think I never had any children, that it was all an illusion, like everything else. For finally, death took away my husband and I was left totally, irremediably alone. The solitude and silence and thousands and millions of years weighed so heavily upon me I was gradually left immobile, with no voice for a dialog with others, with no desire for anything, empty, disintegrating. Now I don't know if others exist. Quietly here, facing this blank wall, I'm only conscious of my gradual disintegration, becoming fine, dark little dust that embraces the earth becoming indistinguishable from it. Quietly, staring steadily at the brick wall, I feel myself stretching out, becoming a prolongation of the earth, an integral, germinal part of it. A long time ago my own voluptuous flesh lost its moisture. Now when I touch my skin, I touch the tenuous dust of the earth; I breath its darkness, an intense, heavy dark color that permeates my bone marrow.

Here I am, immobile. Once—I don't even know when—I used to knit, embroider, hum an old-time tune. It was my way of rebelling against the condition that was gradually beginning to overtake me, and which finally controlled my last actions. That was when I became obsessed by the copper stewpot hanging in the fireplace—I think it still hangs there; the truth is what would it matter to prove it? That was when I identified with the stewpot, with the silent stillness of things forever condemned to immobility, and when the wall began to imprison me. I was pervaded by the emptiness of being useless, the feeling of a thing-that-no-longer-has-a-ritual-in-life-no-good-bauble-that-no-longer -fills-a-home-with-bubbling-aromas-of-vital-nutrition.

I spanned the short-interminable distance between my bed and this spread of brick wall for the last time. Immobile, I mused over the forests of Tapantí and the beautiful parasites that set up house in another plant and with a strong embrace suck out the vital sap and slowly rob them of their being. It's a spectacle that has always left me breathless, perhaps because I sensed in that example of the forest my future condition of no longer being myself, submerged the way I am in this fatal murkiness on which I feed. You who move about beyond the implacable wall, who eat, sing, write, drink and laugh, you can't imagine the horror of this total stillness, a total silence, a completely quiet time, immobile—with no events, no emotions, no desires, time not flowing—shaded by the solid surface of brick. Can you even imagine the boring eternity of the hell permeating my immobility now?—a hell that permeates my entire being, a prolongation, an extension of the earth and its dense, heavy, dark aroma...

Translated by Elizabeth Gamble Miller

From: Vallbona, Rima de. *Cosecha de Pecadores*. San José: Editorial Costa Rica, 1986.

NIGHTMARE AT
DEEP RIVER

Lilia Algandona

With a hurried step Analida walks down a street which is not deserted. The deafening roar made by the cars is numbing her mind, and the people who see her pass turn round seeking beneath the thick golden lashes of those troubled eyes the reason for her hurried pace...If it were not true, she would not feel so wretched now, so alone, so... empty?

"Alone?" Three years ago she had heard that voice.

"Almost," she had answered, not looking at the stranger.

Following the tragic death of her parents in that accident, she was alone. No, she could not ignore Hernando's existence like this; from a very early age he had shown her a disinterested attachment, the affection of a friend, of a brother. That is why she answered, "Almost alone": because of the man who had been there to give her his support just in time, before she could mindlessly throw herself into the abyss of Deep River, her childhood hiding place and paradise, and almost her grave.

She had felt the sharp point of a dagger piercing her soul when, after a four hour wait for her father and mother, she received the news that their car, exposed to the storm on that rainy night, had met disaster crashing on one of the irregular, rocky curves which lay not far from the country house where the happiness of the Abriles family had until that moment been undisturbed.

She had collapsed at his feet before he understood the message she brought with her. Then, she had regained consciousness in Hernando's strong, brotherly arms. She felt his tears mingling with hers. She heard his pleasant, manly voice saying kind phrases to her, words of understanding, gentleness, and affection. But no, the reality was not kind, nor gentle, nor pleasant. They were dead. They no longer existed, and she could not go on listening to him, she simply could not go on living, and she pulled away from him. And she ran and ran as far as her strength allowed. But just in time, before she could carry out her act of madness, the same arms which had had such delicate solicitude for her took her violently by the shoulders, so forcefully that Analida had to fall to her knees on the wet sand.

"Almost alone?" Again the the well-dressed young man with the olive skin and dark eyes posed his question; he insisted on keeping the appealing redhead company. And then, the girl's blue eyes smiled at Juan Raul Narvaez, and her face, still marked by dark circles from uncontrolled weeping, took on a courteous expression for this persistent fellow.

Starting that day, Juan Raul and Analida became friends. His jovial nature reawakened youthful longings in the young woman's life, pleasures set aside because of her recent loss. Recent? Not really. By then it was two years since the tragic accident. For two years also, Hernando had also stayed at her side. They attended the University together and, on weekends, when Analida was in the mood to do so, they would go the beach or to a movie. However, the two seas would cloud over constantly and dampen the good spirits of both young people, because for Hernando happiness lay in seeing her smile, in seeing her free from worry and disappointment. But while he was making every effort to see her happy, in the young woman's mind one scene kept repeating itself over and over: the screeching tires of a car going full speed; raucous laughter; the sea, angry and vociferous, pounding the rocks; a stone falling and sinking down, down, down until it was forever submerged in the depths. And then, the sea would become calm and peaceful once more. Curiously, Analida would grow calm also. She knew the scene would not appear again until the following day— with a little luck, not until the next week. It was a nightmare which tormented her constantly and which she could not understand. That same vision kept troubling her and had not let her be calm since her parents' death.

When Juan Raul showed up in her life, that life took a turn for the better.

"My name is Juan Raul," he had said as he sat down next to her.

"I'm Analida Abriles," she replied, her gaze searching for Hernando, who would be meeting her around that time.

"I'm new here. I come from Puerto Rico," he said with a smile. "I believe you really are alone."

"I'm waiting for a friend."

"Then am I disturbing you?"

"No, of course not. And what brings you here?"

"I love adventure. I wanted a change of scene and—here I am."

"That's interesting." She stood up. "My friend has arrived. I'll see you around, Juan Raul."

"Aha, your memory is good, isn't it?"

"Yes, it is." She was already going off.

"Will I be seeing you again?"

"Maybe. Panama is a small country."

Juan Raul's eyes followed her and encountered a hard, challenging gaze. When Hernando had her before him and he felt her delicate hand take hold of his arm, his eyes recovered their gentleness and with a worried smile he questioned the young woman.

"A stranger. He's just arrived in Panama."

"Oh, I see." And his inner calm was restored. But this did not last long: through unforeseen circumstances, two months later Analida and Juan Raul had fallen in love.

...But now all that is over, and she is very much alone. And she cannot believe it. She seems to see herself still hand in hand on the beach with her adored J. R., running through the wet sand. How different that winter from the one which had brought such bitterness into her life!

"Is something the matter?" she asked when she noticed that he was in the house. Only in an emergency would Hernando use the key which let him into the Abriles home, now occupied by the deceased couple's only child.

"Yes, very much so."

He was in a rage. Analida sat down,

"Well, talk. You're scaring me, Hernando."

"Where have you been?" he shouted.

"Hernando!"

She had never seen him like this. Her voice faded away when he came near her, imperious.

"Are you telling me where you've been?" His voice was harsh.

"You have no right..." she began.

"Neither do you."

"But I don't understand you."

"I implore you to think it over; I want what's good for you, only what's good for you."

"You're self-centered, that's what you are."

"That's not true, Analida. I know what's suitable for you. I know..."

"Nothing...you can't know it all. I have a right to be happy. I have cried so very much!"

"I want the best for you," he said once again in a very low voice. And I'm afraid. Because, you know, I can see what lies ahead..."

"Oh, now, you're a fortuneteller!" And she roared with laughter.

He took hold of her by the arms. He held her imprisoned. He was her brother, her friend. Why was he opposed to her happiness? Analida covered her face with her hands and her roars of laughter turned into sobs.

"At all costs," he said with controlled fury, "I'll keep them from harming you. I'm responsible for you."

And his dark, dark eyes sought hers and made or perhaps confirmed the promise which Hernando had once made to himself when very young.

But now, now...Analida is sobbing in face of the bitter reality. She touches her dress and does not believe what is happening. It's she herself and at the same time it is not. She is twenty-four and she feels she is bearing an old woman's heavy cross.

"You know, Hernando...I too can see what lies ahead...And I hadn't realized," she whispers. She has sat down on a park bench to think. But she has done too much thinking. She has gone back on a road which is already part of the past, a past which is tormenting her, which is beating her down, which....

"I can't go on," she now sobs. Her eyes look without seeing. And now she gets up. She is walking along hurriedly. She is sobbing, laughing, babbling. Then she catches a glimpse of a lovely country estate surrounded by fruit trees, and she hears the roar of the sea...How could she have walked so far? Could she be mistaken?

"The guests must be here already." And she laughs, and the vibrant laugh of a young girl in love fills the air around what had formerly been her beautiful home, where her wedding reception was to have been held. Near her beloved Deep River.

"Deep River!" she remembers. "It's been such a long time since I've been with you, since I've visited you!"

Analida is eager to stand before her favorite pleasure spot. She unfastens the lovely braid holding on the small but graceful veil, takes off her white shoes, and runs toward the edge of the highest crag. Then she gazes off in the distance and, as if in a whirlwind of memory, there passes before her once more, but in slow motion, the scene which time and time again has tortured her and yet now entrances her.

Not far from there a car is moving along at full speed. The highway, slippery from a recent shower, makes the vehicle's tires squeak. Behind the wheel, Hernando drives, his gaze fixed on the road. He had to do it, he couldn't let his beloved Analida marry that fellow. Little by little, and in spite of his determination, he had had to distance himself from her life. Until one day his heart grew light as he noticed the return address on a note and then grew heavy as he realized the letter was an invitation to her wedding, Analida's wedding. And he is almost convinced. He almost accepts it.

"What a surprise!"

"Hi," said Hernando, getting up from the table where he had been approached by Juan Raul, who invited him with a gesture to sit down to his coffee once again.

"Don't leave, Hernando. That is your name, isn't it?"

"Yes, yes."

It was exactly two days before the wedding.

"I imagine Analida has invited you to our wedding."

"Yes, she has."

"Then," he laughed complacently, "You yourself will witness your defeat."

"What do you mean?" He was already leaving.

"No, no...let's not make a scene. I mean that, unfortunately for you, I'm the winner of the contest."

"I really don't understand why you should speak of your marriage to Analida as if it were a game of chance."

"In some ways it is. I have been patient. Two years of semi-engagement. But," and he laughed again, "it's definitely been worth the trouble. Analida is a beauty and her dowry triples her value."

"What the hell are you saying?" exclaimed Hernando, both astonished and indignant.

"What are you going to do about it?...Hit me? Never. Day after tomorrow, I'll be her husband. And I'll tell you, besides thoroughly enjoying a joke at your expense, I'm ending up a triple winner, and I can allow myself the luxury of responding to that possessive look you sent my way two and half years ago. I'm sorry to have frustrated your amorous intentions, I'm sorry...."

He was unable to say more. Hernando aimed a punch at him and before going off said between clenched teeth: "You still haven't won, you swine, not yet! You'll soon see how the struggle turns out. Because I'm more than just someone in love, I'm a brother, a friend, and above all, a man...And that, that's something you'll have a chance to find out for yourself, you scum, even if I have to kill you and her to prove it."

Analida put her hands to her temples. This was something more than the usual nightmare. The tires were coming closer and closer...She saw herself standing before the altar. At her side, her dear J. R. She also remembered Hernando, arrogant, determined. A shot, then....

The car was coming closer now. Behind the wheel, he remembered her kneeling before the lifeless body of the man who would have been her husband, if a bullet had not intervened. Hernando drove with increasing speed. He saw himself looking for her after he had escaped from the policemen who were taking him away under arrest. He would pay for what he had done, but first he had to find her, ask her forgiveness, explain to her. Finally he realized that he had wandered around in a stupor, without remembering that he could find her only in that place.

Analida swung around quickly and made out the car in the distance. She knew everything. She understood everything.

"And now you see," she sighed, "I, too, can see what lies ahead, Hernando."

She noticed that the sea, suddenly furious, was striking the rocks with uncontrollable force. The car was coming closer. She covered her ears with her hands. That screeching sound was quite close.

Life is ironic. Hernando's car entered the estate at full speed. He knew he would meet up with her on the beach. But he could not see her. The car followed its course faster and faster without the driver realizing he had no brakes. When the slim figure, lingering at the edge of the crag, appeared before Hernando's eyes, he tried to stop, horrified. He uttered a shout. She, who in her demented state could comprehend everything, burst into shrill laughter. Then, a sharp blow. Like a heavy stone, a body into the void. This time, he could not hold her back. And momentarily he himself was crashing on the rocky banks of Deep River. And as Analida had seen so often in her nightmare, the sea turned calm and peaceful. And this tranquil sea, or at least the tranquillity longed for by Analida, would be eternal.

Translated by Julia Shirek Smith

From the journal, *Maga*, Number 10, Panama: April-September, 1986.

THE RAIN
ON THE FIRE

Giovanna Benedetti

This evening at six, when my husband comes home, he'll find me slumped behind the shower curtain with my wrists slashed, and, even though I know perfectly well I'll be dead, I think I can tell now what his routine will be, and predict the moves he'll make before he makes them. There will be the calculated touch of a hand checking the brake on the Toyota, then rolling up the windows; the key in both doors, and then outside in the garage the pretentious gesture of letting the world pass through the corner of his memory. His collar will be twisted to the left, making him look as if the outline of the car, instead of being in front of him, were sprouting from his head.

My husband will come home straight from work tonight; there won't be any friends or bars or happy hours. I know because today is Thursday, and Thursday's schedule doesn't include making the rounds.

When he comes home he'll get out of the car whistling "White Magic," a ridiculous song that's been rolling around on his tongue for fifteen years. He'll kick each tire gently and caress the hood, the immaculate finish, the chrome, smiling at the culmination of his labors converted into machinery and blazing blue metal. With music on his lips, he'll open the trunk and take out the bag with the two pineapples his boss's secretary gave him this morning, and when he lowers the lid again he'll remember that he had thought about adjusting a couple of screws "because the lock doesn't catch, there's something wrong with it." I've been hearing him say that for days. He'll immediately look for his tools, the oil can, and a dirty rag, and leave the bag of fruit on the floor.

After spending half an hour on his knees, twilight will give him the perfect excuse to forget the whole thing without having to admit defeat, and he'll come up the stairs whistling "White Magic."

The living room will be dark, without a trace of my shadow, but when he doesn't see me he'll think I'm in another room, in the bedroom, sleeping...peacefully, he'll suppose. (Or, will he be able to tell at that moment that I'm dead? I don't know.) My husband will keep on filling each nook and cranny of the house with his absurd song, unaware of my silence. Through the apartment walls, the neighbor's television set will serve as background noise and inform him that at that moment it is six-thirty. At that point—and although I know perfectly well he doesn't have the faintest interest in what the newscast might say—he'll turn on the set mechanically "because every good executive should give the appearance of knowing what's going on in the world," as the book says. And so, settling down, with his collar unbuttoned and his shoes and socks off, he'll rummage around the kitchen for a can of beer and then remain looking at the screen for a long time.

He won't be thinking of me yet. At most, I'm buried in one of the distant regions of his brain that announces exact times: dinner, for example. But my husband won't be hungry yet; Thursdays he always eats late and besides, he won't be in any hurry. When he begins to feel the first warning rumble in his gut—at eight o'clock or so—the lateness of the hour will remind him of the pineapples and he'll poke around in all the kitchen drawers for the big knife without finding it. Then for the first time since setting foot in the house, my name will explode from his lips, violently, between two goddamns, while he continues to scramble around the pots, yelling and cursing, louder and louder. When the outburst is over, he won't have any choice but to peel the fruit as best he can with the bread knife. It's small and rusty.

Gnawing on a hacked-off chunk of pineapple, my husband will storm into the bedroom, dancing with rage. He'll expect to find me lying in the middle of the bed, fully dressed and ignoring his tantrum. When he doesn't see me, he'll stop and just stand there for a few seconds, getting used to the idea before advancing to the bathroom door. It will be closed, but he won't open it immediately...he'll go up to it, slowly, saying, "Are you there?" and he'll put his ear to it, listening to a strange sound that will reach him from inside, breaking the silence

(...plink...plink...plink...)

my husband will start to turn the doorknob; he'll push it open

(...plink...plink...)

and then he won't say anything. Mechanically, he'll tighten the faucet, turn on the light above the washbasin and unzip his fly to urinate calmly.

Still urinating, he'll look in the mirror at the dark blue of the shower curtain, then he'll turn his head to look over his shoulder for a second (a shadow forming a lump?) but his curiosity won't go beyond the subconscious and he'll turn to face forward again, towards the washbasin, without knowing at that moment that the lump is me, and that I am there, waiting.

When he leaves the bathroom my husband will simply think I'm not home, I'm out, wandering around the shops, or the drugstore, or the supermarket. Or that I'm with my friend Diana somewhere, it doesn't matter where. It'll all be the same to him, judging by the way he'll shrug his shoulders and let a sneer slide down the corners of his mouth as he saws off another chunk of pineapple and pours himself another beer.

Diana's voice on the telephone will tell him that she hasn't seen me all day. She'll be the one calling, asking to speak with me. "No, she's not here, I thought you were together;" and he'll hang up, realizing that it's peculiar, very peculiar...his wife doesn't go out alone, not at this hour, normally. And for the first time, uneasiness will begin to creep into his brain. But, thinking it over, he'll know there isn't any problem—after all, wives always come home.

My friend will call again and he'll say the same things he did before; they'll talk about inconsequential matters. From a distance my husband will position her words alongside each imagined gesture, putting Diana together and taking her apart like a jigsaw puzzle. Then, because both women are blondes, he'll find himself bouncing as if on a trampoline into the figure of Roxana. He didn't want to think of her. And yet...Roxana's hands, Roxana's neck, her neckline this morning, the color of her blouse buttoned at the front; Roxana, her eyes enormous, sitting at the desk on the other side of the hall...Roxana, between one evening and another, looking sideways to see if he's watching her from a distance, or suddenly in a corner, body to body.

Strangely enough, the woman who has been causing him so much turmoil for several months now is none other than the same faceless secretary who for years had been taxing his patience without arousing his interest. She had never particularly stood out from the rest until the day it happened: a gesture, anything...they may have run into each other on the street, they may have exchanged a different word ...and from that moment on there had been the surprise, the mystery, the chemistry which forced him to look for her. To try to read the expression on her face. To prove that she was aware of the games that eyes could play. To sense her coquettishly evading his challenge, proposing her own style as she invited an encounter.

My husband always thought that his secret had remained a secret, and he ended up convincing me that the reality I could guess in his eyes every time he had been with her didn't exist. I withdrew into a world of suspicion and silence, and ended up overlooking what was happening ...as all women do.

And we do it because in these situations—sometimes I think men don't understand it—every woman knows two kinds of truth and two kinds of lie. They are two halves of the same reality which she sometimes learns to combine unconsciously: the truth she learns to avoid in spite of her suspicions and the lie she welcomes because what counts is what's left: that last scrap she can still hang on to by a corner, that remainder of the bond she knows can be broken by a sudden pull. So she plays with it gently, adjusting her grip, holding on with great care when faced with the hideous fear of a break or the impotent terror of loss.

But it's late, and today is Thursday. He will have come home without any problems, without suspecting, his home is the untouchable refuge of the warrior—the last tavern.

Sitting on the couch, my husband will continue to wait for me to show up, pondering his revenge, the kind of welcome I'll deserve. Imagining the dialogue—the jealousy?—and the infallible reasons which protect his rights. But I know his mind will find some excuse or other when his fingers start to drum on the beer can of their own accord, when his feet on the armchair relax into sleep, when the small furrow in his forehead returns to signal an old expression of impatience, or when he begins to discover that the novelty of my absence has begun to lose its edge and is settling in comfortably with the lethargy of his body. At that time of the night, the only thing he'll be aware of will be an immense tiredness and the thought of a warm shower before going to bed.

In the bathroom, he'll look at his nude profile in the mirror. He's not bad, and he knows it: the weight is perfect for the body, the skin tight over muscles defined by the sustained effort of running for an hour, three days a week. Yes, definitely, his skin suits him; it shapes him nicely.

My husband will look for the perfect pose, inhaling deeply to enlarge his chest, one foot behind the other, toes pointed, waist slightly bent, neck straight, eyes forward, lowered left arm gracefully brushing flexed knee, hips suspended in profile—the pose of the Discobolus! He'll stay balanced for a second, then the right arm which begins to rise in an oblique line along his back, squeezing a towel as if it were a discus, will continue its ascent until it finds the exact angle in the play between shoulders and legs.

The third time the phone rings, the discus-thrower will break his pose and pad towards it with the towel draped over his shoulders, but he won't arrive in time. The last ring will leave him frozen half a yard away: "Diana again," he'll think as he goes back into the bedroom. And then he'll stop short when he looks at the bureau and discovers that my brown leather purse is there, the one I always use when I go out in the daytime—it's been there all along.

With his mouth hanging open, he'll undo the clasp. Going over an endless array of incoherent explanations, he'll put his hand inside, carefully, with the eager interest of a child discovering sex: the address book, cosmetics, the change purse and, finally, what he didn't want to find but was afraid he might: the key ring with my sign of the Zodiac and all the keys to the house—the only ones I have and he knows it. Then he'll run naked into the bathroom, grabbing his pants off the floor and throwing them on without bothering with underwear. He'll bound across the living room, run down the main stairway and go outside, where the rain and the darkness will begin to cover his suspicions with dread.

My husband will walk slowly up the block as far as the corner, cross the street and start to go faster, looking for a new rhythm, another stride; he'll adapt his steps to the pace so familiar to his legs. Faster, up the avenue, down the ocean boulevard, finally bursting out onto the cement, he won't be aware of his heels pounding the hard surface or of his toes absorbing the shock. A couple of hours later, the weariness in his legs, the sweat, and the rain will have combined to change his face into that of a stranger (the same face he wears when he comes in from work) and, home again, he'll go up the stairs whistling "White Magic." He'll open the door, call my name a couple of times affectionately, cheerfully; he'll come in limping and sweating, and playfully start to poke around the apartment. He'll look under the furniture, searching everywhere: under the bed, behind the bureau, in the corners...then, going into the bathroom and taking off his clothes, he'll suddenly find the trail of dirt and blood his battered feet have left. My husband will stretch out his right arm and touch the dark blue curtain, sweeping it aside and sliding the plastic liner with it, so he can get into the shower. But when he looks in the only thing he'll find, besides surprise, will be the exact space of time in which to let out a scream—a long scream, a cutting one, like the blade of the knife he had been looking for in the kitchen and couldn't find anywhere, the same long knife that at this precise moment has just finished slitting his throat from ear to ear.

Translated by Gloria Nichols and Robert Kramer

From: Benedetti, Giovanna. *La lluvia sobre el fuego*. Panama: Instituto Nacional de Cultura, 1982.

THE SCENT
OF VIOLETS

Giovanna Benedetti

There are innocent things and naive places and people who don't know—for example—that the knock on the door of an ordinary house on a January morning, when you're dragging the weariness of the mid-day sun down the last block in the neighborhood as far as the corner, and the morning-after face of the golden-skinned woman who opens the door into music and smoke, and you, looking at her and thinking, "No, this one won't work out," can be precisely those elements: innocent things (the book you're carrying and she's looking at), and naive places (the last block of the neighborhood you almost never go to) that are present here, in front of this door, interrupting your routine with an extraordinary event.

You go in.

(first strange happening)

She has let you in after the "Good morning, Señora," without further ceremony, trustingly, and you sit down in the living room, with the briefcase on your knees and the book in your hands. The rhythm of the music begins to creep into your brain from another room: rock, surely; good rock...it sounds like the old days, like the Rolling Stones, Mick Jagger, like windows that shatter with a crash.

She hums the melody, "Ruby Tuesday," the rhythm dominating her movements, and asks you to follow her to the room the music is coming from, a sunny little room. You ask yourself why she is so trusting, but you go in and sit down, noticing that the room smells like violet-scented talcum powder. Or is it the woman? It's useless to try to guess which, because the perfume immediately insinuates itself into your mind along with the green of the plants, the bare walls, the Rolling Stones, the smoke, the first few minutes of the afternoon and, when you leave, when you are out on the street again, the scent of violets is part of the memory.

(second extraordinary happening)

The sounds of Rock. Jagger. The uneven rhythm tearing down the silence and her murmuring voice, amused by your offer, asking you about the book you have in your hand. It's an erotic book, pretty strong stuff...she curls up on the rug and starts to leaf through it, and then you ask for it back, telling her it isn't yours. "It's out of print," you tell her, showing her the catalogue. It's the club's system, you explain; all she has to do is pick out another book. But no, she wants that one, now, and her laughter dissolves into a challenging look—"I'm sorry, Señora" —but she insists and you give in; you'll settle the finances with the company later. What's important, you tell yourself, is that the smile has returned and floats gratefully above the perfume of violets.

You have to charge her for the subscription—"that's the way the club works, Señora, but it's not much." "Of course," she says, getting up with "Ruby Tuesday" on her lips. Before leaving the room she says she'll be back in a minute, don't go away, wait for her, and you follow her body in your mind. It isn't until later when you're out on the street again that you'll realize there isn't anywhere you would have rather have been at that moment than near that suppleness, that skin you felt was almost willing, and you imagine them behind the book you have left.

"Want to know something?" she asks, coming back in the minute she had promised, "This way you don't feel the clerk in the store wondering about you—know what I mean?—and looking at you as if you're thinking the same things they have on their dirty minds."

"Thank you."

Her frankness is surprising. It's as if she wants to go out into the world without permission. And yet, something in her look warns you of a distance in her shadowed eyes, and something tells you that here, with this wonderful luck you're having, this body of a doll is a cold and remote place and that its movements are programmed from somewhere else. It's as if this image of a woman who's been out all night and this scent of violets and this Jagger music and this friendly welcome and that hair and that laughter and that mouth weren't there before: they arrived with you, and began to exist so you would live them.

You feel like a puppet lowering its head.

You smile and get ready to go. When you start to leave, you say goodbye with your briefcase in your hand and you think as you look at her that somewhere in that figure of a doll there must be a hidden button that she pushes to set the stage so she can put on this strange little drama for your benefit.

(third extraordinary event)

She looks over the catalogue. Her forehead is furrowed with interest. You see her start slowly, hesitantly, and then, triumphantly, "This one," she says, pointing on the pink page to Anais Nin's *Delta of Venus*. "I'm interested in this—when it's written by a woman, sex has to be interpreted as a surrender."

"Anais Nin," she says again, and for the first time there is a fresh quality in her voice, that of something very close to being human. The doll vanishes behind her self-composure and you follow her, aware of all your senses, playing with time like a robot that waits or a puppet that's arriving, and when she gets up to change the record, you have the feeling that it isn't the delicate trap that she's setting but your own stifled yearning that is fanning the flames of your desire.

What does she want?

What does it all mean—her smiles, your presence in this house, the way she looks at you, your books scattered all over the rug, her childlike enthusiasm that's looking for something, that's talking this way, as if you weren't a complete stranger selling books?

Or could it be precisely because you are?

Because you're a wandering stranger, not in tune with the complications of her world...a world you feel is about to cross your own and split into two halves, without touching you.

You go back.

(fourth extraordinary event)

Three orders in one week. At the office they ask you what's going on. They realize you're neglecting the customers and they even threaten to change you to another territory. But you go back.

She calls out to you from a distance and you see her in an upstairs window. Her "hello" floats down to you and she comes downstairs, opens the door, and welcomes you warmly. Yes, you're sure she's going to like the book: Miller's *Tropic of Cancer*, a classic already, you explain. And again the scent of violets, the slow rock music like broken sobs...you follow her, like the first time, to the back of the house, the little room filled with plants and music, like before, only this time there is a cup of coffee and a cigarette, and the distance between the two of you is less.

You sit close to her on the rug, near her legs. You study her answers; she's acting like someone who still doesn't accept the game that's being proposed and the doll that is inside her or the puppet in your body are in charge of your movements.

You don't dare.

"Tomorrow," you think when you're back out on the street making the last calls on your route.

The next day you see her in the window, silently combing her hair with her fingers...that hair that falls to her shoulders, black and straight.

You call her from below, but this time she doesn't come down.

"She hasn't seen me," you think, and you wait in front of the door with the package of books in your hand.

You keep on waiting, but then you're confused by the sound of footsteps coming nearer—different footsteps, a man's—and you freeze in astonishment when the doorframe is filled by the husband-boyfriend-lover or whoever the guy is, when he looks you over icily and grudgingly says hello. You look at him steadily and ask for her.

She comes out then, with gracefully intricate movements; she leaves the door open and the house evokes the memory again. But this time there are no languid looks, no rock, no violet perfume—only the calculated body of a rubber doll that asks you what you want and the husband-lover-boyfriend. Your suspicions are confirmed when you open the package and hand her the book: de Sade's *Justine*, a stirring book, you say with a thick voice, and the mask on her face and the puppet in your body vanish, breaking your surprise: "No, Señor, I'm sorry, there must be a mistake." And then suddenly smiling, "Oh, Darling, do you know what? I asked the young man from the book club for a mystery novel, because I know you like ghost stories."

You leave.

And with the sun behind the ocean in the middle of the afternoon you see her, small and fragile, peering out of the empty eye sockets of a gigantic doll when the last delivery on your route and the scent of violets are entwined again, in another house, another book, another unusual event.

Translated by Gloria Nichols

From: Benedetti, Giovanna. *La lluvia sobre el fuego*. Panama: Instituto Nacional de Cultura, 1982.

THE WRECK OF
THE *ENID ROSE*

Rosa María Britton

A pox on he who first sowed the sea
with planks of pine and measured all
its length with frail, brittle wood.

—Tirso de Molina

The wreck of the *Enid Rose* took place off the north coast about two hours out of Portobelo, on the 20th of October nineteen hundred forty-nine. Witnesses on the beach told of hearing a great explosion first, and then they saw the fire that almost devoured the ship before they even had time to tug their boats, beached in the sand, into the sea to go to its aid. The survivors of the tragedy later stated to the appropriate authorities that they were not sure about what happened. The panic had been of such a magnitude that their memories simply flagged; overwhelmed by the memory of the terrible moments they had lived through, they were unable to describe the events well, and each of them told of the tragedy in his own way. Of the fifty-seven passengers who had embarked at Colon, packed tightly in all over the boat like clusters of bananas, only fifteen managed to save themselves. When the disaster took place the sea was quite choppy, and many who threw themselves into the water to escape the flames were dashed against the sharp teeth of the reefs, thrust toward certain death by the violent waves.

The captain of the *Enid Rose*, a fellow named Nicanor Vasquez, who was counted among the survivors, stated that he had been warned of the approaching bad weather by the harbor authorities, but his passengers had forced him to weigh anchor, urged on by the need to get to Portobelo in time to attend the procession of the Black Christ. The boat had been chartered—at a very good price, to be sure—by a group of the faithful who wanted to make the voyage in relative comfort, but Nicanor, opportunistic and greedy, had sold passage to several others as well, among them an archaeologist from the United States who was eager to study the old fortifications at Portobelo and who arrived on board with several assistants and an enormous pile of luggage which was stacked on the poop. With the brusqueness of those of his race he ordered in bad Spanish that nothing was to be touched because the instruments were very delicate, and this provoked the irritation of the other passengers who had settled themselves in the area nearby. But Nicanor Vasquez undertook to placate them because the gringo had paid him rather well.

The archaeologist went down with all his instruments, which brought forth an official protest from the American Embassy. It turned out that the man had been part of a special work group and in fact it was not clear what his real profession was. The governor of Colon demanded a protracted investigation of the unfortunate affair from the appropriate authorities, and for many days afterward politicians anxious for notoriety gave lengthy, fiery speeches over all the radio stations in the country; declarations and accusations that demanded the construction once and for all of a passable road as far as Nombre de Dios in order to prevent tragedies like the one that had taken place. But soon everyone ended by forgetting the whole affair because it was not an election year, everyone, that is, except the relatives of the victims and the survivors of the shipwreck who preached to the four winds their gratitude to the Black Christ for the miracle that had saved their lives. They all vowed to attend the procession the following year, all except Nicanor Vasquez: he didn't believe in all that claptrap.

Besides, the only thing that interested him was convincing the insurance company that the shipwreck had been an accident so they they would pay him the twenty-five thousand pesos in accident indemnity, and he wasn't going to accept a penny less. No sir, he was no dummy! He had three partners in the ownership of the boat who were already going around talking as if the loss of the *Enid Rose* had been his fault. It had just been reconditioned, with brand new engines and everything newly painted blue and white. He suspected that the explosion had been caused by the fireworks he was carrying in the hold, but since the passengers who knew about that business had been drowned, Nicanor prudently kept his mouth shut and didn't mention it, because he knew that the insurance company would seize on any excuse not to pay off. The sea had swallowed the skeleton of the *Enid Rose* and was not going to give it back, and no matter how much the insurance company poked around, they weren't ever going to find anything. Nothing!

Three months after the shipwreck, one Thursday at about noon, the beach at Maria Chiquita was covered with fish that appeared to be leaping out of the water with the high tide. They lay on the warm, black sand until they died, their tails and gills fluttering painfully. Some kids, curious to see what would happen, grabbed them while they were still alive and tossed them back into the sea, only to watch them swim away toward certain death. On the third day, as the phenomenon kept recurring all along the coast from Maria Chiquita all the way to Palenque, the frightened natives, worried that the ocean was about to empty itself of all its inhabitants, informed the authorities in Colon. At first it was only the smaller, brightly colored fish, the timid inhabitants of the reefs, that were leaping out of the water, but later on it was also the porgies, the octopuses, and even moray eels, green or black-flecked, whose lengthy bodies were twisting on the beaches, showing their long rows of menacing teeth that dissuaded anyone who might have dared to touch them. The vultures started feasting on the mass of rotting flesh, but they too began to die within a few hours, writhing about as if poisoned. The ones who arrived later on limited themselves to keeping watch over the beach from a distance, lighting in the shape of a cross on the tops of the coconut trees.

The mayor of Maria Chiquita, who had been on a spree in Colon and unaware of what had happened, finally arrived, holding a perfumed kerchief up to his nose because the stench was so impossible that he could hardly even come near the beach.

"We must call the Health Department right away," he announced through his improvised mask.

"All the beaches are contaminated. Some ship going through the Canal must have thrown something into the ocean that is killing the fish," said the policeman from Viento Frio, and there was some logic to his pronouncement.

"It's the gringos' fault," shouted the deputy who represented the province in the Assembly, without being certain of anything but eager to win votes among his constituents of the leftist worker class, who didn't care for him very much.

*   *   *

The health inspectors arrived in their outboard motor boats, impeccable in their khaki uniforms and sun helmets. They were equipped with gas masks of the kind used by U.S. troops during WWII and they went over the affected beaches with a fine tooth comb, preparing their report. In this first document, which reached even the President of the Republic, the ninety-six known species of fish encountered on the beaches were mentioned, plus just as many others as yet unclassified, attracting the attention of scientists from several continents.

Despite the politically motivated objections of the deputy representing Colon, they had to request the assistance of the U.S. Navy at Rodman Naval Base, the only ones capable of exploring the ocean bottom in search of the precise cause of the north coast fish deaths.

They came with their oxygen tanks and special equipment in three large launches, shouting orders to one another over a P.A. system. The people came out of their homes to watch them, with kerchiefs and rags tied over their faces that made them look like a gang of bandits. Even the black sea urchins, with their rippling spines, were escaping from the sea now, ready to die with the rest of the marine fauna of the area.

The gringos measured everything with scientific precision, the Ph factor and the temperature of the water at twenty different depths, the chemical composition of the water in each of the areas affected, the tidal shifts, the actinic rays, and even the number of chamber pots emptied on the beaches every morning.

"Next they're gonna ask us what we eat every day to see what we're gonna shit," some one in Portobelo complained.

"But if this mess is their fault because of all that stuff they throw in the Canal, you can bet they're not going to say so," the deputy from Colon insisted during a general assembly meeting.

But no one paid much attention because election time was too far away and nobody really cared about the north coast villages anyway.

*   *   *

The final report of the investigation done by the Navy team was handed over to the governor of Colon, three copies in a sealed envelope. One addressed to the Intelligence Service, another to the President's Office, and the third to come to rest in foreign hands. The governor brought together all the mayors of the affected areas to discuss the report, which consisted of seven hundred ninety-eight pages, nineteen maps, forty-four photographs, and a complete scientific bibliography. This document once more filled everyone with respect for gringo know-how.

After much discussion about the best way to present it, the mayors decided to read it out loud, page by page, in order to understand in detail the phenomenon that affected the coastal beaches. Thus, when they got to page twenty-one, they became aware that for the first time in these waters specimens of *Prognathodes aculatus, Halichoeras iradiatus, Histria-histria,* and *Ogcocephalus nasatus* had been observed, and these are species of great interest to marine biologists.

"And what are those, compadre?" the mayor of Viento Frio asked his counterpart from Portobelo in a low voice.

"Fish, compadre, dead fish!"

"So what's all the fuss about, then?"

"Ssshhh...ssshhh..."

Everyone was nodding when the council secretary came to page one hundred and seven where the composition of the water in the affected areas was laid out in detail, a composition that differed in no way from that of the other beaches further away, where the fish had not been given to committing suicide en masse. The reading was suspended when the governor himself began to snore in his seat of honor.

"It's better for all this to be published as soon as possible," he announced before closing the session, which ended in the Blue Boy Bar.

Someone dared to ask if the report included a final summary, because it was urgent that they resolve the problem. No one could stand the stench of rotten fish any longer. The governor thundered with his scorn.

"One must do things in their proper order. We have to read everything, down to the last jot and tittle. This report has taken a lot of work. Do you have any idea of the number of brilliant scientists who have participated in this project? They're talking about the northern coast of Panama the wide world over, now. Don't you realize the interest awakened by this strange phenomenon?"

"I would stay here reading all night long if necessary," said one audacious mayor. "The smell is unbearable in my town, and with all the flies there are we might have an epidemic of diseases."

"We are all as interested as you are," the governor rebuked him, visibly irritated, "but things must be done with all possible calm for them to turn out right."

They agreed to meet the following day at ten o'clock to continue the reading of the document.

"Let's hope there's a quorum," the audacious one whispered as he went out.

Meanwhile the people living near the beach could no longer remain in their homes because of the unbearable stench, which hovered like an evil cloud along the whole coast. Some, more daring than most, began the task of burying the dead fish on the beach, utilizing the excavating machines the gringos had left behind. But while they were digging even more fish arrived on the beach and died there, until the people gave up, defeated. There were those who suggested selling all this putrefaction as fertilizer, a proposal that was taken up with great enthusiasm at first, before the inevitable problems of transporting and marketing the stuff (because of the nature of the product) emerged, and this punctured the balloon before it rose very high.

The stench spread as far as the entrance of the Canal itself, and the pleasure boats had to alter their course in order to avoid the fainting spells which the awful odor produced among the tourists.

*   *   *

"It's the souls in torment that are frightening the fish," announced Tati Tachu, the oldest woman in Portobelo. "The souls from the *Enid Rose*. They never got that affair cleared up. No sirree! It wasn't cleared up. The ocean swallowed all those people and they never found a reason for it. One of my goddaughters was on that boat, and I hear her calling me at night. The wind brings me her words...'Godmother, Godmother.' I hear it so clear."

"Tati Tachu never speaks empty words," several listeners remarked, alarmed.

"Tati Tachu's never wrong."

A large delegation of concerned citizens went to talk to the mayor, but they didn't find him because he was at the meeting called by the governor in Colon.

Tati Tachu...Tati Tachu...The call went from mouth to mouth, traversing villages oppressed by the miasma of death, which was enveloping everyone like the effluvium of evil itself. Green flies came, luxuriating in the rotting mass, discharging eggs that in a few hours turned into a palpitating mass of worms. The dogs were the first to flee into the forest. Perhaps it was because they were not tied down by their possessions that they understood the world was coming to an end before the human beings did. And the gangrene set in along the north coast of the Isthmus of Panama.

The combination of subterranean currents and seismic movements in the continental platform had provoked a rare convergence of factors on the floor of the ocean, raising the Ph factor 0.002 and some fractions, which, when added to the atmospheric temperature of 29.765 degrees C. and the winds from the south southwest, have contributed to the proliferation of an extremely rare strain of Dactylometra physalis. This phenomenon has been observed previously in other tropical and sub-tropical areas, but never further north than 35 degrees latitude and 5 degrees longitude. The last time it was documented was on some localized beaches on the coast of Brazil between Natal and Aracati.

"What page are we on, *compadre*? I can't last any longer, I'm pissing in my pants."

"Ssshhh...ssshhh..."

"They're getting toward the end now."

"Ssshh...ssshhh..."

Consequently, we recommend the following procedures to eliminate the infection of these waters by Dactylometra physalis...

"Dactylometra physalis, what the hell is that, compadre?"

"The bug that's killing the fish. A species of jellyfish."

"Ssshh..."

*...to mix in equal parts nitrous copper with oxy-medroxy-piruvato
-tetrahydrocholorphenil...*

"Where we gonna get hold of them things, compadre?"

"The gringos will do everything, don't worry yourself about that.
They know we don't understand anything about all this, and they love
to show off. The gringos like to brag..."

* * *

"Ears from a white bat, three shark's teeth, leaves from a purple
guandu, virgin's urine, skin of a pied rabbit...What's missing, Señora
Zacarias? Tati Tachu is very demanding in what she needs. If it's not all
here, she won't do the job."

Pastor Lucius Plimpton Jones of the Foursquare Church of the
Round Gospel announces that tonight there will be prayers and tes-
timonials on behalf of all the victims of the north coast. The members
of the choir should be at the service on time.

* * *

On the day appointed by the military scientists, by chance on
Tuesday the thirteenth of January, when the tide on the north coast was
at its lowest, the launches left the port of Cristobal, loaded down with
their cargo of NOF-345, the substance capable of eliminating the infestation of *Dactylometra physalis* from the ocean.

A group of politicians went to see the expedition off, and there
were several who offered to go along with it.

"I get seasick, compadre. I wouldn't get on that thing even if I
were crazy."

"No one can go along," the governor announced. "NOF-345 is
quite toxic and they don't want any problems with the civilians."

"Gringos like to make themselves look like the only men who can
really do things."

"All the better. Let 'em screw themselves."

In Portobelo they took Tati Tachu on a stool down to the beach
and left her there alone near the water with her ingredients on a large
plate. She didn't want them to clean up the dead fish around her. "They
can tell me where the souls in pain are," she declared in a weak voice.

"Tati Tachu is very demanding, but this is very hard work. We
have to pick her up at three on the dot because she says that after that
the sea's going to rise, and she's not responsible."

Everyone fled, and there they left her with her new red and yellow
dress and a hat loaned to her by a neighbor so she wouldn't be so much
in the sun. After Tati Tachu reached the age of ninety, she stopped

counting the days. Her flesh was gradually getting blended with her bones, and the gold tooth her third husband had given her was the only one noticeable in the middle of a face stretched tight as a drumhead. Only her eyes betrayed the fact that she remained alive—glowing eyes that never missed the slightest detail of anything around her.

At five in the afternoon a vaguely threatening wind began to bend the tops of the coconut trees down. The sea turned a livid blue while the gringos finished spreading their NOF-345 up and down the the whole coast. The sky was gradually darkening and from Maria Chiquita to Palenque the force of the wind was picking up. The tempest came down from the north northeast, with lightning bolts that bounced angrily off the surface of the choppy sea. The people of the coast crossed themselves and prayed in fear; the wind blew away the sheets and roofs of corrugated iron, and many houses were destroyed.

"The end of the world!"

"Tati Tachu announced this. There is no reason to worry. The ocean is purging itself."

"It's the souls climbing out of their tombs in the ocean," Tati Tachu chanted, almost asleep because the effort had been really too much.

Near midnight it began to rain heavily, sheets of rain all over the north coast, drowning out the noises of the storm. For the first time in eleven days, since the whole affair had begun, in fact, the terrible stench disappeared from the atmosphere and at dawn the birds began their flirtations as if nothing had happened. The people of the coast began poking their heads out cautiously, not anxious to witness a new catastrophe. A tranquil sea received them, the intense blue color of the festal Caribbean on all the post cards. The beaches—absolutely clear of putrefaction and flies!

"Praise be to God!" pastor Lucius Plimpton Jones of the Foursquare Church of the Round Gospel intoned.

"Those gringos are really something, compadre."

"No one can ever tell *me* that they weren't the ones who got this whole mess started in the first place," the deputy proclaimed.

"Those souls rest in peace now," Tati Tachu belched as she awoke from her deep slumber, rubbing the sleep from her eyes.

NOF-345 has proven to be an effective compound against the infestation of Dactylometra physalis on the coast, read the final report.

*   *   *

ESTRELLA DE PANAMA, 14 January 1950:

Last night, after a heavy storm on the north coast, the remains of the shipwrecked Enid Rose were discovered on the beaches of Maria Chiquita. As our readers will recall, that ship went down with great loss of life on October 20th. After examining the remains of the hull, the experts comfirmed that the explosion which brought on the catastrophe was caused by combustible material which the ship was carrying illegally in the hold. The authorities are searching for the captain, Nicanor Vasquez, in order for him to respond to the charges, but until now all efforts made to locate him have been fruitless. Captain Vasquez collected a rather large indemnity for the accident and since has disappeared.

Translated by Leland H. Chambers

From: Britton, Rosa María. *La muerte tiene dos caras*. San José: Editorial Costa Rica, 1987.

ONE MINUTE

Griselda López

It was a black street, obscure, with rickety houses of rotting wood and wretched wooden barrels, with women who were reproducing in eyes, nostrils, thighs, in quiet and gentle wombs which fearfully awaited a multiple delivery.

It was a long night, sinuously long. A night which held all men and all suffering, just as those wombs held all the pre-ordained lives, the men and women who were born and who died in a brief gasp.

Natalia was born during an infinitely long minute, on that lifeless street, full of muffled sounds, in a smooth and small womb. Through a wall of blood, flesh and bone, vibrant voices reached her, strange and previously unheard voices that she was nevertheless predestined to understand.

"I'm not going to pay you anything. You're shit. I've wasted time with you."

The one who was shouting left. All that remained were cries, shouts, recriminations...and the wailing of a little boy.

Natalia tried to see the external world. She saw a dilapidated room. Dark. Incredibly dark. She saw with eyes she did not yet have, with eyes that would have to develop. That one she was in started to move. She felt suddenly nauseated, like she was spinning around in the dense liquid. "That one" began walking, moving, shifting...

Little by little she was hearing other things, with ears she did not yet have...with ears that would have to develop. She heard the barking of dogs, the rolling of barrels...voices: some high, others low; some soft, others rough; none of them sweet, all bitter.

"How many have you got tonight?"

"Only one, how about you?"

"I've already had four. My body can't take it. I'm bitten all over. I've gone to bed with the most savage ones. And none of them wants to pay."

"I don't feel anything now," another voice says. "It's like I'm sleeping."

Silence took over the voices. Natalia heard a different voice, more serious.

"How much?"

"Two dollars."

A pause. And "that one," where she was, began to move again. Natalia liked the gentle swaying. She fell asleep. A powerful jolt woke her up. She felt "that one" jerk around violently. She had no way of understanding...but she understood. Suddenly she found out about everything that was out there. In one second she lived many years. Many more than "that one." And she decided to die. Natalia only lasted one minute.

Translated by Marinell James

From: Jaramillo Levi, Enrique. *Antología crítica de joven narrativa panameña*. Mexico, D.F.: Federación Editorial Mexicana, 1971.

I'LL EAT THE LAND

Griselda López

She was desperate. Her memories had gone away and in vain she tried to hang onto them. She felt empty: horribly alone and empty. The cold light of the afternoon (and Pedrito's forever—suspended laughter, beating at her temples) slipped in through a large, old window. They had all gone away. They had all left her. Time, the humidity, the rains and the immense solitude of the plain that carried them off. She was the only one left. She and her memories. Memories that came and went and sometimes escaped her, slid through her fingers and left her inert and empty. She and her memories. (Pedro's face that visited her at night, with his huge smile and his wide hands, smile and hands that stayed dead). But now, her memories had escaped her for good. One day she was careless, she attempted unsuccessfully to detain them.

The neighbors had gone away. Clotilde, Juan and even Mateo and Teresa, the best people on earth, had gone away. They had all gone away. They sold the cows, the chickens, the pigs. They said: "Maria, come with us. Run from the bad weather and loneliness."

But she didn't want to go away. She couldn't go away. One day she told them: "I'll eat the land before I go away." They all laughed. "Maria, don't stay here alone," they repeated. And Maria already didn't answer. She watched them go away, crying or laughing. They all walked toward new joys or toward new bitterness. With their children and their suffering on their backs, their exhausted lives on their backs.

Maria remained, mistress of the immense empty plain. She sowed the ground and fed her hens. She had lived there since childhood. Her parents had also loved this land, they had scratched at her, eagerly seeking her mystery, feeding themselves from her, drinking from her large, dark teats....

Ever since she was small, she'd said to her parents: "I'll eat all this land before I leave here. Little by little. I'll swallow all of it."

Those who listened to her laughed. The boys said: "Maria the dirt-eater. Let us have a little."

Much later Pedro came. To her he represented the land. His dark, infinite skin embodied everything she loved. The strong tenderness of his arms made her love grow and grow. Maria felt full, full of that vastness she couldn't hold, which escaped through her eyes to be reflected in Pedro's.

During the deep, still nights, lethargic with sleep, possessed to the depths of their souls by earthly emotions, Maria repeated to Pedro: "When you leave I'll feel very alone. When you're no longer here for me, there will still be Pedrito...If Pedrito leaves me, there will still be the land..."

"...and you'll eat all of it," Pedro finished, laughing with his full-moon laugh.

Pedro went away, sadly and inevitably. His laughter was cut off brusquely. Later on, Pedrito was silenced as well, to go and join that dark and never cherished land....

And now...she was without memories. Pedro's face had faded away. Pedrito's laughter no longer echoed. She had to leave, because nothing was left for her. Her eyes were tinged with infinity...

"I won't go away," she said.

She sat down on the patio and with a spoon, began slowly to eat the land.

Translated by Marinell James

From: Jaramillo Levi, Enrique. *Antología crítica de joven narrativa panameña*. Mexico, D.F.: Federación Editorial Mexicana, 1971.

A HEAVY RAIN

Moravia Ochoa López

A mean sadness opened its mouth in each one of her steps. Death was surrounding her inversely to the way she always thought death would be. Brought up good as a child, it was always there, half-concealed inside her skin and bones—the sadness. It could be seen, little by little, that she had that mean streak of sadness inside. Such was death. A little bit of sadness, just enough so as not to say it is happy, so as not to say, so as not to think "it comes empty-handed," "without warning" whenever.

She heard the rain as it fell. "A heavy rain," she remarked and no one made any comment—lately no one had made any comments. Besides, it was obvious. It was raining. "At least if they'd said," she thought, "if only they'd said, 'Look, it's true, it's raining' or 'it certainly is raining a lot.' " Only Dvorak said, "What's happening" very sweetly, and without looking at him she knew that Dvorak was concerned about her, that he was trying to find out, that he could see her, that Dvorak...

Later on she realized that Dvorak had loved her. He brought white carnations that afternoon telling her "These are the ones you like." Yes, she smiled then, finally she would smile for Dvorak's eyes to see. She had not done that in a long while. She cautioned him about holding back tears, that she had not seen him smile and she tried to tell him her illness was a lie, that she was well, that ever since this morning when it started to rain, everything had seemed to change and she was feeling happy. He added to her sense of well-being, her smile, and without thinking about it much, she intended that her voice would be very clear from afar so he could hear: "Dvorak, thank you, Dvorak, I'm well. I think I've made it through the worst." And she saw that her mother had kept the windows open this afternoon—weren't they always closed, ever since she'd become ill? And she saw the color of the ferns in the tall fernstand, and the sky, clear like Dvorak's eyes that now were looking at her without blinking, eyes that desired to cut through the gloom. She heard him say clearly and though not moving his lips, he repeated, "These are the ones you like." Her mother sensed this and said somewhat harshly, "Get out of here, you're going to wind up crying..." She wanted to know what he was trying to do and then he blurted "What does it matter?" and again repeated, "your flowers." "Dvorak," she mused, then something strange happened so that everyone looked at her lips. Almost inaudibly, the plumpish women who was her mother said, "God." She kept on admiring her mother's agility, her enthusiasm to take care of everything. She marveled how the word "God" had passed momentarily through lips that never mentioned him. Dvorak would talk to her, it was true, but Dvorak in his sorrow seemed to be lonely, scrutinizing her, loving her—that is, while the fragrance of the carnations swelled throughout the bedroom. Upstairs, her brother was coming and going—she could tell by his footsteps. The mother was busy with friends who kept on arriving. Suddenly it seemed as though the house was full. When the mother started to sob she asked herself, "Why have they come," and asked her mother, "Who has brought the bad news?" She got up slowly. Dvorak stayed seated watching the bed. The nightgown of white silk was perfumed by the carnations as was the bed. She saw her mother. "Mother!" she cried out, waiting. You could say that the visitors were "close friends." Her mother did not hear her. She was dressed in dark grey, and the visitors, in white, or violet greys. She felt cold. Through the wide open door she saw the hearse. She thought, "Who could it have been?" "People die," she murmured. "I'm also going to die," and, turning around, she went back to bed, saw Dvorak crying over a body laid out on the bed. "Me" she said not gazing at herself for too long. Then again she turned her eyes toward the hearse that brought the casket which was so beautiful, and now, as if totally synchronized, she saw her father. He'd just arrived, now he was being told, he looked like he was grieving. He was a good man who aged the instant anyone whispered, "I'm sorry." And the flowers, that huge pile of flowers, so many flowers.

She walked toward the bed and entered her being anew. Now she was aware that the last flashes of her existence had been those that morning when she was gazing at the heavy rain coming down, toward the end and because of that, she felt so much sorrow and so much wonder at feeling calm and rage simultaneously. For the first time, dead as such, she felt for Dvorak, when he realized that her mother, in spite of everyone's opinion, wanted to personally wash and dress her. Dvorak had to wait outside. That made no sense. Dvorak, who loved her.

Later Dvorak took her by the hands and wouldn't let them take her or put her inside the casket, not there. Soon after, the darkness, the voices, the flowers, the flowers, that huge pile, that terrible and enormous pile on top, that silence. Dvorak

Translated by Zoë Anglesey

From: Ochoa López, Moravia. *El espejo*. Panama: Imprenta Nacional, 1968.

THE DATE

Moravia Ochoa López

Although it may seem quite vulgar, I can tell you again that I loved him. Not with my heart but with my whole being, with all the copious generosity he learned to tap into, also copiously. Want me to tell you about it? At times I've thought about looking for him, but I was afraid of what could happen given it's been so long since we've seen each other. In the middle of all this—the great things the two of us could have done together. It's conceivable these things happen when what's happening is defined. But I can't admit it, I'll figure out all the reasons!

I'm going to start from the beginning.

Without realizing it I was letting myself carry on foolishly. That was, without a doubt, what he expected of me. At least that's what I thought. But what excuse would I have after everything happened? Maybe it's better, perhaps not, because the truth is, I don't like to be straightforward with myself and an excuse would indicate a great sacrifice on my part. It would have been better to leave things as they were. But how they were going was not to my satisfaction, either.

"If I wasn't at work, here, inside this enormous hole-in-the-wall ice cream parlor, I'd know what to do. One night I thought, "Let me look" scrutinizing each section of the whole place. "Hey kid! You wanna make twenty cents? Deliver a message close by!" I yelled.
"For twenty cents, okay, a deal. What do I have to do?"
"You get the twenty cents when you get back. Take the note to this place. It's all written down. Can you read?"
"I'm old enough. Sure I can. What else?"
"You'll tell me what he tells you. That's all."

Now the matter was half-settled. Why was that? The vulgarities that hit us. If a person can predict everything that happens, life would be too easy and monotonous. There are these blessings and small circumstances that teach us the most fascinating things. Even though what happened doesn't have me too convinced. Finally when all was said and done, I kept on loving him with nothing else mattering to me. Clever connoisseur of the weaknesses of a woman like me, he allowed for my every demand. I do not have moderate tastes. I loved him. He was not going to be deterred from going out the way I wanted.

So at 7:30 I finished my shift. Before arriving at the meeting place I walked up and down different streets to give myself time. I needed to know if what was mine was truly so. I realized I wasn't exactly dressed to the hilt but I didn't give that any importance. My flirting was now very secondary. I'd put on my first miniskirt which didn't fit too badly. Good enough! I was a bit on the slim side and reasonably attractive. I could tell when I walked by the huge mirror of a picture window at the movie house. Looking into it, I could easily see perpetual motion in the street with people coming and going. The huge window reflected everything, clearly and variegated.

That's when I saw him. He was part of the whole scene which still didn't bore me at all. I focused all my attention on him. If he'd seen me right off, he didn't let on to anyone. Later he came toward me slowly and distracted, not only extending his hand to me with forced politeness, but with eyes that I know were looking at me with all their eloquence. His was such a shameless courtesy I could hardly keep from getting angry, but everything about him was infinitely better than not seeing him. A grand prize of pleasure in the midst of a vast effervescence. Where did we go from here? Since he looked so elegant, I recall suggesting we might as well go somewhere fun and swanky. For the ambiance of "service with distinction." A fine place where we could experience worthwhile moments. Everything is a question of "art" and knowing how to make the worst things pass as the world's most impeccably divine.

I let him take my arm, with the gratitude of a puppy that gets a pat when it feels abandoned and masterless. I would look at him one, two, three times and for a long while—with complacency, so he'd have to go through all the turbulence that left me in a whirl the first time we went out together. He seemed very satisfied and I was promising myself to be very condescending. The kid I'd sent had done everything right. That night I would have the opportunity of being his, even though Luis Antonio had never actually asked me to. But when it came to him, he had the means of making me happy. It was a state of mind I relished. I would pass the test and no one could reproach me for it without being unjust.

As an insistent drizzle was falling, he took me by the hand and quite rapidly, we crisscrossed the city—a city of cramped streets even though they might have names like Central Avenue. We also ventured into very narrow alleyways, so narrow they seemed to be scrunched into place. We only heard the light patter of rain falling on us and the sound of our feet, his and mine, on the wet cement.

"They are my friends," he told me as we arrived at our destination.

Part of the itinerary was a huge place almost closed up for the night. It was a house with exit and entrance. So we also entered. A dozen men were drinking in silence under a blue light. Rooms could be seen to the side with closed doors. Some had keys in them waiting to be opened. Others remained mute and keyless. Every once in a while a ruckus or argument flared up behind the walls. A little later I learned about the matter related to the keys. They were for rent. Where there was a key, the room was available. For whatever exercise.

"Wait for me. I'll be right back. I'm going to get a match." Luis Antonio urgently announced. He had never been like this before with me. His face looked animated and flushed. I took note of this under the light blue light, the darkness of his eyes and the brilliant color reflected by his skin. I assumed he was this way because he was in my company and furthermore he'd had more than a few "whiskeys." Only whiskey at the moment. The "friends" hadn't talked to us much. A lean and complacent guy went with him and for a long time, I kept wishing they'd return.

"Are the matches very far from here?" Mortified, I asked a woman who came out of a room with a sleepy face.

"Depends," she said disagreeably.

Depends? What an answer! I stood up and searched in my purse again. How could I have I forgotten! I carried a small blue lighter. I took it and calmly returned to my sofa, sitting down nonchalantly. To me everything was turning out intelligible and overwhelmingly disturbing.

Quite a bit of time passed before he came back. The ruckus subsiding in a room sounded like drumbeats—dry and sparse, separated by vast, intervening spaces. Even with a certain serenity in his contorted face, he came back transformed and looking sickly. I felt disgusted. Someone had said something before. But I couldn't believe it then. I just looked at him until he could no longer look at me. I felt like an enormous wave of some sort of emptiness came over my body. I couldn't identify it because it was terrible. Now I no longer had him, but whose fault was it? The friend looked at me nervously. No one smoked and I hid the lighter in my hand with remorse.

"A drink?"

His voice sounded overly masculine. It was better I thought that because I felt like laughing and I laughed as hard as I could until I felt relieved. I became afraid of what struck me as a revelation. And as a great disconsolation. I straightened his tie. What more could I do? When he looked at me, I felt some sadness. Would he understand? What do I know. Under the circumstances I needed all my wits, then and there, to resolve the whole affair.

"If you want, yes, but not in this place," I answered.

I didn't say a word about the matches. His friend had stayed in the chair, staring at us as if he were too sick to move. When I was ready to leave, Luis Antonio meekly followed me. He really didn't have much energy and I myself felt better in the fresh air.

"You want something to drink?"

"I just wanted to get out of there," I answered.

"You're leaving?"

"Going home. And by myself."

"Excuse me," he said.

"It's okay. It hasn't been anything, believe me. If I had only known...but who's to blame for this kind of thing!"

"Did you figure things out?"

"Of course. Goodbye."

"Forgive me," he responded guiltily.

I felt small when I pulled away crying.

We hardly care to ponder things, if all of a sudden the night suspends itself over us like a nimbus of misty rain.

Translated by Zoë Anglesey

From: Ochoa López, Moravia. *Yesca*. Panama: Departamento Nacional de Cultura/Ministerio de Educación, 1962.

ELIO

Bertalicia Peralta

I never remember anything, I don't try to look for or get myself involved with things that have already happened. If something hurts me, really hurts me, then yes, I remember, then I love to remember. I try hard not to forget. Yes, I must be a masochist,

like when...

I don't know why but sometimes I think:

It's better not to exist, not the way other people want you to exist. One day they say I love you, I adore you, and I too say it, afterwards they repeat it, likewise I repeat it and then there are innumerable occasions when I keep on saying it, until I don't know whether it's truth or fiction, but I have to say something positive.

With Elio it's different.

Since he's arrived, I've changed; yes, definitely I've changed. When it comes to him, I do care. Sometimes the mere thought that I can hurt him, hurts me. I don't want to. I love him too much. I love him so very much, that if I had to choose between him and my family, I know I'd choose him; just Elio. This is what they can't understand at home, I'm fond of them. We've lived together long enough. I don't want to be part of their lives anymore, I want to live, just like I live now, even though at times I lack some stuff I'd like to have: Elio has what's his, and no, we won't marry, we don't want to. I don't understand why people have to get married if they love each other a lot. I know many people who are married and they don't love each other. I don't understand it; this is what I really don't understand. Once I was at the point of doing it myself, but my eternal indecision about doing things prevented me from going through with it. A lack of faith in others or in myself, I don't know which, but now I feel good about not having done it. I wouldn't have been able to have the life I have now, I wouldn't have known Elio or if so, I would have had to play cat and mouse.

Now

I have to go to work, as always; eight hours, unbearable heat, constant dehydration, bad pay. I'm thrilled by children, I love them. Not Elio. He says they're a nuisance and that's the last thing he wants.

We don't fight about that. We hardly fight at all. He has a personality you'd call intense, he's irascible, he can lose his temper at the drop of a hat over any foolishness (for example, when he tries to put a roll of film in his camera and he can't and I see how he struggles and sweats and then I see how he looks at me as if to ask for help), and he uses some grandiose words for maximum impact and I sometimes get to thinking they even suit him, that without them, I wouldn't know who he is (or when he has been studying hard and then at exam time he doesn't get the grades he expects, because he worries too much about his grades, they obsess him, and then he blames the professors, or when he's depressed and he decides to "cure himself" with cheap rum, because in this state he can drink more and get even more drunk, and then he starts to cry). Each day I feel he grows within me, that I could never be without him, that if he left me now for sure, I'd be missing something—missing a great deal. No, I hope he doesn't do it, not now,

because I know that

when we met each other

my life didn't have the worth it has at the present time. After many attempts, I was deceived, to the degree I thought it was better to disappear from the map but I really didn't want to die. When we met it wasn't via the classic Cupid's arrow or love at first sight, not in my view at least. I know he put some effort into convincing me—he eventually won me over, demonstrating to me day by day, hour by hour it was me who he was looking for. I didn't let him; it was like grabbing a cat by the neck, watching it try desperately to get loose, and I dug my claws in more and more, always with my trite face and air of superiority that began to melt with every blow of Elio's love. Afterwards I don't know what happened. I went on giving in, giving in. I began to yearn for his voice, miss it during the hours I was used to hearing it, (gruff and tender up against my body, his eyes taking me all in, he licking my ears softly, lovemaking with our hands lonely on the small white tablecloth in our favorite cafe, feeling as though nothing could mean more than his caress, that everything of interest came from him, his laugh, his refined and studied aloofness, his way of inhaling a cigarette and passing it to me blowing a kiss, his way of embracing me when we met in the evening.

I was never happy before I met him. I'm positive.

Nor afterwards, I'm sure of that.

But I did get closer. Positively.

Like previous to this, we didn't share an apartment, nor life, nor this warm happiness that drenches us. I continue yearning to be with him, to go to the movies with him, to listen to records with him, to get together with our friends to celebrate the publishing of a new book of poems even though they might be bad, to chat, to immerse myself in

Bach or Vivaldi—one and the same to me, contemporary as we are—or to simply walk on the beach at the sea, with our arms around each other, walking for hours to the sound of water, me tickling his skin, caressing his head during the night, waking him up in the mornings when he doesn't want to get up, rolling over, and I have to gently tease him, kiss him and kiss him until he finally smiles still half asleep, and his mouth lets out its little trace of sourness and I feel the vapor of his breath on me and me I love it and I never want to go back to the life I had before.

Translated by Zoë Anglesey

From: Jaramillo Levi, Enrique. Ed. *Antología crítica de joven narrativa panameña*. Mexico, D.F.: Federación Editorial Mexicana, 1971.

AND THIS BLUE
SURROUNDING ME AGAIN

Bessy Reyna

At times, the simplest of things become even simpler. Like calling someone who lives far away, just to tell them you miss them. Simple gestures, like opening a door and entering a room we have been in so many times before. Like the night I went back to her house and entered that blue room for the first time in five years. It was hot and the clothes I was wearing, long-sleeve shirt and heavy pants, made it so much worse. She opened the door, wearing a tank-top and baggy shorts. I walked in pretending not to be uncomfortable, and we sat making small talk, looking at each other and trying to guess if we really had become immune to one another. Without a word, she got up and walked away. I sat, listening to the jazz record she had been playing when I walked in. "Here, why don't you change into these clothes, you will be more comfortable," she said, handing me a pair of old shorts and a T-shirt. A simple gesture. The simple gestures of this person I once loved who was now handing me clothes, her hand touching mine when I reached for the clothes, as if nothing had happened. As if time had not been. As if the years in between never existed.

I wanted to believe it was the simple gesture of her love surfacing when she smiled. Me, wanted again, years later in this room where I now sat surveying my surroundings making an inventory of things replaced, remembering lying here on the same worn-out blue carpet, blue light, blue furniture. I never really paid attention then to how blue this room was. Even the paintings hanging on the walls are done in blues. The wallpaper used to be light blue but now, covered with water stains, is mostly peeling pieces of blue. The moonlight coming in from two sides makes the room look even bluer.

I want to stop all the memories flashing in front of me, aware of how this room is affecting me, merging with my mood, infecting me. Can I fight this? She probably wants me here tonight because there is no one else around, what has she done in the last five years? I found clues in her bedroom when I went to change my clothes, new faces smiling from elaborate picture frames. I found myself smiling back at me from one of them, each frame carefully placed like those in a gallery. Did she love them?

The night I left her bedroom, five years ago, I thought would be the last time I would be in that room. Did she plan for the hate? For the dryness of her sex? Lifting her body abruptly in the middle of making love, looking amused, "You think for a moment that I enjoy sex with you? You must be kidding!" Her face was so full of contempt "I am fed up with you, I have someone else now," she shouted at me, "You are just like nothing to me now," she kept saying while I was still panting from make-believe love-making that a short time back had seemed like caring. After that, every movement hurt me, getting dressed and leaving seemed to take place in slow motion. Earlier that day, we had gone to visit some friends for dinner, only I didn't know I was supposed to be the chef. They had bought lobsters, "We hear you are a great cook" they told me, daring me. "Sure! Just give me a cookbook and I can do anything!" I never believed they would take me seriously. I had never cooked a lobster before and this one was alive. I chose the fanciest french recipe I could find, one with cognac, hoping they wouldn't have the ingredients I needed, but they did. We were all impressed when I lit the sauce at the table. The meal was a great success, but I just couldn't eat it, not after cleaning it and letting all the gunk spill out into my hands. I didn't even taste it.

After dinner we sat talking to each other, the way people do when they get together, not wanting to sound too controversial or too boring. She got up from the living room, went to make a phone call and stayed away for the longest time. Who was she whispering to on the phone? I sat pretending to enjoy my after-dinner drink. "Sorry it took so long," she said casually, trying to smile, sitting next to me, touching me. I resisted her touch wondering who was at the other end of the line. Was I so jealous because I recognized the signs?

It was not the first time we broke up; this time it took longer for me to return, that's all. We liked pretending it was entirely the other's fault. Can I hate and keep on wanting? (She was right, these clothes are more comfortable.) The simplest gestures making the hurt come back.

It is so still outside. I turned off the lights and sat in the darkest corner, she will probably notice my absence after a while and will try to talk me into returning to her bed. I can't, not tonight, tonight I want to be part of this blue room which my mind converts into a stage set where, at the end of the play, one character moves away to another city.

I didn't hear her walk into the blue room. Next thing I knew her hands were caressing me and our fingers were searching and I couldn't stop this need from developing inside of me once again as if nothing else mattered, as if I had stopped caring about anything but feeling her touch. On again, off again love, like changing radio stations when you don't like the music. Only it was me this time, me being changed. Does it really matter here in this blue room? Fingers not daring to rush, to be too obvious, to get too carried away, centering on each touch, because nothing else matters but the blue warmth surrounding us and the room encouraging us to touch and to forget having left it, to forget I now have someone else who loves me, and who I am loving most of the time, except for this one moment when all this blueness surrounds me and I must find out why she left me, and why she hurt me so much and she is not going to tell me, just like before, and it does not matter because in this blue room nothing matters but her touch and the warmth around us.

She had carefully orchestrated my return, planning how to get me back. She searched for me, found me and brought me back. A message left on an answering machine, reaching out, "I had to talk to you, no one else would understand, you are the only one who understands, I have to see you." The past skillfully avoided, coming back to entice me.

She glides expertly next to me, as if she owned the space I occupy, her body surrounds me, overcomes me and I follow her rhythms losing myself for an instant and then I struggle to recapture my body as if it had been invaded. But it wasn't really, I let it happen. She was giving me something I wanted but didn't want to have, because I was used to knowing how it felt when I didn't have it and now I wish I didn't know how it feels having it again. But now I do.

I had to find out, no, didn't have to, simply wanted to.

Translated by the Author

(Original publication)

WINGS

Graciela Rojas Sucre

"Ding dong
Ding dong
bread and coffee
for the curate
pretty girls like bread
Ding dong
Ding dong
The old ladies to seven o'clock Mass they go.
ding dong ding dong ding dong
The young girls to the twelve o'clock Mass they go.
ding dong ding dong ding dong."

Pepito, was walking lively and noisily, singing along with the happy song of the village bells, his closed fists imitating the rhythmic motion of the clapper. Joy bouncing all through his body. Whenever the bells rang that way, they were announcing a fiesta. And their mother would dress them in their new outfits and would take them to church looking very elegant. It was really worth it to go to church! The flowers and lights and the smell of incense; the Padre would be dressed in golden vestments and the altar boys would bow and jump while sounding the small bells and Brother Anselmo would create strange music on the pipe organ.

Upon their return from Mass, the cook would have made a special meal; and after lunch, all the children in the house would be granted permission to visit their grandmothers' or uncles' houses. And it was so wonderful to be out in the street and to misbehave in somebody else's house. The uncles and grandmothers were wonderful and would never tell on them, and the little cousins, even if they had a fight, and were angry with one another, would always make up at the end...

"ding dong ding dong
ding dong ding dong
bread and coffee

for the curate."

Viva the Mass and Sunday!

Approaching his older brothers, he started nagging them to hurry up:

"Get dressed quick. There is Mass and fiesta."

"Ha, ha, ha! The others responded."

"This one does not even know the days of the week. Look at how silly he is. Don't you see today is Saturday?"

"Liar! The bells are ringing and calling us to Mass."

"Silly," one of the older ones exclaimed. "It's because somebody died."

"Died? Listen to the bells, as if the bells would sound that pretty if someone died. The death knell sounds ugly. Dong dong ding dong."

"True! But that's when someone important dies, when a nobody dies, the bells ring as they do for Mass because they're happy."

"Yes, why is that?"

"Because when a child dies they say another little angel has gone to Heaven and that's why we must be happy."

"Who said that?"

"The Padre."

"So tell me, who's a little angel today?"

Everyone looked questioningly at him. Turning into an angel was really important. The thought of having wings and flying among the clouds filled them with envy. Pepito had been so envious, so many times, while watching the vultures make big circles and flying high up to the sun so gracefully. He felt jealous of those big, ugly birds that everyone hates.

Once—and he remembered it so well now—they wanted to fly so badly that they decided to learn how to fly anyway. After discussing this subject for a long time with their friends, they agreed to try it one Sunday in the vacant lot where a neighbor was building a house. They promised each other not to say anything to their parents. To learn how to fly would be their secret, so, in case they were ever going to be punished for something bad they had done, they could, to the great surprise of all, start flying together and escape, to roam free any-where...and they would return only when their parents, after much crying and waiting for them, would no longer have the strength to scold them...

And when the day arrived, Jorge, who was the gang leader (Jorge always had to be in charge of everything...) told them to climb on one of the empty wagons that had been left at the lot next to the piles of sand, stones and gravel. After they climbed, they formed two lines, creating an angle in which Jorge placed himself at the front, with his back to everyone, and almost at the border of the wagon. He told them not to cluster around but to spread out, so the wagon would not tilt. Furthermore, forming an angle like that, they could more easily imitate the birds flocking in great groups with a leader in the front. Jorge would be the "leader-bird". Who else could do such a thing? Who could be better than him in that role? He made them extend their arms on both sides, and move them as if they were wings. Then, in an authoritarian tone, he started giving orders: everyone, when told, would have to imitate him. When he started flying and leading the way, and said: "one, two, three" all must follow him, but without bumping into each other and making sure that they kept the line. Their ears must be open because the orders would be coming from the air and they must remember one thing: not to go away from the lot, they could not be seen by anyone...Now, ready! And...and one...and two...and three!

And, in a second, like a flash, Jorge crashed against the ground, with the rest of the gang watching in horror, while trying to hang-on as the wagon overturned unexpectedly, because of the excessive weight. They all started screaming. They were terrified, panic-stricken, particularly when they saw Jorge's blood stains and were unable to get up and save him. Jorge, was asphyxiating under their weight. They started screaming so loudly that the everyone in the neighborhood came running toward them. Jorge was stunned, he was taken away with a broken skull and the rest of them were left with scrapes and bruises all over their bodies. The neighbors, in their rush to help them, never asked what had happened. Crazy kids, that's all!...But, the failed attempt cost them several days of being forced to stay home, covered with ointment and bandages...Of course, they did not feel like repeating the attempt. And that's how their flying escapade came to an end...But their secret desire to fly never ended. The blue and high sky, was a continuous temptation. And the white playful clouds, like heavenly streets, were even more tempting. And all the birds, big ones and little ones, from the ugly vultures to the hummingbirds, the butterflies and the flies, were always making them so jealous....But what of becoming an angel?!...Why didn't they think of that before? That was really easy to accomplish, if it was true what the priest said: Just a matter of dying, that's all...But how does one manage to die? And who was the fortunate person who died today?

"Hey, who's the new angel?" In unison, they asked their older brother.

"Zorrita. She died yesterday."

"Zorrita?" And, they shook their heads in disbelief. Who was going to believe that? Ugly and skinny Zorrita, the washer woman's daughter, now an angel...And she was such a cry baby, stubborn and always asking for things. They had started calling her "Fox-face", because she would steal any food she found around her, and her face was so long and protruding. Zorrita, an angel! That was laughable. Angels should be graceful and have some meat. Zorrita was all skin and bones and dirty and spoiled...How could she have turned into an angel? So, to make sure, they asked again:

"Is it true that Zorrita is the new angel?"

"True."

"And how do you know?"

"The Padre said it in catechism class: All children who die turn into angels, and one must be very happy and run to ring the bells."

"But have you seen her? Zorrita herself turned into an angel, wings and all?"

"No, I haven't but, I'm real sure that it is true; Don't you know that priests never tell lies? Besides, we can ask the cook: Doña Eulogia, she knows everything..."

And sure enough, the eager group headed toward the kitchen. They surrounded Eulogia, who was a very patient woman, showering her with questions.

"Eulogia, is it true that Zorrita died?"

"Listen, is it true that she turned into an angel?"

"Tell me, how does one die and turn into an angel?"

"Where is Zorrita? We want to see the wings and watch her fly."

"We want to become angels too, how do we do it?"

Eulogia started by calming them down. She made them sit on the large bench in the kitchen, then, she started to explain:

"Well, yes, it's true. Zorrita died yesterday afternoon. The wake lasted all night and now they are going to bury her. And they have already rung the church bell. She died because God wanted her to. One does not die when one wants, but when God feels like it. Zorrita was very sick and she suddenly got worse and that's why she died."

"What is dying, Eulogia?"

"Well, turning stiff and without breath, you can't talk, or eat or move. It is like a heavy dream from which no one wakes up. All Christians who die lose their color, their eyes get sucked-in and their noses stick out and they must be buried before they decompose and break up."

"And that's what happened to Zorrita?"

"That same, same thing!"

"Uhm! And, doesn't Padre say that when kids die they turn into angels?"

Eulogia seemed to be searching for an answer, so she tried to come up with something really good:

"El Padre, he is right. But it happens like this: When a little one dies, right at the last moment, when the soul is in agony, a little white dove comes flying out of their mouths and goes straight to the sky, and up there it turns into an angel."

"But Eulogia, tell us, where is Zorrita right now?"

"Dead, at her mother's house, where the wake is taking place."

The children did not understand all that business of Zorrita being at her house and the dove in the heavens. And with their faces full of wonder, they were just about to ask more questions when Eulogia, who had guessed their intentions, beat them to it:

"Ah, if you are such know-it-alls and don't believe me, go ask your father who is a well-educated man, or ask the Padre, who knows about theology; because as far as I am concerned, I don't have time for your silliness. I am a Christian and very busy."

Having finished, Eulogia turned around noisily in the kitchen, moving pots and pans and lighting the stove with great fury. The kids didn't have any choice but to take their long faces elsewhere. They regrouped on the porch, and decided to go to Zorrita's house in search of better information.

Sophia, Zorrita's mother, had a small house, it was poor and almost void of furniture. It was in the outskirts of the town and had a little yard with fruit trees in the back. They had been there once before, when their mother had given them permission to go visit that house and pick up oranges and mangos from the trees. Now, they were going back without permission, and, if anyone asked them, they would say that their mother had sent them to find out if it was true that Zorrita had died.

When they arrived, they noticed that some of the town's women were coming in and out, talking secretly, their heads covered by a black veil like when they went to church. They waited for a moment when no one was entering or leaving to peek in from the back door. The room was completely empty, creating a strange scene: The walls were adorned with wreaths made of fresh flowers, and, at the center of the room, there was something like a table covered in white, and a tiny body on top of it, with many decorations and flowers around. Four big wax candles in tall candlesticks were placed on the ground next to the corners of the table. Was that the angel? They had to find out. And looking around them, they sneaked in, one by one. There was a great silence inside. They could hardly make out the whispers coming from the next room, where women were trying to keep their voices lowered as they spoke. Tiptoeing they got closer to the table. Zorrita was there! It was Zorrita, dead, just as Eulogia had explained. But she was so changed. Very quiet and pale with her eyes opened, without blinking, as if fixed on the ceiling. Her small hands over her chest, tied with a white ribbon and holding a small palm leaf of the same color. Over her yellowing forehead they had placed a small crown of wax flowers. She was dressed in a full length dress with a white silk shirt and a great display of laces and ribbons had been spread out all over the table. There were roses and jasmines all over her body and the table. Zorrita was very clean and smelled of the perfume of the freshly cut flowers. When had anyone seen Zorrita that well-dressed and smelling so good? They could not explain her unusual luxurious appearance, knowing that Sophia had hardly any money.

Carefully, they looked at her neck and her back to see if she had wings. Nothing! Not even a trace. They realized that they had not been able to look at her feet. It would be good to look at them—those dirty little feet of Zorrita's that had crawled on the floor all twisted and bent as if they were rags—one of them dared to lift up her skirt and with great surprise they found that Zorrita had her little feet nicely covered by white socks and shoes. She had very clean legs and her whole body was clean!...And, under that beautiful dress, she had even more new clothes.

They looked at the door again and because no one was coming in they got closer to her to examine her better. They touched her, she was cold and heavy. Then they looked at her glassy eyes and limp mouth, there was no trace of the dove feathers that Eulogia had described. Pepito, who could no longer contain his curiosity about everything he was seeing, got really close to Zorrita and tried to whisper in her ear.

"Zorrita! It's us. Is it true that you are going to become an angel? Come on, tell us! Don't be so stubborn. I am Master Pepito, the son of your mother's mistress, *la patrona*. Don't you remember all the candy I always gave you?"

Not one word came from the dead little girl's closed mouth. Zorrita couldn't even hear and she was there sleeping with her eyes open, and unable to do or say anything for Heaven's sake! That business of dying is a serious business, isn't it? They looked confusedly at each other. They were intrigued by Zorrita's quietness and the silence around them, and those flowers that were starting to fade, and the hissing of the wax candles twisting because of the heat. There was a strange smell, everything looked strange there...The sound of the bells starting their round startled them. They stampeded out toward the fruit trees outside, trying to hide behind the bushes, they started discussing nervously. What was all that? Why was poor Zorrita so dressed up and made up? And why didn't she have wings, nor was there any evidence of the dove in the room? Who was right after all? Eulogia or the Padre? Juan kept saying that almost everything Eulogia had foreseen had happened; but that he wasn't sure about that business of the dove. Pedro the older one, suggested that when they took Zorrita to the church, she would turn into an angel right then and there in front of the altar...

"That's it!" was Albertin's suggestion. All they had to do was to go to the church to convince themselves...They thought it was a great idea. They were just about to leave when they heard great cries coming from the room where Zorrita was. They looked in and were able to see Sofia held back by two neighbors, screaming with anguish and exclaiming "Daughter of my body! Treasure of my heart, soul of my life. They're taking you to the cemetery and I'll never see you again!...And this horrible life that gives you children that one learns to love, to take them away without warning and without rights!"...and that it was better if she also died.

All the women in the neighborhood cried with her, blowing their noses and eyes with a handkerchief or the hems of their skirts. A man came in and took his hat off, as if he had entered a church, and taking Zorrita by the arms, gently placed her in a small white box someone else was holding for him. They arranged her clothes and covered her with flowers. Sophia, managed to run free from the hold of the neighbors and threw herself on top of the box, crying hysterically, kissing her daughter's stiff small face and covering it with tears...The neighbors' sobs grew in intensity. Even the two men started crying while struggling to pull Sophia away from the box. The women finally were able to pull her away from the box, and took her to her room, while the two men placed the top on the box and started to nail it shut. The crying increased, and the sound of the hammering, mixed strangely with the sad cries, making the happy sound of the bells seem as if they had gone purposefully crazy...And without being able to contain themselves the boys also started crying. Poor Zorrita, unable to speak, or move, or breathe, locked up like that in that small box! She would never ever be awake again! Never ever see her mother again, gone somewhere who knows where. Unable to turn inside that box even though she had loved to walk and play in the street!...

Four young men entered hat in hand, lifted the small box, grabbing it by the handles on the sides, and carried it away. Some children came in with wreaths and flowers. In their eagerness to see everything, our little boys had come into the room forgetting about themselves. Some of the women must have noticed them because they started to comment:

"Would you look at that! Those are the children of Sophia's mistress, *la patrona*. Would you look at that! How respectful that white woman is, even sending her kids to the wake!"

"That's nothing" said one of them, "the best part is that she even paid for the funeral shroud. Did you see how pretty it was? The best anyone has seen around here, full of lace and ribbons...and, *la patrona* did more than that: she even paid for that pretty white and silver casket, like the caskets of high quality. I'm telling you that sometimes there are some white people out there who're really good to us poor folks."

"Listen, neighbor" said another, "do you know what Zorrita died of?"

"Well, they say," and at this point the woman lowered her voice "that she died of...hunger! She got sick from lack of food and when Sophia managed to save enough money to buy medicine, it was too late. That woman has always been so obstinate. She never asked anyone for help when she needed it."

So, Zorrita had died of hunger and instead of feeding her, when they had a chance, they had let her die, and now they were dressing her up like a doll, and sending her to the cemetery inside a nice white and silver high quality casket! And, instead of helping Sophia on time, the white woman was satisfied enough to send the money for the funeral arrangements and the casket. And the *patrona's* children became angry. Rage that such strange things should happen for no reason, and that the grown-ups did not pay any attention. Rage upon finding out that Sophia was so poor, and that the neighbors called her obstinate. Rage that Sophia's *patrona* was distributing all these benefits so late...

The children rushed out of the room, just in time to join the group forming two lines on the way to the church. They were so overcome with pity and love for Zorrita, that they tried to get as close as possible to the casket. And the little white children, greatly admired by all, walked with long faces and tearful eyes, at the very beginning of the funeral procession, behind the casket, as if they, too, were grieving relatives. Zorrita really needed this because no one knew who her father was and Sophia had no family, no brothers or other male relatives, not one man to be in charge of the pain, of the funeral...

At the church, the ceremony was very simple: The padre sprinkled holy water over the box, and said some things in Latin and then, the group walked toward the cemetery. As they left the church, the four young white boys noticed the proud figure of their father, crossing the park toward their house; so the boys figured that very soon it would be lunch time and that their absence might be investigated; and they started to tremble...It would be better to go home once and for all, and leave the funeral. But, would they ever find out about Zorrita? Wouldn't it be better to be punished rather than not know? So they asked an old man who was walking at the end of the line.

"Is the cemetery far away?"

"The same distance it always was."

"How long will it take to get there?"

"One hour more or less."

"And what happens when they get there?"

"They bury her in the grave I dug early this morning. I am the gravedigger."

"Wow!"

"And then?"

"Then, they shovel dirt on top of the box and cover it and push it down, and put a small white cross on top by her head to remember her by."

"And, that's all? What happens after?"

"Only God knows!"

"But, is it true that Zorrita is going to turn into an angel?"

"Sure, if the Padre says so."

"Have you ever seen anyone turn into an angel?"

"Nope! Those are God's tricks which he doesn't let the humans see. The joke is to do it without anyone knowing."

And, the children, now fully informed, did not see the need to continue all the way to the cemetery. And because they had started feeling hunger pains and remembered lunchtime, the "mourners" turned their backs on the funeral and deserted it, running toward their house.

They made it just in time to rest a little, without being seen. They went to the garage so they could discuss the matter in private and so they could talk and think about what they had seen that morning. So everybody was right! So it was true about becoming an angel but God was the one keeping the secret. How did he do it? So they started to make all sorts of conjectures about it.

"I am sure that at night, when people are sleeping God will send a big angel to look for Zorrita. And the angel will take her out of the box and fly her to Heaven with him, and there, God with his magic wand will turn her into an angel."

"Well, I believe that it is Saint Peter who will come for her, because he is a very old and serious person, and he can better take care of her..."

"It can't be Saint Peter, he doesn't have wings, or time for such things. Don't you know he is the Heaven's gate keeper and he is always busy?"

"I know, I know!" said Albertin, happy with his discovery.

"Well, tell us!"

"Don't you remember the song:

"To get to Heaven
all you need
is one little ladder
and one really big...?"

So, that's it! God tells Saint Peter to put the little ladder (the big one is for big people) at the entrance and it reaches the cemetery and he will send an angel to help Zorrita go up the little ladder, and Saint Peter will hold her hand to come into Heaven."

"Ah!" said Pepito triumphantly, "Now I know why they dressed her up like that, and made her look all pretty. Because to get to Heaven and see God and Saint Peter and the other saints you have to be clean; otherwise they won't let you in! How can you get in if you are ugly and dirty?"

"That's right!"

It seemed to them that they could see the little ladder, moving in the sky like the circus trapeze, and they could see Zorrita rising covered in flowers and they could see her in the moonlight, climbing to the sky, beautiful in the funeral dress that Sophia's *patrona* had given her, Zorrita holding the hand of a beautiful and shining angel. And the white dove carrying the message of Zorrita's death to the heavens kept flying, lovingly, around her head...

And at Heavens' gate, Saint Peter, very alert, and with his keys making a great noise, would open the gate wide and he would extend his arms to help Zorrita come in, just in case she stumbled over all the lace in the hem of her funeral dress...And, after that, they would have a party in honor of the new angel: All the big angels and the little new angels forming groups of four and the cherubs, the archangels and seraphim—who are the grown-up angels—will be singing psalms and making music with harps and flutes, from the balconies in Heaven and the saints and the martyrs will be at the balconies and in a special balcony in the back there would be the Holy Family—the Virgin Mary, Saint Joseph and Baby Jesus—and in another special balcony would be Jesus Christ and his apostles; and the Holy Spirit with all the messenger doves that brought the dead children to Heaven, who would have a special silver bird cage suspended from the sky's ceiling; and God the Father would be in the middle of the sky and his throne of gold placed really high on a great golden platform. Saint Peter would be accompanying the newly arrived child and introducing her to God the Father and to everyone around just by saying "This is Zorrita!..." And, at that moment, the celestial court would start applauding in honor of Zorrita, Sophia's daughter, the white woman's washer-woman...And God the Father will make her climb the stairs to the throne and would take out of his pocket two small brand-new and shining wings and with a bit of spit will stick them onto Zorrita's back. Then, everyone would applaud again, and the heavenly orchestra would play a very happy "paso doble" while God the Father, would order to change that ugly name of Zorrita into another more dignified one, a shorter and prettier name: Ita (from Zorrita) Angel, yes, Ita-Angel...and every choir in the sky will sing: Glory, Glory to Ita-Angel! and, at the end of the party, God the Father will give the order to break the ranks and have a good time and will send Saint Peter and Saint Paul with other helpers to pass out sweet rolls...and all the angels will be surrounding Ita-Angel filled with curiosity about her and asking her all kinds of questions, and because she just arrived, she will be shy, and at the beginning she will be tongued-tied, but very soon they will all become friends and will tell her all about things to do in Heaven and later (and this was the main thing) they will take her flying, flying, with her own wings, to go to all corners of the sky.

How lucky Zorrita was! Don't you agree?

Translated by Bessy Reyna

From: Rojas Sucre, Graciela. *Terruñadas de lo chico*. Santiago, Chile, 1931.

THE BIRTH

Isis Tejeira

I am an employee of the civil registry. There, I'm a file clerk. Day after day, I file papers and more papers in enormous metal furniture that no one pays attention to. In this profession, which I've been practicing for fourteen years, everything is alphabetically exact. Papers from job applications, birth certificates, death certificates, and they all ask for the same information: age, sex, occupation, marital status; age, sex, occupation, marital status, and the names are repeated again and again.

I don't know if I'm explaining myself. For example, you're planning to travel, okay, you have to apply for a passport; on the form they ask you, each time, your age, your sex, your occupation, your marital status. Then, for the vaccinations, the same questions, to buy the ticket, the same questions, on the plane they give you a paper for customs with the same questions. I use the trip as an example, but at each stage in life one must fill out forms. And on the death certificate, also the same questions. Well, somebody makes copies of each one of those papers, and my job consists of filing them. From A to Z they must be ordered and separated according to their category and kept in huge shelves. This I do from seven in the morning to five in the afternoon, with two hours out for lunch.

Since I have no greater ambitions, I am resigned to my lot. More than that, I love these papers, filled out by anonymous human beings, to which, every now and then, someone attaches a photograph.

I am a very punctual woman, and very honorable. In the fifteen years I've been here, I haven't missed a single day, and they even gave me a certificate for never arriving late. I began working at eighteen and I'm still here. And if they ask me how it's going, well just fine, I usually answer.

And, above all, no complications. Very peaceful. Well, once I had some emotional entanglements with a colleague at work, whom they transferred, and then he married someone else. My papers don't allow me time for that sort of thing. That happened ten years ago. How time flies!

But now, suddenly, things have become complicated, and I'm worried. Even though I haven't yet come to the change of life, it's been four months since I've had a period. This bothers me. I've thought about going to the doctor and I'll do it as soon as I have time. Besides, I've felt nauseated, my waistline has grown and I have an anomalous belly. When I press it or I put on a girdle, it crackles and flattens and rises again as if...

Well, thinking about it carefully, it's best to go to the doctor. Pregnant? Impossible. I haven't even been with a man, something that seems to bother everyone else, but I'm not worried about it. "Girl, why don't you get married? Girl, a woman alone..." In short, on the many papers I've filled out in my life, the only thing that ever changes is my age.

Now it's four o'clock in the afternoon and I have filed away exactly one million papers that everyone will forget, everyone except me, because they are part of my life.

I go down the stairs with my bulky abdomen, which for some unknown reason has grown, and I cross the street. Facing my building is a doctor's office.

"Come in, ma'am, sit down," says the friendly nurse, and takes out a piece of paper, like the ones I live with. "Name, age, marital status..."

"Single," I say.

She looks at me pityingly.

"Oh, don't you worry...It's just that it's been four months since I've had a period, and I have unmistakable symptoms, so I've come to see the doctor. It well may be hydropsy."

The nurse smiles benevolently, and I sit down, worried. So she thinks that...Oh, no, what will mom and dad say, and my aunt who lives in the provinces, so chaste, so pure, so pious. But there's a solution for this.

I sit and begin to settle my abdomen in its place. The noise makes the nurse turn around. But I've managed to gather it up and almost, almost recapture my old figure. The other patients who are in the waiting room are also looking at me. I smile and after a while I go into the examining room.

Without examining me, seeing the enormity of my abdomen the doctor asks:

"How many months?"

"Months? Doctor, I have hydropsy."

"Yes, that's what they all say."

"I'm telling you the truth. Examine me. I haven't even been to bed with anyone, I swear to you."

He smiles patiently.

"Take these pills to calm your nerves. You're very strong and you'll have a beautiful child."

"Doctor, I..."

"Calm down, calm down. Does your family know?"

"But I'm not..."

"Okay, okay, if you persist in trying to hide what is obvious, I have no choice but to wish you good luck. I don't have time to waste." And he got up sternly and solemnly from the chair.

I have heard or read somewhere words like desolation, melancholy, abandonment, despair, anguish, anxiety...moods that have nothing to do with the orderly papers of my strict files. But that's the way I felt. Me...me pregnant!!! And the son of a...didn't believe me. And, who will? No one, no one, but I'm not pregnant. I swear it. Well, I'll just lock myself in my room and I won't come out for five months. If it's a virgin birth, if it's the Antichrist, if it's whatever, no one will find out. My God!, this happening to me, to me! And I can't even say that it's been bad luck, it simply hasn't been. I swear it, I swear it not once but a thousand times. I haven't even been tempted. My bath is private and anyway sperm can't swim. And no one visits me. Only, at times, when I'm behind at work, I bring my papers home to put them in order and then return them the next day. I don't even have friends, nothing. Oh, I don't even have anyone to tell my shame to.

All that night and the days that have followed I've done nothing but think. I stopped going to work. My boss called me, worried. By that time the papers had piled up into the millions. I told him my mother was sick and I had to go to her. Who could tell when I might return? And here I am, stretched out on my bed playing with my abdomen. How it crackles! And how well it adapts to the pressure of my hand. I go out to the corner from time to time, when hunger strikes. Fortunately, I've been methodical enough that I have savings to see me through the months remaining. Then I'll return to my files. This can't be true. But, okay, let's say that the virgin birth has come to pass. When the Holy Spirit did it—that was twenty centuries ago—besides, no angel has come to me to announce any birth...

Oh!, I hadn't thought about it carefully. Maybe it *is* the Antichrist. With the Antichrist comes the end of the world. Wouldn't it be a good idea for me to tell my story so the world would stop sinning? I hadn't thought about it. The end of the world is near. Okay, this has to be done rapidly. I've wasted two months locked up and I haven't thought of humanity. The end of the world. Oh! Yes, of course, it can't be anything else. But what barbarity! what irreverence! Besides, no one would believe me. I would look ridiculous. On the other hand people must be very busy filling out sheets of paper. I'll call my office.

"Mama is still sick."

"But, my child, the papers keep piling up here. And we're approaching a billion. We have a young man, but it's not enough. You don't know how much we appreciate you now. You're a wonder with the papers."

I've gone to bed tired. My voluminous abdomen has been dropping for some time now. And I feel a little colicky, as if I were going to get sick.

And now pains...So it was true!

Oh God!... I'll heat water...Oh, and some scissors to cut the umbilical cord. Oh, God, how much it hurts to have a child. And a fatherless child. Once I heard that you have to push...and if I were to call my neighbor...? And if I die...? Oh, no! A life as useful as mine, they said so in my office. No one is as efficient as I am. Look at how the work is piling up. Oh! Oh! My child's coming! I'll call my neighbor...

"Please, help me, doña Sol."

"But child, I didn't know you were in this condition."

"Help me, doña Sol."

"I've brought several children into the world. But, what a strange-looking abdomen!"

"Doña Sol, I can't stand it."

"Come on, child, come on."

I was frightened. My insides were crackling more than ever, as if...

"Push, girl, push..."

"Nothing yet?"

"Push, it's coming..."

Now doña Sol has turned white as a wall, as a...but it's what she's seen come out of my womb. Enormous pieces of paper, lumps of paper, sheets of lined paper, ready to be written on. One each for even the most distinct institutions. Doña Sol was frightened.

"But, child, what on earth made you eat paper..."

"But I haven't eaten paper!"

"Of course, of course...If you had eaten it, it wouldn't be...You, young lady, have become a paper factory, an application form factory, a bureaucracy factory..."

"Doña Sol, please, call my office, and ask when they replace me that they not hire a woman..."

"You're right. But I recommend that you not tell anyone about this. Don't you realize, if they discover that you gave birth to paper, the state will put you to work?"

Translated by Linda Britt

From the journal, "Alfa", Number 2, Circulo Lingüístico Rícardo J. Alfaro, Panamá, 1977. Also published in the journal "Imagen", Revista de Extensión Cultural de la Universidad de Panamá, 1985.

THE PIANO
OF MY DESIRE

Isis Tejeira

It is good to remember dreams: dreams about Brahms, about my Panamanian life, and about everything that can be evoked from a childhood, perhaps too distant, in which all things were possible, because everything happened as in a dream and all of a sudden you find you have too much gray hair, but I remember those long lights, stretched out in the sky, which were marking the way for the warplanes, and I remember the story of the nightingale and the rose, that rose the bird colored red with its blood and then was flattened by a carriage, and the one about Pérez Mouse, who fell in the boiling pot, and the little cockroach that sings about him and cries over him. The childhood that, in spite of everything, lingers like the last ember of purity you discover one day when you're waiting for someone or something that doesn't arrive, on one of those afternoons that's as long as the lights illuminating the skies during the war.

But of all my hopes, the one that hurt me the most was because of the movie *The Unforgettable Song*, about that tuberculous musician who, while playing his revolutionary etude, was spilling red bloodstains on the keys, and who loved his country, then occupied by representatives of the czars. That was when I thought I would become a pianist. Perhaps the best in the world and yes, I told my parents, I want a piano.

That was the miracle. Of course, if she wants it she'll have it, mama and papa said to each other and they told everyone else that I, the girl with the big eyes, wanted a piano. They would make all the arrangements, they told me, while they knitted my two braids, then so fashionable, with their two great many-colored bows, and put on my tidy white uniform for school.

One day they gave me the news. You will have your piano and you will be the best pianist in the world. Mr. López, who brings us our laundry, will get one for us. It had to be a used one, because at that time the few new pianos that existed were very expensive, impossible on our poor budget.

"Mr. López has already asked us for a deposit and next Monday your piano will be here and you'll be the best pianist in the world."

And my dream began, the most beautiful of dreams. Naturally, my second-hand piano couldn't be carried up through the stairway. They would hoist it over the balcony, as in that movie I had seen about the life of a jazz musician, where they had lifted the piano up, lashed securely, and the whole neighborhood would come out to see it, everyone happy, and I, as though inspired by the Holy Spirit, would play and play, especially that pathetic revolutionary etude so pathetic, and the polonaises. What a pity that even though I was very thin, I wouldn't leave my bloody stains on the keys.

And the wait began: Thursday, Friday, Saturday, Sunday, Monday...How I wished for classes to end on those days, so I could leave, running as fast as I could, crossing the streets, taking short cuts, and see the space that mama had left free in the living room occupied by my piano!

And I arrived, throbbing. I climbed the stairs. Downstairs there was no one. They had told mama it would arrive at three and it was three-thirty, they're already finished!, I had thought I was going to see it as they raised it up over the balcony, no doubt it had already arrived, I was thinking, while I knocked impatiently at the door. There was mama who was also waiting, but nothing else, the space was empty.

"Don't worry, child, your piano will come and you'll be a great pianist, the best in the world."

That afternoon papa arrived carrying Venezuelan cookies, so delicious!, and out of pure sadness and the urge to cry I devoured cookie after cookie.

Well, who knows what would happen, maybe tomorrow, Tuesday, or Wednesday, Thursday; Mr. López appeared and was interrogated by mama.

"Nothing to worry about, ma'am, I thought the deposit you gave me was sufficient, but the owners won't give it to me if you don't send them a hundred dollars more," and of course, a hundred dollars was a lot of money and they'd have to see where it would come from, but I would have my piano, yes my daughter, and you will be the best pianist in the world.

Oh, that crazy desperate love of my young heart. Papa bought me *Teaching Little Fingers To Play*, so that I would have, at the very least, my first book of music, and I looked again and again at those hieroglyphs, those round signs in black and white, and the keys of G and F.

And they dressed me up each morning to go to school, with my braids and my multi-colored bows and my tidy white uniform, in those days when along with the stars some long, long lights illuminated the sky to show the airplanes their way.

Across from my home there was a long, narrow park, with its great tall laurel trees from India, leading us almost to the sea. The war was reaching its end. The bomb shelters that had been built beside the residences across the narrow park looked like hills and had been fixed up as terraces, with beautiful wrought-iron chairs and great pots of overhanging flowers, and I used to think that's the way the famous Babylonian gardens would look. And I returned from school day after day through that park plaza, so long and narrow. How I loved that house almost directly across from mine, with its terrace, and I used to sit outside on a bench to see it better. But now all I wanted was to be the best pianist in the world, and I waited all over again the following Monday, Tuesday, Wednesday; and the space waited, and that Thursday when I was coming home from school, very slowly, walking, tiptoeing, I saw a truck carrying a beautiful piano. Now, yes, finally it had arrived, and the truck was crawling along like a turtle, as if the men were looking for the place they were going, and perhaps they don't know where it is, I'll walk along beside them and tell them, look, that's where I live, there where those men in uniform are climbing those stairs to knock at the door, where mama will open it and say yes, it's here, come in, those men are, undoubtedly, the ones that will help me realize my dream, and how lucky I am, I will experience the thrill when they tie it up very securely and hoist it up over the balcony, just as I had dreamed it, but the truck continued on its way and they've gone too far, no, no, don't make a mistake, please, I was telling them from deep inside me, don't get confused, look, by now the uniformed men must be talking with mama, and the truck stopped exactly in front of the house with the terraced bomb shelter, and a blond woman with blue eyes came out and I watched, from that park of my childhood, as they carried the piano to the wrong house, to the garden house. But what about those men I saw going up to our home? Of course, perhaps they had gone up to collect payment for the transportation, probably the piano had arrived while I was still at school, which I had left, walking, tiptoeing, trying to see the truck that would bring my happiness, but they had delivered the piano and they would be there, putting it in the place Mama had prepared.

I got up from my bench, where I had been sitting, worrying. My eyes wouldn't even let me see the road; I had feelings of happiness and sadness, a prolonging of my desire that it be there, and I climbed the stairs very slowly, until I arrived at the door. A mixture of hope and hopelessness, of yes and no, of a daisy losing its petals in a he loves me, he loves me not, just as sad and just as happy. Mama opened the door when she heard my steps. There were the men I had seen, very serious and circumspect. But no, I'm sure there is also my long-awaited dream, the one that would turn me into the best pianist in the world and

I saw, almost without looking, the space cleared by mama, because my piano had to be there.

"Really, Madam, we are very sorry about what happened..." No, it wasn't possible, my clouded eyes won't let me see, that sensation like when they steal your doll from you, and you look for it and look for it, because it has to be there, right where you left it...

"It isn't the first time this has happened with that man," and they continued talking and talking endlessly, those uniformed men, but the space is empty, an emptiness as simple as the empty spaces that occupy all spaces. In that moment I couldn't see any more. I clung to my mother trembling with fear, ravaged of all my hopes.

"What we do promise you, madam, is that he will return every last dime to you."

Translated by Linda Britt

From the journal, *Maga*, Number 10, Panama: April-September, 1986.

ABOUT THE WRITERS

COSTA RICA

DELFINA COLLADO

She has written many books for children and has won several national prizes. Collado has published the following books: *Mundo de Tipirito; Tierra Oscura; Yiguirro Real; Los geranios; Bajo la luna de jade; El sapito dorado; La vaca que se comió el arco iris; El unicornio y sus estrellas; Las fierecillas mágicas.*

CARMEN LYRA

Pseudonym of María Isabel Carvajal (1888-1949). She became famous for the stories published in the most important Central American journal, *Repertorio Americano,* edited for many years by the Costa Rican writer Joaquín García Monge; and because of her left-wing ideas, for which she suffered exile in Mexico, where she died. *Los cuentos de la tía Panchita,* a book of stories for children, is her best-known work. Lyra also published a novel: *En su silla de ruedas.* All of her literary work has been compiled as: *Obras completas de Carmen Lyra.* (San José, Costa Rica: 1973). *Los fantasías de Juan Silvestre* (1988, 2nd edition); *Relatos escogidos de Carmen Lyra* (1977); and *Los otros cuentos de Carmen Lyra* (1985), are her other books, the last two published after her death.

EMILIA MACAYA

Born in San José, Costa Rica, she went to college in Europe and earned a degree in Spanish Philology in Costa Rica. Macaya teaches Greek and Latin Literature at the Universidad de Costa Rica, in San José. She is at present the Dean of the College of Humanities at that university. She has published one book of short stories: *La sombra en el espejo* (San José, Costa Rica: Editorial Costa Rica, 1986).

ROSIBEL MORERA

Born in 1948, in Alajuela, Costa Rica. She studied theater and Philosophy of Education. Morera teaches History and Art Theory at the Universidad Nacional, in Heredia, Costa Rica. She has twice won the "Alfonsina Storni Latin American Poetry Prize" of Buenos Aires, Argentina: 1986 and 1988. She has published the following books: *Cartas a mi Señor* (poetry, 1974); *La proyección escénica: Hierofanía y Maná del arte del actor* (1983), for which she won the Universidad Nacional essay prize; *Las resurrecciones y reencarnaciones de Lázaro Fuentes* (short stories, 1988); *Los nombres con que quiero* (poetry); and *Testigo interior* (novel).

CARMEN NARANJO

Born in Cártago, Costa Rica, in 1931. Naranjo holds a M.A. in Liberal Arts from the University of Costa Rica. She has been her country's Ambassador to Israel (1972-74), Costa Rica's Minister of Culture (1974-76), and is presently the director of Editorial Universitaria Centroamericana, the Central American Federation of Universities Press, in San José, Costa Rica. She has won all of her country's important national prizes for literature. Books published: *La canción de la ternura* (poetry, 1964); *Misa a oscuras* (poetry, 1965); *Los perros no ladraron* (novel, 1966); *Camino al mediodía* (novel, 1968); *Memorias de un hombre palabra* (novel, 1968); *Responso por el niño Juan Manuel* (novel, 1971); *Diario de una multitud* (novel, 1971); *Hoy es un largo día* (stories, 1972); *Por las páginas de la Biblia y los caminos de Israel* (essay, 1976); *Mi guerrilla* (poetry, 1977); *Cinco temas en busca de un pensador* (essay, 1977); *Ondina* (stories, 1985); *Sobre punto* (novel, 1987); *Otro rumbo para la rumba* (stories, 1989). Naranjo teaches literature at the Universidad de Costa Rica, in San José.

EUNICE ODIO

Born in San José, Costa Rica, in 1922, she lived in Guatemala, Cuba, the United States and Mexico, where she died in 1974. She became a free-lance journalist, writing articles for various Central American and Mexican newspapers. She first won recognition as a poet in 1948 in Guatemala, where she was awarded first prize for poetry with her book *Los elementos terrestres* (1948). Her other books of poems are: *Zona en territorio del alba* (1953) and *El tránsito de fuego* (1958). Other works she published, in prose: *El rastro de la mariposa* (story); *Los trabajos de la catedral* (essay); *En defensa del castellano* (essay). Books published after her death: *La obra en prosa de Eunice Odio* (1980), by Rima de Vallbona; *Eunice Odio en Guatemala* (1983), by Mario Esquivel Tobar, which documents most of her writings published in that country; *Antología: Rescate de una gran poeta*, Juan Liscano, Ed. (1975); *Territorio del alba y otros poemas* (1974). She is one of the greatest poets of Costa Rica, overlooked by the intellectual community of her country until her death.

YOLANDA OREAMUNO

Born in San José, Costa Rica, in 1916, Oreamuno lived in Chile, El Salvador, Guatemala and Mexico, where she died in 1956. Many of her writings remain scattered in the magazines and newspapers of these countries, while others are lost. It is believed that she wrote at least one other novel: *La ruta de su evasión*, that won an important prize in Guatemala and was published in that country in 1949. There is another edition, published in 1984, in her country, by Editorial Costa Rica. After her death, her short stories, articles and letters were collected in the book: *A lo largo del corto camino* (1961), and a selection was made by Costa Rican writer Alfonso Chase in the book: *Relatos escogidos* (1977). Victoria Urbano, a Costa Rican writer who lived in the U.S., produced the first study of Oreamuno's work: *Una escritora costarricense; Yolanda Oreamuno* (1968), published in Madrid, Spain. And another Costa Rican writer who lives in the U.S., Rima de Vallbona, published a study: *Yolanda Oreamuno* (1971).

JULIETA PINTO

Born in San José, Costa Rica, in 1922, Pinto earned as a B.A. in Philology from the Universidad de Costa Rica. She founded and has been the chair of the Department of Literature at the Universidad Nacional, in Heredia, Costa Rica. Books published: *Cuentos de la tierra* (stories, 1963); *Si se oyera el silencio* (stories, 1967); *La estación que sigue al verano* (novel, 1969); *Los marginados* (stories, 1970); *A la vuelta de la esquina* (stories, 1975); *El sermón de lo cotidiano* (1977); *Abrir los ojos* (stories, 1982); *El eco de los pasos* (stories); *Historia de Navidad* (story, 1988).

VICTORIA URBANO

Born in Costa Rica in 1926, Urbano studied English and Business in San Francisco in 1945. In 1952 she enrolled in Spain's Royal Conservatory of Dramatic Arts, where she graduated with honors. Two of her plays were produced in Madrid, with excellent reviews: *Agar, la esclava* (Teatro de Bellas Artes, 1952) and *La hija de Charles Green* (Teatro de Cultura Hispánica, 1954). She earned a B.A. and a Ph.D. at the University of Madrid. In 1966 she began teaching Spanish at Lamar University (Beaumont, Texas), where she was awarded the life title of Regents' Professor, in recognition of her outstanding teaching and research activities in 1972. She won many international prizes and honors. Books published: *Marfil* (stories and poetry, 1951); *La niña de los caracoles* (prose, 1961); *Platero y tú* (prose, 1962); *Juan Vásquez de Coronado y su ética en la conquista de Costa Rica* (history, 1968); *Una escritora costarricense: Yolanda Oreamuno* (essay, 1968); *Los nueve círculos* (poetry, 1970); *El teatro español y sus directrices contemporáneas* (1973); *Y era otra vez hoy* (stories, 1972); *El teatro en Centroamérica, desde sus orígenes hasta 1975* (essay, 1978); *Freeway to Italian* (grammar, 1977).

RIMA DE VALLBONA

Born in San José, Costa Rica, in 1931, Vallbona obtained an M.A. in Liberal Arts from the University of Costa Rica, and a Ph.D. in Modern Languages from Middlebury College (Vermont). She also earned a "Diploma of French Teacher" at the Sorbonne (France), and a "Diploma in Hispanic Philology" from the University of Salamanca (Spain). Vallbona has been on the faculty of St. Thomas University (Houston, Texas) since 1964, teaching Spanish and Literature. She was the organizer of its Spanish Department and served as its first chair (1966-1971). She is a member of numerous national organizations related to literature and teaching. Books published include: *Noche en vela* (novel, 1968); *Polvo del camino* (stories, 1971); *La salamandra rosada* (stories, 1979); *Las sombras que perseguimos* (novel, 1983); *Mujeres y agonías* (stories, 1982); *Baraja de soledades* (stories, 1983); *Yolanda Oreamuno* (essay, 1971); *La obra en prosa de Eunice Odio* (anthology, 1981); *Cosecha de pecadores* (stories, 1981). She has been awarded many Costa Rican and international prizes and honors.

PANAMA

LILIA ALGANDONA

Born in Panama City, in 1968, Algandona is a Bilingual Secretary, now in her fourth year of Law School at the Universidad de Panama, in Panama City. As a high school student she won many national student writing awards. She has only published two short stories (one included in this anthology), four years ago, in the Panamanian cultural magazine "Maga," founded, edited and directed by Enrique Jaramillo Levi.

GIOVANNA BENEDETTI

Born in Panama City, in 1949, Benedetti earned a B.A. in Law from the Universidad de Barcelona, Spain; and a Ph.D. in Autorial Law from the Universidad Complutense de Madrid, Spain. Benedetti has won the "Ricardo Miró" national literary prize as a short story writer and as an essayist. Books published: *La lluvia sobre el fuego* (stories, 1982); *El sótano dos de la cultura* (essays). She has also published poetry in magazines and anthologies.

ROSA MARIA BRITTON

Born in Panama City, in 1936, Britton lived in Cuba for many years. She studied Medicine in Madrid, where she specialized in Gynecology. In New York she studied Oncology, and lived there for 12 years. Since returning to Panama in 1973, Britton has been the Director of the National Oncology Institute, in Panama City for over 10 years. She has won the "Ricardo Miró" national literary prize several times as a novelist, short story wirter and playwright. Books published: *El ataúd de uso* (novel, 1983); *El señor de las lluvias y el viento* (novel, 1985); *La costilla de Adán* (articles, 1985); *Quién inventó el mambo?* (stories, 1986); *La muerte tiene dos caras* (stories, 1987); *Esa esquina del paraíso* (theater, 1987).

GRISELDA LOPEZ

Born in 1938, López studies journalism in Mexico. She has been director of Channel 11 Educational TV in Panama, and teaches journalism at the Universidad de Panama. Many years ago she founded, together with writer Bertalicia Peralta, the literary magazine "El Pez Original." She has published two books of short stories: *Piel adentro*; and *Sueño recurrente*.

MORAVIA OCHOA LOPEZ

Born in Panama City, in 1939, Ochoa López has won the "Ricardo Miró" national literary contest several times for poetry. She directed the literary magazine *Itinerario*. She has been included in several anthologies, both as a poet and as a short story writer. Poetry books published: *Raíces primordiales* (1960); *Cuerdas sobre tu voz de alba infinita* (1964); *Las savias corporales* (1965); *Donde transan los ríos* (1975); *Ganas de estar un poco vivos* (1975); *Círculos y planetas* (1977); *Hacer la guerra es ir con todo* (1979). Books of short stories: *Yesca* (1968); *El espejo* (1971).

BERTALICIA PERALTA

Born in Panama City, in 1939, Peralta was Co-founder of the literary magazine "El Pez Original." She has won the "Ricardo Miró" national literary prize several times for poetry. Some of her books of poetry are: *Canto de esperanza filial* (1961); *Sendas fugitivas* (1963); *Dos poemas* (1964); *Atrincherado amor* (1964); *Los retornos* (1965); *Un lugar en la esfera terrestre* (1971); *Himno a la alegría* (1973); *Ragúl* (1976); *Libro de la fábulas* (1976); *Casa flotante* (1979); *En tu cuerpo cubierto de flores*; and her books of short stories are: *Largo in crescendo* (1967); *Barcarola y otras fantasías incorregibles* (1973); *Puros cuentos* (1988). She has won many national and international prizes, and has been included in many anthologies, both as a poet and as a short story writer. She is now the Director of Public Relations for the University of Panama.

BESSY REYNA: (Note: Double listing—author/translator)
Born in Cuba in 1942, Reyna moved to Panama at an early age. She has published *Ab ovo*, (short stories, 1978) and *Terrarium*, (poetry, 1975). Reyna received an individual writer's award from the Connecticut Commission on the Arts in 1990, and has participated extensively in poetry readings in the New England region. Editor of *El Taller Literario*, a bilingual literary magazine, her work has appeared in numerous literary magazines and anthologies, including: *Breaking Boundaries: Latina Writings and Critical Readings*, (Horno et al. Eds., University of Massachusetts Press, 1989); *Clamor of Innocence: Short Stories from Central America*, (B. Paschke & D. Volpendesta, Eds., City Lights, San Francisco, California, 1989) and *IXOC Amar-Go: Central American women's poetry for peace*, (Zoë Anglesey, Ed., Granite Press, Maine, 1987). Reyna is a graduate of Mount Holyoke College and the University of Connecticut School of Law.

GRACIELA ROJAS SUCRE
Born in Aguadulce, Panama, in 1904, Rojas Sucre devoted her life to teaching. A graduate of the Escuela Normal de Institutoras, she continued graduate studies in Santiago, Chile and at Columbia University, N.Y. She taught high school in Panama, at the Instituto Nacional and was part of Panama's diplomatic mission to Washington, D.C. The story in this anthology is taken from her book *Terruñadas de lo chico*, (short stories about children; Santiago, Chile, 1931).

ISIS TEJEIRA
She teaches Spanish and literature at the Universidad de Panamá. Tejeira has been an actress in national theatre for many years. She has published one novel: *Sin fecha fija* (1982), and published stories in national magazines, such as "Maga" and "Imagen."

ABOUT THE TRANSLATORS

ZOE ANGLESEY, poet and fiction writer, has been traveling and living intermittently in Central America since 1968. She was invited to participate in the Rubén Darío Festival in Nicaragua, the Dominican Writers Congress in 1986 and the Central American Writers Congresses held in Costa Rica (1985) and Guatemala (1988). Her translations appear in issues of *The Massachusetts Review, The Maryland Poetry Review, Tamaqua, Fiction International, Poetry East, Crosscurrents, Green Fuse, Onthebus, The Underground Forest,* and many other literary magazines. Anthologies with her translations are *And We Sold The Rain* (New York: Four Walls Eight Windows, 1988); *Woman Who Has Sprouted Wings* (Pittsburgh: Latin American Literary Review Press, 1987); *Women on War* (New York: Touchstone/Simon & Schuster, Inc., 1988) and the bilingual *Ixok Amar Go: Central American Women's Poetry for Peace*, which she edited (Penobscot, Maine: Granite Press, 1987). She has translated *Poems from the Erotic Left* by Ana Maria Rodas of Guatemala; *Death and Other Ephemeral Wrongs* by Ana Istaru of Costa Rica; *My Guerrilla* by Carmen Naranjo of Costa Rica; *Sudden Death* by Etelvina Astrada of Argentina and *Military Secret* by Roberto Sosa of Honduras. She compiled and coordinated the translation of *Women by the River* (Tegucigalpa, Honduras: Ediciones Paradiso, 1990) a bilingual collection of contemporary multicultural women's poetry from the United States.

LINDA BRITT is Assistant Professor of Spanish at the University of Maine at Farmington. Her previous translations include a collection of short stories by Carmen Naranjo, *There Never Was a Once Upon a Time* (Pittsburgh: Latin American Literary Review Press, 1989). She has also published critical articles on Naranjo and on Cervantes and García Lorca.

LELAND H. CHAMBERS is a professor of English and Comparative Literature at the University of Denver. He has published scholarly articles on the *Quijote,* Baltasar Gracián, and the English Metaphysical poets Richard Crashaw and Henry Vaughan, as well as on André Gide and Miguel Angel Asturias. For six years he was editor of *Denver Quarterly*. His translations of fiction by Spanish and Latin American writers have appeared in *Mississippi Review, Black Warrior Review, Sequoia, New Orleans Review, New Letters, Translation, Arte, Anaïs, Fiction,* and others. His translation of three novellas and a short story by the Argentine Ezequiel Martínez Estrada, *Holy Saturday And Other Stories*, was published by the Latin American Literary Review Press in 1988.

IRENE DEL CORRAL was born in New York, N.Y. in 1929. She has a B.A. in Spanish from Hunter College of the City of New York (1950), and an M.A. in Humanities, from The University of Texas at Dallas (1984). Del Corral is currently in the Ph.D. program in the area of translation at the University of Texas at Dallas. She teaches Spanish at Richland College, of the Dallas County Community College District. Del Corral has published a translation of a novel by Mexican playwright and novelist Jorge Ibarguengoitia: *The Lightning of August* (New York: Avon, 1986; London: Chatto & Windus, 1986); and an article in *Translation Review* (University of Texas at Dallas, No. 27, 1988); "Humor: When Do We Lose It?"

VIRGINIA EDWARDS was born in St. Louis Missouri. She received a B.A. in English from Vassar College, Poughkeepsie, N.Y. in 1964 and a master's in urban and regional planning from the University of D.C., Washington, D.C. in 1980. She is accredited by the American Translators Association (ATA) for Spanish to English translation. She translated literary articles and poetry for *Americas* magazine, published by the Organization of American States, from 1968-70; has been on the U.S. State Department list of translators and interpreters for many years. Edwards is currently involved in translating articles on breeds of wild and domestic horses descended from Spanish and Portuguese breeds. She lives in Texas where she breeds and trains mustangs and is writing a novel.

ELIZABETH GAMBLE MILLER is Associate Professor of Foreign Languages and Literatures at Southern Methodist University. She has introduced the poetry of Hugo Lindo and the fables of David Escobar Galindo to English readers in three bilingual editions with her critical introductions. She is currently translating these and 15 other Salvadoran authors of the 70's and 80's for an anthology which will include short fiction and poems. Her translations of numerous poems and short stories of Central American authors have appeared in journals and anthologies. She is editor of ALTA Newsletter, the newsletter of the American Literary Translators Association, and on the international board of *Translation Review*, an associate member of the Academia Salvadoreña de la lengua and an honorary member of Asociación Prometeo de Poesía of Madrid. Book publications are *Hugo Lindo, Sólo la voz/Only the Voice*, a poem of forty-seven cantos, a bilingual edition, (Mundus Artium Press, 1984); *The Ways of Rain and Other Poems*, a translation of the twenty-eight cantos of *Maneras de llover* and selections from eight other volumes by Hugo Lindo. An essay introducing "The Ways of Rain," an essay, "The Poetry of Hugo Lindo," and a "Translator's Note." A Foreword by Rainer Schulte and an Afterword by David Escobar-Galindo. A record sheet of the poet reading. (A bilingual edition, Latin American Literary Review Press, 1986.) Prose: *The Enchanted Raisin*, Jacqueline Balcells, a translation of seven short stories by the Chilean author, (Latin American Literary Review Press, 1989); *Fábulas/Fables*, David Escobar-Galindo, one hundred twenty-one fables translated in partial collaboration with Helen D. Clement, a bilingual edition, (Editorial Delgado, San Salvador, 1985.)

MARINELL JAMES is a free-lance writer, editor and translator. James has translated *Deviations*, a book of poetry by Enrique Jaramillo Levi; she is currently translating poetry by Latin American women poets.

ROBERT KRAMER is Associate Professor of Modern Foreign Languages at Manhattan College, where he teaches German, classics, world literature, and art history. He is the author of *August Sander: Portraits of an Epoch* and *The Art of Kasak*, as well as of numerous articles on art and literature. He is also a poet, playwright, and literary translator. He was formerly director of the New York Poets Cooperative. He has received a Fulbright fellowship, a Swiss Government grant, and four awards from the National Endowment for the Humanities in the fields of literary history, art history, and literary translation.

SABINA LASK-SPINAC was an Assistant Professor of English at Rockland Community College in Suffern, N.Y. She has translated Spanish short stories from Honduras (to be published by the University of Texas) and Yiddish and Hebrew poems, published in *Domension* (1980), and *Tikkun* (1989). Her scholarly articles include "Old Cry, New Shofar: The Poet-Prophets of Jewish Modernism," in *Midstream* (1988); "The Alienated Art Critic," in *Spontaneous* (1987); "The Literary Kaleidoscope" *Reading, Writing and Interpreting Literature*, (1988); "A Hunt for Tennyson: Teaching Poetry Through Painting: (ERIC, 1986); and "Fryeing Freshmen in the Pool of Humanity" (*English in Texas*, 1985).

GLORIA DE MOYA NICHOLS is a translator and interpreter, and has also been a teacher of English as a Second Language. She has been an interpreter for the U.S. State Department and the Federal Court system, and has worked for the United Nations. Born in Havana, Mrs. Nichols has traveled widely in Central and South America. She is also a professional photographer.

DON SANDERS is a singer/songwriter who was born in Houston, Texas in 1943. In addition to touring and recording, he has served as an artist in residence for many school districts and has worked as an actor.

His translation of Emilio Carballido's one act play, *Nora*, was jointly produced by Main Street Theater and Teatro Bilingue de Houston in 1988. His translation of Osvaldo Dragún's *Los de la mesa 10* and *Historias para ser contadas* was given a staged reading by Main Street Theater in 1989 and is scheduled for production.

JULIA SHIREK SMITH has an M.A. in Spanish from New Mexico Highlands University. She has been an Instructor of Spanish at that University since 1988. She was accredited as a Spanish-to-English translator by the American Translators Association in 1987. Smith has published Chapter One of the novel *Dos Crimenes*, by the late Mexican novelist and playwright Jorge Ibarguengoitia in *Translation*, Volume XIV, Spring 1985.

BIRGITTA VANCE was born in Austria. She obtained her Ph.D. from Wayne State University in Detroit, Michigan and is at present an Associate Professor of Spanish at the University of Michigan-Flint where she teaches grammar, translation, and courses on Contemporary Spanish and Latin American fiction. Among her publications is: *A Harvest Sown by Death: The Novel of the Spanish Civil War.* She translates from German and Spanish to English.

SAMUEL A. ZIMMERMAN, after obtaining his B.A. and M.A. from Ohio State University and a Ph. D. from the University of Florida, Zimmerman has taught Spanish language and literature for 26 years at Southern Methodist University, Dallas, Texas. He had translated and written critical articles on the short stories of Carmen Martín Gaite and Enrique Jaramillo Levi. Zimmerman received the Poste d'Assistant award from the French government and received a Fulbright Travel Grant.

CLARK M. ZLOTCHEW is a Professor of Spanish, SUNY College at Fredonia; and Faculty Exchange Scholar of the State University of New York. He is the author of *Libido into Literature: The "Primera Epoca" of Galdós* (Borgo, 1990), and of *Voices of the River Plate* (Borgo 1992). Translator of Fernando Sorrentino, *Seven Conversations with Jorge Luis Borges* (Whitston, 1982), of *Falling Through the Cracks: Stories of Julio Ricci* (White Pine, 1989) and *The House in the Sand: Prose Poems by Pablo Neruda* (Milkweed Editions, 1990). Zlotchew is also the author of numerous articles on Spanish and Latin-American Literature; author of interviews with Borges, Denevi and other Argentine writers; translator of Spanish-language fiction and poetry. His original short stories in Spanish have appeared in literary journals in Argentina, Uruguay, Mexico and Costa Rica. One of these stories appeared in Italian translation in a Milan magazine.

ABOUT THE EDITOR

ENRIQUE JARAMILLO LEVI, born in Colón, Panamá, in 1944, is a short story writer, poet and essayist. He has published five books of short stories, the most acclaimed of which is *Duplicaciones* (Mexico: 1973, 1982. Madrid: 1991). He has also published four books of poetry, the most recent *Extravíos* (Costa Rica: 1989); three anthologies of Panamanian literature, including *Poesía panameña contemporánea* (Mexico: 1980, 1982); two anthologies of Mexican literature: *El cuento erótico en México* (Mexico: 1975, 1978) and *Poesía erótica mexicana 1889-1980* (Mexico: 1982; and has compiled and written the prologue for three books of essays on the Panama Canal by Panamanian scholars. Founder, director and editor of "Maga", a literary journal (1984-1987; 1990-). At present he is director of the Department of Literature at the "Instituto Nacional de Cultura" in Panama. Jaramillo Levi was a Fulbright scholar at the University of Texas at Austin (1987-1989), and taught Latin American literature at California State University, San Bernardino (1989), and at Oregon State University, Corvallis (1989-1990). Two volumes of his short stories and two books of poetry have been translated into English. He has been translated and published in German, Portuguese, Polish and Hungarian. *Puertas y ventanas (Acercamientos a la obra literaria de Enrique Jaramillo Levi)*, a book of over 40 essays and reviews of his writings has recently been published in Costa Rica by EDUCA, with a prologue by Costa Rican writer Carmen Naranjo.

STUDIES ON LITERATURE FROM COSTA RICA:
A GENERAL BIBLIOGRAPHY

Albán, Laureano. "Poesía femenina contemporánea costarricense," in "Ancora" (*La Nación*), San José, Costa Rica, April 25, 1976.

Baeza Flores, Alberto. *Evolución de la poesía costarricense* (1574-1977). San José, Costa Rica, 1978.

——."La poesía femenina costarricense: breve balance y perspectivas," in *Káñina*, No. IX, San José, Costa Rica: July-December, 1985.

Bonilla, Abelardo. *Antología de la literatura costarricense*. San José, Costa Rica: Studium, 1981.

——.*Historia de la literatura costarricense*. San José, Costa Rica: Studium, 1984.

Cortés, Carlos. et al. *Para no cansarlos con el cuento: narrativa costarricense*. San José, Costa Rica: Editorial Costa Rica, 1989.

Chase, Alfonso. (2 tomos). *Narrativa contemporánea de Costa Rica*. San José, Costa Rica: Ministerio de Cultura, Juventud y Deporte, 1975.

Duncan, Quince. et al. *Narrativa costarricense: una interpretación socio-histórica.* Heredia, Costa Rica: 1985.

Duverrán, Carlos R. *Poesía contemporánea de Costa Rica*. San José, Costa Rica: Editorial Costa Rica, 1978.

Kargleder, Charles J. and Warren H. Mory. *Bibliografía selectiva de la literatura costarricense*. San José, Costa Rica: Editorial Costa Rica, 1978.

Martínez S., Luz Ivette. *Carmen Naranjo y la narrativa femenina de Costa Rica*. San José, Costa Rica: Editorial Universitaria Centroamericana, 1987.

Menton, Seymour. *El cuento costarricense: estudio, antología y bibliografía* México: Ediciones de Andrea/University of Kansas Press, 1964.

Miranda Hevia, Alicia. "El cuento contemporáneo en Costa Rica," in *Káñina*, San José, Costa Rica: January-June, 1981.

Núñez, Francisco M. *Itinerario de la novela costarricense*. San José, Costa Rica: 1947.

Portuguéz de Bolaños, Elizabeth. *El cuento en Costa Rica*, 2 ed., aum., San José, Costa Rica: Lehmann, 1964.

Sandoval de Fonseca, Virginia. *Resumen de la literatura costarricense*. San José, Costa Rica: 1978.

Sotelo, Rogelio. *Escritores de Costa Rica*. San José, Costa Rica: Lehmann, 1942.

Soto Soto, Jorge. *Galería de valores femeninos costarricenses*. San José, Costa Rica: 1975.

Urbano, Victoria, ed. *Five women writers of Costa Rica*. Beaumont, Texas: Asociación de Literatura Femenina Hispánica, Lamar University, 1978.

Valdeperas, Jorge. *Para una nueva interpretación de la literatura costarricense*. San José, Costa Rica:1979.

Vallbona, Rima de. "Trayectoria de la poesía femenina en Costa Rica," in *Káñina*, No. V, San José, Costa Rica: July-December, 1981.

STUDIES ON LITERATURE FROM PANAMA: A GENERAL BIBLIOGRAPHY

Aguilera, Luisita. *Leyendas panameñas*: 1949.

——.*Leyendas y tradiciones panameñas*: 1952.

Alvarado de Ricord, Elsie. *Escritores panameños contemporáneos*: 1962.

Arosemena de Tejeira, Otilia. *La mujer en la vida panameña*. Panamá: EUDEP, s.f.

Avila Castillo, José. *Cuentos panameños* (2 tomos). Bogotá, Colombia: Instituto Colombiano de Cultura, 1972.

Cabezas, Berta María. *Narraciones panameñas*. México: 1956.

Del Saz, Agustín. *Nueva poesía panameña*. Madrid, España: Ediciones Cultural Hispánica, 1954.

——.*Antología general de la poesía panameña Siglo XIX y XX*. Barcelona: Bruguera, 1974.

Fernándes Cañizales, Victor. *La patria en la lírica panameña*. Panamá: Editorial Universitaria, 1971.

Fuentes, Cipriano. *Narradores panameños*. Caracas, Venezuela: Doble Fondo Editores, 1984.

Garay, Narciso. *Tradiciones y cantares de Panamá*. Bélgica: Sorti des Presses J' Expansion, 1930.

García S., Ismael. *Medio siglo de poesía panameña*. México: 1956.

——.*Historia de la literatura panameña*. México: UNAM, 1964; 1972.

González Ruíz, Sergio. *Veintiséis leyendas panameñas*. Panamá: 1953.

Herrera Carmen D., et al. *Bibliografía de obras escritas por mujeres panameñas*. Panamá: Asociación Panameña de Bibliotecas, 1976.

Jaramillo Levi, Enrique. *Antología crítica de joven narrativa panameña*. México: Federación Editorial Mexicana, 1971.

——.*Poesía panameña contemporánea*. México: Editorial Liberta-Sumaria, 1980; Editorial Penélope, 1982.

——.*Poesía erótica de Panamá*. México: Editorial Signos, 1982.

——.*Para contar el cuento (Cuentistas de Centroamérica: 1963-1991)*. San José, Costa Rica: Editoral Costa Rica/UNESCO, 1991.

Korsi, Demetrio. *Antología de Panamá. Parnaso y prosa.* Barcelona: Casa Editorial Maucci, 1926.

——.*La mujer y la poesía en Panamá.* Panamá: Instituto Nacional de Cultura, 1977.

Miró, Rodrigo. *El cuento en Panamá.* Panamá: Impresora de la Academia, 1950.

——.*Aspectos de la literatura novelesca en Panamá.* Panamá; Impresora Panamá, 1968.

——.*La literatura panameña (origen y proceso).* San José, Costa Rica: 1972.

——.*Itinerario de la poesía panameña.* Panamá: Librería Cultural Panameña, 1980.

Miró, Rodrigo y Aristides Martínez Ortega (comp.). *Antología de la poesía panameña.* Bogotá, Colombia: Convenio "Andrés Bello" - SECAB, 1985.

Pitty, Dimas Lidio. *Letra viva.* Panamá: Ediciones Formato dieciseis, Universidad de Panamá, 1986.

Revilla Argüeso, Angel. *Cultura hispanoamericana en el Istmo de Panamá.* Panamá: ECU Ediciones/Convenio de Santo Domingo, 1987.

Riera, Mario. *Cuentos folklóricos de Panamá:* 1956.

Ruíz Vernacci, Enrique. *Introducción al cuento panameña.* Panamá: Biblioteca Selecta, 1946.

Sepúlveda, Mélida Ruth. *El Canal en la novelística panameña.* Caracas, Venezuela: Universidad Católica "Andrés Bello"/Centro de Investigaciones Literarias, 1975.

Torrijos Herrera, Moisés. *Ancón liberado. Antología poética.* Panamá: 1979.

ANTHOLOGIES OF (OR INCLUDING) LATIN AMERICAN WOMEN WRITERS IN ENGLISH & SPANISH

Agosin, Marjorie, ed. *Landscapes of a New Land: Short Fiction by Latin American Women.* Buffalo, N.Y.: White Pine Press, 1989.

Arkin, Marian and Barbara Shollar, eds. *Longman Anthology of World Literature by Women 1875- 1975.* New York: Longman Inc., 1989.

Barradas, Efraín, ed. *Apalabramiento: cuentos puertorriqueños de hoy.* Hanover, NH: Ediciones del Norte, 1983.

Bassnett, Susan, ed. *Knives and Angels: Women Writers in Latin America.* London: Zed Books, 1990.

Caistor, Nick, ed. *The Faber Book of Contemporary Latin American Short Stories.* London & Boston: Faber & Faber, 1989.

Erro-Peralta, Nora, & Caridad Silva-Nuñez, eds. *Beyond the Border: A New Age in Latin American Women's Fiction*. Pittsburgh: Cleis Press, 1991.

Gómez, Alma, Cherrie Moraga and Mariana Romo-Cardona, eds. *Cuentos: Stories by Latinas*. New York: Kitchen Table, Women of Color Press, 1983.

Guerra-Cunningham, Lucía. *Splintering Darkness: Latin American Women Writers in Search of Themselves*. Pittsburgh: Latin American Literary Review Press, 1990.

Handelsman, Michael H. *Diez escritoras ecuatorianas y sus cuentos*. Quito: Casa de la Cultura Ecuatoriana, 1982.

Lewald, H. Ernest, trans. and ed. *The Web: Stories by Argentine Women*. Washington D.C.: Three Continents Press, 1983.

Luby, Barry J. and Wayne H. Finke, eds. *Anthology of Contemporary Latin American Literature 1960-1984*. London-Toronto: Associated University Press, 1986.

Manguel, Alberto, ed. *Other Fires: Short Fiction by Latin American Women*. Avenal, NJ: Clarkson N. Potter, 1986

Menton, Seymour, ed. *The Spanish American Short Story: A Critical Anthology*. Berkeley: University of California Press, 1980.

Meyer, Doris, and Margarite Fernández Olmos, eds. *Contemporary Women Authors of Latin America: New Translations* (Brooklyn: Brooklyn College, 1983).

Meyer, Doris, ed. *Lives on the Line: The Testimony of Contemporary Latin American Authors*. Berkeley: University of California Press, 1988.

Miller, Yvette, ed. *Latin American Women Writers—Yesterday and Today*. Pittsburgh: Latin American Literary Review Press, 1977.

Ortega, Julio, ed. *El muro y la intemperie: el nuevo cuento latinoamericano*. Hanover, NH: Ediciones del Norte, 1989.

Partnoy, Alicia, ed. *You Can't Drown the Fire: Latin American Women Writing in Exile*. Pittsburgh: Cleis Press, 1988.

Picón Garfield, Evelyn, ed. *Women's Fiction from Latin America*. Detroit: Wayne State University Press, 1988.

Rojo, Grinor, and Cynthia Steele, eds. *Ritos de iniciación*. Boston: Houghton Mifflin Co., 1986.

Santos, Rosario, ed. *And We Sold the Rain: Contemporary Fiction from Central America*. New York: Four Walls Eight Windows, 1988.

Sefchovich, Sara, ed. *Mujeres en espejo*. México: Folios Ediciones, 1983. *Mujeres en espejo 2*. México: Folios Ediciones, 1985.

Silva-Velásquez, Caridad L., and Nora Erro-Orthman, eds. *Puerta abierta, la nueva escritora latinoamericana*. México: Joaquín Mortiz, 1986.

Urbano, Victoria. *Five Women Writers of Costa Rica.* Beaumont, Texas: Asociación de Literatura Femenina Hispánica, Lamar University, 1978.

Vélez, Diana. *Reclaiming Medusa: Short Stories by Contemporary Puerto Rican Women.* San Francisco: Spinsters/Aunt Lute Book Co., 1988.

Vigil, Evangelina, ed. *Woman of her Word: Hispanic Women Write.* Houston: Arte Público Press, 1984.

Rodríguez Monegal, Emir. *The Borzoi Anthology of Latin American Literature.* New York: Alfred Knopf, 1977.

Zapata, Celia Correas de, and Lygia Johnson. *Detrás de la reja: Antología crítica de narradoras latinoamericanas del siglo XX,* Caracas: Monte Avila, 1980.

Zapata, Celia Correas de, ed. *Short Stories by Latin American Women: The Magic and the Real.* Houston: Arte Público Press, 1990.

GENERAL BIBLIOGRAPHIES OF (OR INCLUDING) LATIN AMERICAN WOMEN WRITERS

Alarcón, Norma and Sylvia Kossnar. *Bibliography of Hispanic Women Writers.* Bloomington, IN: Chicano-Riqueño Studies Bibliography Series No. 1, 1980.

Cortina, Lynn Ellen Rice. *Spanish-American Women Writers: a Bibliographical Research Checklist.* New York: Garland Publishing, 1983.

Corvalán, Graciela N. V. *Latin American Women Writers in English Translation: A Bibliography.* Los Angeles: California State University Latin American Studies Center, 1980.

Dolz-Blackburn, Inés. "Recent Critical Bibliography on Women in Hispanic Literature." *Discurso Literario* 3, 2 (1986): 331-34.

Flores, Angel. *Bibliografía de escritores hispanoamericanos. A Bibliography of Spanish-American Writers* 1609-1974. New York: Gordian Press, 1975.

Freudenthal, Juan R. and Patricia M. Freudenthal. *Index to Anthologies of Latin American Literature in English Translation.* Boston: G.K. Hall & Co., 1977.

Knaster, Meri. *Women in Spanish America. An Annotated Bibliography from Pre-Conquest to Contemporary Times.* Boston: G.K. Hall & Co., 1977.

Lindstrom, Naomi. "Feminist Criticism Of Latin American Literature: Bibliographic Notes." *Latin American Research Review* 15, 1 (1980): 151-59.

Marting, Diane E., ed. *Spanish American Women Writers: A Bio-bibliographical Source Book.* New York: Greenwood Press, 1990.

——.*Women Writers of Spanish America. An Annotated Bio-bibliographical Guide.* New York: Greenwood Press, 1987.

Ramos Foster, Virginia. "La crítica literaria de la profesoras norteamericanas ante las letras femeninas hispánicas." *Revista Interamericana de Bibliografía/Interamerican Review of Bibliography.* 30.4 (1980): 406-12.

Resnick, Margery and Isabel de Cortivron, eds. *Women Writers in Translation: An Annotated Bibliography.* New York: Garland Press, 1984.